Ghosts of Saint-Michel

Also by Jake Lamar

Rendezvous Eighteenth

If 6 Were 9

Close to the Bone

The Last Integrationist

Bourgeois Blues

Ghosts of Saint-Michel

Jake Lamar

St. Martin's Minotaur ✷ New York

This is a work of fiction. All of the characters, organizations, and events portrayed in this novel are either products of the author's imagination or are used fictitiously.

www.minotaurbooks.com

Library of Congress Cataloging-in-Publication Data

Lamar, Jake.
    Ghosts of Saint-Michel / by Jake Lamar.—1st ed.
        p.   cm.
    Sequel to: Rendezvous eighteenth.
    ISBN-13: 978-0-312-28925-6
    ISBN-10: 0-312-28925-1
    1. African American women—France—Paris—Fiction. 2. Triangles (Interpersonal relations)—Fiction. 3. Restaurateurs—Fiction. 4. Missing persons—Fiction. 5. Paris (France)—Fiction. I. Title.

PS3562.A4216G47 2006
813'.54—dc22

                                                                          2006040537

First Edition: June 2006

10 9 8 7 6 5 4 3 2 1

For Dorli

Acknowledgments

I'D LIKE TO THANK a few wonderful people I know; some of them might not realize how much they helped me during the writing of this novel; others have provided invaluable support over many years: Joyce Marie Doucette Lamar, Bert and Cindy Lamar, C. K. Williams and Catherine Mauger, Diane Johnson, Mavis Gallant, Salim Akil, Almeta Speaks, Ellery Washington, Robert-Charles Chemoul, Hisham and Diana Matar, André Figueiroa, Natasha Bryer, David Van Taylor, Holley Stewart, David Tanzer and Kris Dahl, a magnificent ally in this crazy vocation.

PART 1

La Mère

One

MARVA DOBBS LOVED THE *rentrée*. She loved the way the French spoke of the end of summer as a reentry. Like a high-flying space voyager reentering the earth's atmosphere. After the intoxicating pleasures of a month-long vacation, the whole country was supposed to return to practical everydayness. Back to school, back to business, back to reality. From summery hedonism to autumnal seriousness. The unofficial start of the *rentrée* was the first Monday in September, like Labor Day in the United States of America, the country Marva had abandoned four decades earlier. But while Labor Day Weekend was a three-day holiday, the *rentrée* was a three-week mini-season. Early *rentrée* was the last week of August. Late *rentrée* was the middle of September. French people even wished each other a *"bonne rentrée."*

Have a good reentry: sort of like saying "happy end of holidays." For Marva, there was something festive about this time of year, the collective sentiment that it was time to get back to work.

Marva was *rentrée*-ing early this year. Following the habit of the past thirty-nine summers, she had spent most of August in Brittany, with the family of her husband, Loïc Rose. As usual, she'd had a pleasant time, sailing along the rocky shores of France's northwestern coast, drinking white wine and eating juicy langoustines—those tiny, needle-clawed crayfish that were a Breton *spécialité*—and going for long walks across the dramatic cliffs, arm in arm with the man she had loved for two-thirds of her life. Loïc would have been happy to stay in Bretagne, as they often did, until after the first weekend in September. But Marva insisted on a somewhat premature return. Because, through all those pleasant walks and meals, during all the engaging conversations she had had with Loïc and his—after thirty-nine years it was really *their*—relatives, Marva had been thinking incessantly, obsessively, about one person: her young lover back in Paris, Hassan Mekachera.

Monday, August 27, 2001. The Boulevard Saint-Germain still had its sleepy, late summer feeling. There were couples and clusters of tourists wandering up and down the broad avenue but not much traffic. Many of the classy fashion and furniture shops were closed. The hustle-bustle that energized this main artery of the Left Bank most of the year was, for Marva, eerily absent. Like much of Paris in the dying days of summer, the Boulevard Saint-Germain had a half-deserted air about it. Lots of visitors, but precious few residents. As she walked to the garage that housed her silver Audi, Marva savored the unfamiliar stillness of the street. She felt a funny, illicit thrill to be breaking with her routine. She saw the surprise in the eyes of the fat and sweaty garage attendant, imprisoned in his little cubicle, behind the clear plastic wall, when Marva showed up a week ahead of schedule. Being a Parisian, he was far too discreet to inquire as to why she had returned unexpectedly from her summer vacation. He just nodded and said, *"Bonjour, madame."*

Pulling out of the garage, turning onto the rue du Bac, Marva had the childishly delicious sensation of doing something naughty. She had not told her employees that she would be returning early. And she took a certain cruel pleasure in imagining the shocked looks on their faces when the boss came sauntering into the restaurant a week *en avance*. Everybody knew that Marva Dobbs was a creature of habit. At least that's what they thought they knew. But they were all in for a surprise today.

All of them, except for maybe Hassan, the cook Marva had hired only last May. Marva doubted that anything she could do would shock Hassan. He had known her mainly as a lustful and impulsive lover. Would he be happy to see her this morning? Had he thought about her, reminisced and fantasized about her the way Marva had obsessed on him during the past three weeks of separation? Much as she tried, Marva couldn't stop remembering Hassan: the smell, the touch, the taste of him. She saw him in her dreams: his hazel eyes and light brown hair and creamy coffee skin. Every day and night in Brittany, Marva heard a ghostly echo in her head, the memory of her own voice saying her lover's name as they ravished each other, the name that sounded first like a sigh, then, as she said it faster and faster, turned into a delirious hiss, then finally a gasp, repeated over and over again as she reached a mind-shattering climax: *Hassan-Hassan-Hassan-Hassan-Hassan....*

It would have to end. Marva knew that. It was late August now. The *rentrée*. Midsummer's mad passion was over. She had had three weeks in Brittany to consider the situation. And she knew, on this dazzling Monday morning, as she drove north toward her famous restaurant, that she would no longer be fucking her cook in the small bedroom above the kitchen. Today, order would be restored. That was what the *rentrée* was all about. She would explain to Hassan that their brief affair was finished. Marva had wondered if maybe she should fire him. But she couldn't do that. Hassan Mekachera had seven children to support. At least, Marva *hoped* he supported them.

Driving across the Seine, bold sunlight shimmering on the water,

Marva let go a deep, contented sigh. How she adored this city. Even after thirty-nine years, she never took the beauty of Paris for granted. Zipping along the Avenue du Général Lemonnier, the vast Tuileries garden on one side of the road, the magnificent expanse of the Louvre museum on the other, Marva wondered for the ten thousandth time if it was fate, God or sheer blind luck that had led her, a poor girl from the Bedford Stuyvesant section of Brooklyn, to make a life for herself in this most glorious of European cities. And what a life! She was one of Paris's most celebrated *restauratrices*. She hobnobbed with folks who used to be known as the "international jet set." She had a sweet, smart husband who worshiped her. And a beautiful, gifted daughter who had not only excelled in the European educational system but who had then gone on to graduate with honors from an Ivy League university in America.

So what the hell was wrong with Marva? What had compelled her to have an insane fling with the number-two cook in her restaurant? For Christ's sake, she was sixty-two years old! Hassan was only twenty-eight—a mere five years older than her daughter, Naima. Marva felt a sudden nauseous surge of guilt. What would Naima say if she learned of her mother's affair? Would she be horrified, disgusted, tickled, blasé? Marva had been so preoccupied with thoughts of Hassan all through August that she only now recognized how much she had missed Naima in Brittany. This was the first summer ever that her daughter had not spent any time in France at all. Naima said she was just too busy on her movie shoot in New York. Driving up the rue des Pyramides, Marva shook her head in bittersweet wonderment. For most of her life, she had felt lucky to escape America. And now look what had happened: Marva's only child, the precious daughter she had sought to protect from that violent kingdom of grinning hypocrisy, had decided to make her home in the U.S. of A. Naima even said she loved it there, in the very city that Marva had left and never missed.

Maybe, Marva thought, when Naima came home to Paris for

Christmas, long after this affair with Hassan was dead and buried, she would confess everything to her daughter. There was a time, not so long ago, when Marva and Naima had been the best of friends. But once Naima left for Brown University, back in 1996, inevitably they had drifted apart. Maybe if Marva opened up to Naima, told her all about the loony passion with Hassan, this would bring them closer again, reestablish that special mother-daughter intimacy. Of course, once Marva talked about Hassan, she would have to reveal much more. Naima had always been an inquisitive child and she would demand to know. But would she really, truly, want to hear all the details of her parents' sexual past, of the chaotic years Marva Dobbs and Loïc Rose had spent together before their miracle of a daughter was born?

From 1962 to 1978, Marva and Loïc were a glamorous and child-less married couple. She was the charismatic African American, tall and voluptuous, with a velvety smooth voice that only slightly blunted the edge of the clever quips she liked to dispense, in perfect English and fragmented French. He was the genial Breton with blond hair, blue eyes and a delicate-looking bone structure. Marva was a genius of black American cuisine, whose fried chicken, barbe-cued spare ribs, black-eyed peas and gumbo tasted, in the words of a famous French chef, like "culinary orgasms." Loïc, meanwhile, brought an acute business sense to the franchise that, soon after its opening in 1965, became one of Paris's landmark restaurants: Marva's Soul Food Kitchen.

Marva and Loïc were completely and utterly devoted to each other. Their emotional commitment, however, did not deter them from engaging in the movable, and fuckable, feast that was Paris in the 1960s and '70s. For the better part of two hyperkinetic decades, Marva and Loïc both engaged in one-night stands, torrid affairs and awkward on-again, off-again sexual friendships with an array of partners, some famous, some infamous, most totally obscure. But they always came home to each other. Many couples they knew well did not survive those turbulent times. But the marriage of Marva Dobbs and Loïc Rose was seemingly indestructible. Outsiders were sometimes suspicious of the couple's enduring bond. They suspected it was primarily a business arrangement. Marva knew better. She believed that she and Loïc were literally made for each other, that even if she had never come to Paris and found him, he would have gone to New York to find her. No matter how many recreational infidelities they indulged in during the wild first act of their marriage, Marva knew she and Loïc would be together forever. This was a fact beyond questioning, like an iron law of nature. It was just the way it was.

Then, at the age of thirty-seven, Marva learned she was pregnant. And the infidelities came to an abrupt halt. For sixteen years, Marva had been convinced of her barrenness. She had had two traumatic "back-alley" abortions when she lived in the States. By the time she arrived in France, her body had stopped following normal monthly cycles. She had never used birth control with Loïc or any of her other lovers in Paris. Three different obstetrician-gynecologists had informed her there was little need to. When Marva told Loïc that a child was growing inside her, they held each other and wept with joy for a full hour. There was never any doubt about paternity: The baby had been conceived in mid-August, when Marva and Loïc were alone together in Brittany. And so began the second act of their marriage: the eighteen years of raising Naima.

While Marva remained an incorrigible flirt, she no longer made love with anyone but her husband. She simply didn't have the desire, the time or the energy for affairs. And, though she had no way of knowing for sure—since she would never dream of asking him— Marva assumed that Loïc, too, had given up his extracurricular adventures. They were both too busy making a living and looking after their daughter. Besides, the sex between Marva and Loïc had always been great. Giving up sex with others was no sacrifice. It was more a conservation of energies, a concentration of appetites, an appreciation of the pleasures of monogamy. When Naima left for college,

Marva and Loïc began the third act of their marriage. Even as they entered their sixties, they were still blissfully horny for each other.

That was one reason why Marva's liaison with Hassan had come as such a shock. As ladies her age went, she was sexually satisfied, not some lonely spinster, widow or divorcée. Driving up the grand Avenue de l'Opéra—which was unusually uncongested, this being the last week of August—Marva started laughing to herself. Or was it laughing at herself? She remembered the saying, "There's no fool like an old fool." It was usually applied to some lecherous codger chasing after a gold-digging young slut. But here was Marva, a distinguished woman of a *certain âge*, as the French liked to say, obsessing on some young hunk. "Giiiiirl," she said aloud, "have you lost your mind?"

Staring up the wide boulevard at the enormous green and gold crown that adorned the top of the Garnier Opera House, Marva felt her vision turn bleary. She wondered if the brassy sunshine glittering on the crown was somehow hurting her eyes. Then she realized she was crying, weeping softly even as she continued to laugh at her foolish old self. It was her husband she was crying for. Now that they had returned from their holiday, she finally recognized the hurt that was etched on his face during those three weeks in Brittany. If Marva had occasionally noticed Loïc's sadness, she quickly forgot it, her mind returning to thoughts of Hassan. Only now did it dawn on her how painfully attentive and solicitous Loïc had been with her in Brittany. How he had behaved like an anxious suitor, almost courting her, seemingly worried that he had fallen out of her favor. Yes, Marva saw it now, saw the low-wave anguish that had gnawed at her husband all through their vacation. How could she have been so oblivious to the obvious reality? Loïc *knew*.

"Do you know, my love, how much I cherish you?" That was what Loïc Rose had asked his wife less than half an hour earlier, as she was rushing out of their apartment. He sat in the breakfast nook of the kitchen, wearing his terry cloth bathrobe, a tiny cup of espresso in front of him. "I cherish you more than anything in this world."

Marva was surprised that he had spoken to her in English. For the past five years, they had mainly communicated in French. She was in a hurry, gulping down a glass of orange juice before she walked out the door, wondering exactly what she would say to her young lover. The tenderness of Loïc's words, the words he spoke in Marva's mother tongue, caught her off guard. He smiled sadly at her, the crow's-feet at the corners of his sea blue eyes crinkling. Loïc was still a handsome man, even if there were only a few threads of blond left in his silvery head of hair.

"I love you, too, baby," Marva said, giving her husband a quick, almost absentminded peck on the lips. Then she strode out of the kitchen, her high heels clicking on the hard tile floor.

"Over, over, over," Marva said out loud, sniffing back tears and banging an open palm against the steering wheel, more determined than ever to end her affair with Hassan, even to fire him if that was what it took to kill her obsession, to spare her husband any more agony. With the *rentrée*, she had returned to her senses. She was climbing the long, steeply inclined rue Pigalle now, leaving the Paris of sparkling magnificence and entering the Paris of tawdry charm. While Marva Dobbs made her home in the elegant, *très bourgeois* Seventh Arrondissement of the city, just south of the Seine, Marva's Soul Food Kitchen had always been located up north, in the funky hills of Montmartre, the heart of the roiling, multicultural, eternally bohemian Eighteenth Arrondissement.

Marva pulled into her specially reserved parking spot, right in front of the restaurant, on the rue Véron. It was exactly 11:30 A.M. She stepped out of the car, took a deep breath, composed her face into a mask of serenity, then walked through the front door. All morning, Marva had hoped to shock her staff. As she entered the restaurant, she could see that she had succeeded. The hell of it was that Marva was as shocked to see all of them, clustered in front of the bar, in a semicircle around a strange visitor, as they were to see her.

"Oh my sweet Jesus," Jeremy Hairston said. He was an un-abashedly gay brother from Arkansas, a head-held-high drama queen who was also the most reliable manager Marva had ever hired. As she had for the past eleven years, Marva had trusted Jeremy to run the restaurant while she was away. She had known he would be upset by her showing up early like this, but from the desperate tone in his voice, she knew that something else was going on.

Jeremy was flanked by the two waitresses: Véronique, from Viet-nam, and Mylène, from Montpellier. Standing slightly apart from the trio, but still facing the doorway Marva had just stepped through, was Benoît, the Guadeloupian number-one cook. Benoît was supposed to have been on vacation until the end of August, leav-ing Hassan in charge of the kitchen. But Hassan was nowhere in sight. Marva knew damn well that Hassan was not the man with his back to her, the short, squat figure the other staffers had partially surrounded.

"Bonjour," Marva said warily.

The stranger slowly turned to face her. Marva recognized him immediately but could not find a name to attach to the face. He had a pasty complexion and greasy black hair atop his perfectly round head. He wore a beige polyester-looking suit, a wide-collared yellow shirt and a tacky, awkwardly knotted brown tie. Holding a little spi-ral notebook in one hand and a ballpoint pen in the other, he flashed a sickly, somehow insinuating smile. Then he began to sing.

"Wheeeen oh wheeeeen will you be miiiiiiiiiiiine?" the ugly lit-tle man warbled.

The line was from the one hit song recorded by Marva and the Marvalines, the bewigged and satin-gowned early-sixties quartet Madame Dobbs had fronted before going into the restaurant busi-ness. That was when Marva remembered who the stranger was: In-spector Denis Lamouche, one of the top cops in the Eighteenth Arrondissement. Marva and Jeremy usually referred to Lamouche, behind his back, of course, by the English translation of his surname: the housefly. A fan of American pop music and all-around pain in the ass, Lamouche appeared in the restaurant about once every six months—but never at eleven thirty in the morning.

"Hello, Inspector," Marva said coolly, knowing that Lamouche enjoyed speaking English.

"Oh, *madame,* I am so happy to see you zis day."

"And to what do we owe the pleasure of your visit?"

Nodding his pale melon of a head and still smiling his creepy smile, Lamouche said, "I am here to inquire about an employee of your."

"Yes?"

"Hassan Mekachera."

"I see." Marva maintained a polite and studiously neutral expression. "Isn't he here?"

"No, *madame.* According to your ozer employees, Hassan has not been here since three days."

"Oh really?"

"Really. And I have reason to believe zat zis Hassan Mekachera, he was—how do you say?—working anozer job. Moonlighting."

"Moonlighting?" Now Marva could not conceal her surprise. "As what?"

Inspector Lamouche tilted his perfectly round head, practically leering at Marva. "A terrorist."

Two

WHY THE HELL WOULD anybody want to blow up the WORTHEE building?

Marva's attention was split between the images on the TV above the bar and the nattering of Inspector Lamouche.

"Zis is what I tell you," the cop said. "Ze Wurzee was assaulted."

Now Marva got it. She saw the twisted, faintly smoking carcass of the automobile. At first she thought it was a suicide bombing or the result of some helicopter gunship attack in Israel, the daily dose of madman violence from the Middle East. Then she saw the blackened façade of the building, the door-sized windows with the glass blown out. She recognized the street, barred off by police barricades, a stretch of Avenue Victor Hugo in the ultraposh Sixteenth Arrondissement,

crammed with the shining red vans and engines of the *pompiers*—
France's proud, silver-helmeted firefighter/rescue worker/emergency
response corps—a blue-and-white ambulance, cop cars and camera
crews. She got a good look at the mansion that had obviously been the
target of the car bomb. She knew it well, the headquarters of the World
Organization for Research into Technology, Health, Education and
the Environment, more commonly referred to by its acronym:
WORTHEE.

The television news reporter pronounced the name of the non-
profit organization in the usual French manner: *"Wor-TAY."* But Inspector Lamouche, wanting to speak English with Marva, had tried
to say it like an American. She hadn't understood what he was babbling about, what "Wurzee" was or what in God's name Hassan
Mekachera, a dreamy, mild-mannered sous-chef, would have to do
with any terrorist attack anywhere.

But Marva had always had cordial relations with the local police
so she offered Lamouche a seat and a cup of coffee, said she'd be
happy to answer any questions and tried not to show how completely
discombobulated she felt. She hadn't even had a chance to greet her
staff. Jeremy had hustled Benoît, Véronique and Mylène into the
kitchen, then went behind the bar and set about making two cups of
espresso.

"What a disgrace zis is," Lamouche said, shaking his head. On
the TV screen, a camera panned across the lobby of the WORTHEE
building, lingering on the shards of glass scattered across the marble
floor. Marva was trying to listen to the reporter's voice-over but Lamouche kept talking. "Fortunately," he said, "ze blast come at four in
ze morning. Imagine if zey strike at ze busy time of ze day. Zere
would be catastrophe. A bloodbaz. As it is, all ze same, zere was one
casualty. A man who happen to be on ze sidewalk. His condition is
critical."

Before she could control it, choke it back, Marva gasped. "Not
Hassan!"

Inspector Lamouche seemed to suppress a smirk. "No. Not him."

Jeremy sashayed over to the table, set down the two cups of coffee and gave Marva a discreet wink. *"Voilà,"* he said softly.

Marva and Lamouche both said, *"Merci."* As Jeremy disappeared into the kitchen, Marva wondered what, if anything, he had told Lamouche about Hassan. About Hassan and her.

"Zis Hassan Mekachera disappear on Friday and Monday morning, ze Wurzee is assaulted."

Marva managed to stifle a nervous laugh. "I'm sorry, Inspector, but maybe I'm missing something here. What's the connection?"

Lamouche's eyes narrowed as he raised the coffee cup to his lips and said, "Zat is precisely what I try to discover."

The TV reporter, standing in front of the snarled hunk of burnt metal that had once been a four-door Fiat, said that the target of the attack was a twenty-nine-year-old institution devoted to "nonpolitcal research." What he did not say was that WORTHEE had always been considered by the United States government to be a suspicious but relatively harmless tool of the United Nations, a think tank of liberal bent but little influence that hosted academic seminars where like-minded people talked at each other about the need to create a world of technologically advanced, robustly healthy, well-educated persons who would breathe pristine air and drink pure water, and cultural events where the diversity of the earth's peoples was assiduously celebrated. WORTHEE's main purpose, however, was producing massive piles of earnest studies that nobody anywhere ever read. Over the years, Marva had known scores of WORTHEE employees. They came from all over the planet but all tended to share similar traits. They were brainy dilettantes, people who wished to do good but were not overly motivated. They wanted to do their part to make the world a better place—but they wanted to do it from within the confines of a plush Paris office. With lots of benefits and leisurely lunches. All in all, they were awfully nice folks. In fact, Marva had just catered their Fourth of July celebration eight weeks earlier.

Marva said out loud what she had been thinking since she saw the images on TV: "Why the hell would anybody want to blow up the WORTHEE building?"

"Did you and Hassan ever discuss politics?" Lamouche asked.

"We only ever talked about food," Marva replied. This was more or less true. Food and fucking had been their twin passions during their four-week affair.

"Would you say he was a friend? As, say, Jeremy is a friend?"

Lamouche's question was freighted with insinuation but Marva couldn't understand what he was insinuating. Did he think she was boffing Jeremy, as well as Hassan? Didn't he know Jeremy was gay? Or was he asking if Hassan was, like Jeremy, gay, and if Marva had some kind of fag hag fixation on both of them? Whatever the innuendo, Marva was pissed. Who the fuck did Lamouche think he was? Marva leaned back in her chair, put her fists on her hips and eyeballed Lamouche long and hard. She saw tiny pearls of sweat pop up across the cop's oily forehead.

"*Qu'est-ce que tu veux dire?*"

It was gutsy enough for Marva to have asked Lamouche, "What is it you want to say?" but she had also addressed him using the informal *tu* instead of the formal *vous*. As an American, this meant nothing to Marva. But she knew that, to a French cop like Lamouche, she had just fired a gooey gob of spit in his eye. Lamouche's face was turning a deep, bruised-looking shade of pink. He continued to address Marva in English. "I would like to see all ze paperwork you have on Hassan Mekachera. Paysheets, et cetera. If you please."

Marva rose from the table, climbed the stairs to her office, quickly pulled Hassan's thin dossier from the file cabinet, went back downstairs and handed the folder to Inspector Lamouche. "That's all I've got," she said. "He was only hired four months ago. I can't say I really knew Hassan." This, too, was more or less true.

Lamouche was all clammy politeness now. "Oh, zank you very much, *madame*. Iz only too kind."

"Don't hesitate to call if I can help you in any other way, Inspector," Marva said, mimicking his manner.

"It looks like you will have to find anozer cook."

"For the time being, perhaps."

"Oh, I almost forget to mention to you, zis person, who was very badly wounded in ze car bombing zis morning. . . . He was not just nobody. . . . Zis was a very important personage."

"Who was it?"

"Ze name has not been released to ze public."

"Oh, come on," Marva cooed. "You can tell me."

Lamouche leered. "All I can tell you is . . . whoever was responsible for zis bombing, I pity zese mens. Zey don't gots long to live." Lamouche extended a sweaty palm. Marva shook it. "See you soon, *madame*."

"*Ciao.*"

It must have been sometime in early June, that night when Jeremy had tried to bust Hassan. Benoît had had to return to Guadeloupe for his father's funeral. A sudden tragedy. He would be gone for a week. Marva's number-one cook for six years, Benoît had always been responsible for hiring his assistant in the kitchen. Marva had learned to respect Benoît's judgment. Though Hassan Mekachera had joined the staff only a month earlier, Benoît had trusted him to run the kitchen while he was away. Marva had hardly ever noticed Hassan. It always took several months for her to feel familiar with a new cook or waitress. But if Benoît had had enough faith in Hassan to leave him in charge, Marva was not going to worry about it. She planned to spend her evenings at the restaurant the way she usually did, charming the customers, flitting from table to table or sitting at the bar holding court with old acquaintances, first-time clients and/or tourists who had heard the myth of Marva Dobbs and were now thrilled to meet the *grande dame* in the flesh. If, in Benoît's absence,

there was any problem, Jeremy Hairston, who ordinarily managed
the place, dealing with seatings, bill paying and all the unpredictable
nightly hassles of running a restaurant, could help out in the
kitchen. Jeremy had, after all, started out as a cook at Marva's. But
on those nights when Jeremy was forced to labor over a hot stove,
Marva had to fill his usual role, actually overseeing the joint instead
of doing the job she had grown to love: simply being the celebrity
hostess, telling anecdotes, flirting like mad, exulting in her unique
Marva-ness, her special status as a local legend, a walking, talking
piece of Afro-American-in-Paris history, a living, breathing tourist
attraction.

That night in June had been crazy busy. Jeremy had spent the
entire evening in the kitchen and was none too happy about it.
Marva, having to take Jeremy's place as manager, was equally
grouchy. Then, at the peak of the near pandemonium, Jeremy came
storming out of the kitchen, his floppy white pillow of a chef's hat
askew, his apron splattered with grease and barbecue sauce. "Hassan's been fucking with the fried chicken recipe," Jeremy huffed.

Entering the kitchen, Marva got her first really good look at the
new cook, truly saw him for the first time, though he had been working in the restaurant for a month already. He stood beside one of the
massive stoves, his hands behind his back, the faint trace of an insou-
ciant smile on his lips. One row of buttons on his white, high-collared,
double-breasted chef's blouse was undone to the midpoint of his
chest, the flap hanging open, revealing a sheer white undershirt.
There was a mischievous schoolboy aspect about Hassan. His head
was slightly bowed and Marva could see his eyes twinkling beneath
the ragged curtain of light chestnut hair that fell across his forehead.
His eyes were hazel and somewhat sleepy, giving him the distracted,
not-all-there look of certain saints and sociopaths. And that sweet
honey gold skin he had. But more than the looks, it was the vibe he
emitted that staggered Marva. Staring at Hassan, absorbing his concentrated energy, Marva experienced an erotic rush of a visceral, a
glandular, power that she had not felt in a couple of decades.

Jeremy raised a drumstick, holding it gingerly between thumb and forefinger like some sort of contaminated specimen. "Here, Marva, taste this," he said, glaring accusingly at Hassan.

Marva took hold of the chicken leg and, keeping her eyes on Hassan, bit into it. Her teeth cracked the paper-fine layer of crusty batter, sank into the plump hot flesh. She felt the juiciness spread in her mouth, all the time keeping her eyes on Hassan, who seemed to look back at her, under the cover of his light brown bangs, in bemused insolence. That was when Marva tasted it, the tang, the pungent, vaguely Oriental flavor. Not soy sauce or sesame oil but something sharp and surprising and definitely not part of Marva's classic recipe, the secret formula that every cook who worked there was required to replicate, dish after dish, night after night. In fact, Marva Dobbs was known to fly into plate-smashing rages if a cook dared to deviate from the recipe.

Marva looked at Jeremy as she chewed, savored the startling new flavor. Her right-hand man had both eyebrows raised expectantly. Jeremy was waiting for Marva to explode at Hassan, then thank him for exposing this insubordinate little punk.

Marva swallowed, returned her gaze to Hassan, who continued to look both bad and bashful. "I try some new spices," Hassan said in liltingly accented English.

Marva turned to Jeremy. "I love it."

Jeremy started blinking rapidly. "Say what?"

"I appreciate initiative in my employees. Give Hassan a ten percent raise."

Marva whipped around and strode out of the kitchen, leaving Jeremy flabbergasted and Hassan still half smiling insolently.

"GIRLFRIEND!" Charisse Bray shouted. "What are you doing back so soon?"

Monday, August 27, 2001; 11:50 A.M. Inspector Lamouche was hardly out the door when Charisse came sweeping into the restaurant, a couple dozen African-American tourists in tow. Charisse wore a billowing purple linen tent dress and an elaborate hair weave, long black braids curled and twirled around each other, piled high atop her head like a ropy crown. An ebullient fifty-something divorcée from Buffalo, New York, Charisse had lived in France for six years. Nevertheless, she spoke very little French, had practically no French friends and only the vaguest notion of what was going on, at any given time, in French political or cultural life.

Charisse associated almost exclusively with other Americans in Paris and made a decent living as a sort of professional black American expatriate. She gave visiting black Americans guided tours of Paris neighborhoods where famous black American expats had lived and worked, ran a Web site offering helpful hints to black Americans who planned to come to Paris for long or short stays (where to hear the best jazz, meet other black Americans) and organized lectures and discussion groups about black American expat perspectives on political issues that affected black Americans back in America: all profit-making endeavors for Charisse Bray. Though a lot of black folks in Paris considered Charisse a crass and shameless hustler, others, like Marva, figured every American in Paris had a hustle, be it translating texts, running a restaurant, singing the blues or greasing the wheels of globalized markets in some corporate gig. As American expat hustles went, Charisse's was, at least, educational. And, as no tour of black American Paris would be complete without a meal at Marva's Soul Food Kitchen, Charisse Bray was always good for business.

"I thought you weren't coming back till next week!" Charisse cried as she threw her arms around Marva.

"The weather in Brittany was miserable," Marva lied. She kissed Charisse once on each cheek. "So we decided to come back early."

"Everybody! Everybody!" Charisse waved frantically at the tourists still streaming into the restaurant. "She's here! She's here! This is Marva Dobbs! This is her! My homegirl Marva!"

On cue, Marva went into her *grande dame* act—which was not

artificial, just a specially selected aspect of her personality, a flamboyant garment she could easily put on or take off—meeting and greeting the good people of the Los Angeles chapter of the African American Book Lovers Association. Their six-day literary tour was focused on the various old stomping grounds of Langston Hughes, Claude McKay and Gwendolyn Bennett, of Richard Wright, James Baldwin and Chester Himes. And Charisse had arranged meetings for the group with the two living giants of African-American literature in Paris, James Emanuel and Barbara Chase-Riboud. While a lunch at Marva's Soul Food Kitchen was part of the package deal they'd signed with Charisse, the L.A. Book Lovers thought they'd missed their chance to see Madame Dobbs herself. Now here she was, every inch the diva in her sleek midnight black Yves Saint Laurent pantsuit, but still down-home and utterly unpretentious, hugging and kissing folks, making everybody feel comfortable. No one among the twenty-four guests would have imagined that Marva's mind was reeling, that all she wanted to do was find her young lover, to know that Hassan Mekachera was alive and well and not a fugitive terrorist.

Jeremy Hairston came striding out of the kitchen to meet and seat people but before he could say hello to anyone, Marva sensed his presence behind her, spun away from the tourist she had been speaking to and grabbed her manager by the arm, sinking her fingernails deep into his left triceps.

"Ow!" Jeremy squealed.

"We need to talk," Marva hissed.

"I know, I know," Jeremy said under his breath. "But right now we have two dozen hungry Negroes to feed, so lemme go!"

"Have you tried to call Hassan?"

"Of course I have. I called the only number I have for him, his portable, all day and all night Friday and Saturday and there was never any answer. I was freaking out, Marva. You don't know what a busy week this is gonna be. It was just lucky I was able to reach Benoît and he came back from his vacation. Speaking of which, what are you doing here anyway?"

Marva ignored the question. "Why didn't you call me in Brittany to tell me?"

"What? About Hassan?" Jeremy smirked. "I thought maybe he was with you." He pulled away from Marva and plunged into the crowd, smiling broadly.

Marva smiled too, smiled through the appetizers and main courses, smiled for photos with the guests she always loved the best, the sisters and brothers from back home. But all the time, she was screaming inside, shouting abuse at Hassan, who had disappeared; at Inspector Lamouche, who had been so insinuating and suspicious; at Jeremy, who had so smugly assumed more than he knew; at Loïc, who had looked so pathetic this morning in his terry cloth bathrobe, clutching his tiny coffee cup and telling Marva, cryptically, in English, how much he cherished her: at all the men who were making her feel suddenly afraid.

"So Marva Dobbs was over here in the summer of sixty-three, on a ten-city European tour, with the Marvalines," Charisse Bray informed a table full of Book Lovers as the waitresses came around with dessert: trays full of cheesecake, ambrosia, chocolate mousse and watermelon. Marva stood nearby, not bothering to correct Charisse yet; to tell her that it was a six-city tour in the spring of '62. "And the group's manager, Sy Abraham—"

"Sid Abromowitz," Marva interjected.

"He dropped dead of a cerebral hemorrhage," Charisse continued, undeterred.

"Actually, it was a heart attack."

"In the middle of the . . ." Charisse paused, trying to remember.

"Boulevard Saint-Germain," Marva said. It was *her* story, after all, but Charisse obviously wanted to tell it.

"Exactly!" Charisse said. "And the four—"

"Three."

"Marvalines, they bugged out. The ambulance took Sy away and he had all their money and their passports and none of them spoke

French. But God was watching over Marva and the Marvalines because the assistant manager at their hotel, Laurence—"

"Loïc," Marva said.

"He spoke English and saved the day. And, of course, he fell
madly in love with Marva," Charisse continued.

"And Marva with him."

"The Marvalines went back to the States but Marva stayed in
Paris and one day, Laur . . . I mean, Loïc, asked Marva to marry him
and Marva said, 'I ain't marryin' no assistant hotel manager. You're
gettin' your butt back in school.' "

"Or words to that effect."

"And Loïc went back to school and became an investment
banker."

"Tax attorney," Marva said.

"And they're still married to this day," Charisse concluded.

"*Happily* married," Marva clarified.

The Book Lovers applauded enthusiastically.

Marva's thoughts raced. How could Hassan be a terrorist? He
was a spacey, irresponsible boy-man who loved food, fucking, and
children. Yes, he did love children. Making them at least. As Marva
began saying good-bye to the Book Lovers, she wondered how she
might track down one of the four mothers of Hassan's seven kids.
Had she ever known any of their names? Could any of them tell her
where he had been the past two or three days? Maybe there had been
a family emergency, a problem with one of the kids, a subsequent
communications breakdown with his cell phone. That didn't mean
he was a terrorist! So far as Marva could tell, Hassan was apolitical
and areligious. There certainly didn't seem to be any violence in him,
any desire to blow things up. But what did Marva really know about
Hassan? She needed to find him. Just as soon as the tour group was
out of there.

"Oh, mercy, mercy, mercy buckoo," Charisse said, squeezing
Marva in her arms. Marva knew that Charisse wanted to be a closer

friend to her, to be taken into her golden circle. They had a lot in common, including daughters the same age living in New York City. But as much as Marva liked Charisse, she'd always been wary of getting too chummy with her. Not out of any distrust but just because of the transience of so many Americans in Paris. It had happened to Marva countless times over the years: Just as a friend had come to feel as tight as family, she would migrate back to the States, returning only to visit Paris, never to live here again. Despite constantly saying how in love she was with France, Charisse Bray was precisely the sort of sister who always, sooner or later, moved back to America.

Still embracing, Charisse whispered in Marva's ear, "So what's this I hear about you and Hassan?" Marva jerked away as if Charisse had just bit her. Charisse, unfazed, flashed an admiring grin. "You go, girl!" she said. Then she turned around and followed the last of the Book Lovers out the door.

Now Marva was really mad. Nobody—not Jeremy and certainly not Charisse—could have known, really known, about her affair with Hassan.

More lunchtime customers walked in. Marva couldn't think straight. She had to get away, go someplace where she could calm down, gather her thoughts. She rushed out of the restaurant and got into her car. Driving south, heading home, Marva pulled her cell phone from her handbag and punched in Hassan's number. She listened to six beeps, then was cut off—nothing but dial tone. Just like Jeremy said. And, like Jeremy, Marva had only this one cell phone number for Hassan. *Merde.* She remembered the address he had given her: It was in one of the grittier sections of Montreuil, a suburb just east of Paris. Hassan said he shared an apartment with his cousin, Ramzi, a garbage collector. But Marva didn't have a phone number for Ramzi. She didn't even know if he had the same surname as Hassan. *Merde merde merde.*

Marva felt a migraine coming on, expanding painfully in her head like a balloon. She needed to lie down, to be alone. She drove faster, taking a tight, almost reckless turn around the towering

Egyptian obelisk at the center of the Place de la Concorde. Marva wondered if Loïc would be home. No, there was little danger of that. If he had been too lazy to go to his office, then, on a fine August afternoon like this, he would have strolled over to the Jardin du Luxembourg to play *boules*. Good, Marva thought, Loïc wouldn't see her so distressed, wouldn't be there to ask prying questions. Her head throbbed. She began to wonder again just how much Loïc knew. If he had indeed guessed that she had a lover. Maybe she should confess, tell her husband about her dirty deed, her betrayal. Admit that right now she was more obsessed than ever with Hassan, obsessed with tracking him down, finding his—

E-mail! Yes, she could try to find Hassan that way. She suddenly remembered how he was always going off to cybercafés to check his electronic letterbox. Marva had noticed these shops popping up all over Barbès, the sprawling African-Arab neighborhood just a few blocks from her restaurant. The cybercafés were usually not cafés at all, since most of them didn't serve food or beverages. They were grim little joints where people paid hourly rates to sit in front of computer screens. Like many other immigrants and children of immigrants in Paris in the early twenty-first century, Hassan couldn't afford a computer—but he had found e-mail indispensable. Once, in July, during the dead late-afternoon hours between the lunch and dinner seatings, Hassan was heading out into the pouring rain in search of a terminal. Marva offered to give him an old computer of hers.

"I have a PowerBook I never even use anymore," she said. "Think of all the money you'll save if you don't have to rent time at a cybercafé."

But Hassan had politely refused. Marva, figuring he did not want to feel like a charity case, didn't press the issue.

Now, as she whipped past the imposing Assemblée Nationale building and turned onto the Boulevard Saint-Germain, Marva realized she could locate Hassan via the Internet. The only problem was that she had absolutely no idea what his e-mail address was. *"Merde,"* she hissed.

Head pounding, eyes beginning to water, Marva was startled to
see the traffic light she was approaching, at the intersection of Saint-
Germain and the rue de l'Université, change from green to yellow.
She knew she was going too fast to stop short. She would just have to
race through the light as it flashed red. Had it not been for the migraine and the tears in her eyes, she would have spotted the motorcy-
clist sooner, before he came roaring out of the rue de l'Université and
directly into her path. Marva managed to swerve away from the man
on the moto, missing him by inches. She heard the screech of tires as
she tried to keep control of the Audi. She saw a group of tourists scat-
ter as her car careered across the bus lane, toward the sidewalk.
Marva let go one last cry of *"Merde!"* as the car smashed into one of
the plane trees that lined the elegant boulevard and the airbag exploded in her face.

Three

NAIMA ROSE WAS AFRAID of the Place Saint-Michel. Or, more specifically, of the grime-covered statues that decorated the huge fountain at the center of the square. It had gotten to the point where she begged her parents, when they walked through the Latin Quarter, to take side streets in order to avoid passing the statues. "The place gives me nightmares, let's go the other way," she would whimper-whine in that implacable manner of a seven-year-old child. Marva and Loïc had always given in to Naima's demand for a detour, however impractical or inconvenient it might be. But late one autumn afternoon, Naima's papa decided to banish his daughter's fear by explaining Saint-Michel to her.

"He was an archangel, the prince of all the other angels in heaven," Papa said.

Naima and her papa stood right in front of the fountain, the jets of water swooshing loudly and splashing into the stone pool. The sky was turning orange, the same color as the leaves that whipped around Naima and Loïc as they stared up at the looming statues. Already, just standing there before the fountain, the wind biting pleasantly at her plump little cheeks, Naima felt somewhat less scared of the eerily lifelike, soot-encrusted figures towering above her.

"There was a great battle in heaven," Papa continued, "and Saint-Michel led the angels in fighting Satan and his army of demons and dragons. And here you see him in victory: Michel, or, as you would call him in English, Michael."

Only then did it occur to Naima how odd it was that Papa was speaking to her in English. Ordinarily, when Maman was not around, Papa spoke to her in French. Naima spoke both languages equally well but she had a fairly rigid sense of when to use one or the other. French was the language of the classroom and the playground, the language of the streets and shops. English was the language of the home, the language of Maman's faraway country, America, the language of Maman's family and closest friends and many of the people who ate at Maman's restaurant. Maman and Papa and Naima together spoke English but Papa and Naima alone did not. Until this afternoon in the Place Saint-Michel. Somehow, Papa's using English made what he said more, rather than less, intimate; more tender and meaningful.

"See," Papa said, "Michael holds his sword in his right hand while his left hand points up to heaven."

Naima gazed at the archangel's long, blackened wings and his impassive dirty face. "Is that the devil he's standing on?" Naima asked her papa, following his lead and speaking in English.

"Yes, it is," Papa said with a chuckle. "And doesn't old Satan look ridiculous with his sour expression?"

"He does!" Naima said, letting out a little squeal of a laugh. Satan was curled beneath Michael's feet, arms crossed in vexation, scowling miserably. He was a grotesque man-beast, with a bare, human chest, horns like little bumps growing out of his forehead, small batlike wings and a long, fat, reptilian tail. But this was the first time Naima had ever found the grimacing, hook-nosed statue funny instead of frightening.

"He looks like he's thinking, 'Oh, brother!' " Papa said. " 'Now I have to go back down to hell.' "

Naima giggled. "Saint-Michel kicked his behind!"

Papa smiled and shook his head. "You sound just like Maman."

"What about those monsters?" Naima asked, turning suddenly serious, as if remembering that she was still very much afraid of the two fierce and massive creatures that flanked the statues of Saint-Michel and Satan. They were twins, each bearing the head of a lion, wings of a bat and coiled lizard's tail—but with a far broader and scarier wingspan than Satan's and tails longer and fatter than his as well. Violent streams of water gushed out of the creatures' gaping, long-toothed jaws.

"Those were Satan's dragons," Papa said knowledgeably, reassuringly. "Saint-Michel conquered and tamed them so they pose no danger for people."

"*Ah bon?*" Naima said, nodding and lapsing into French, responding to Loïc with the equivalent of "Oh really?"

"Let us read the plaques under the two dragons," Papa said, staying in English. "Can you read the Roman numerals written in the stone there?"

Naima spelled out the letters slowly, trying to remember the number that corresponded to each one: "M . . . C . . . M . . . X . . . L . . . I . . . V . . . Um, one thousand . . . uh . . . one hundred . . . er . . ."

"It says nineteen forty-four," Papa said gently. "What year is it now?"

"Nineteen eighty-five," Naima quickly replied.

"Exactly," Papa said. "And how many years difference is there between nineteen forty-four and nineteen eighty-five?"

Naima paused, patiently watching the equation take shape in her mind's eye, like figures on a blackboard. "Forty-one."

"Precisely," Papa said, with just the faintest flicker of pride in his voice. "They could not fit many words on this stone tablet. But it tells what happened on this very spot forty-one years ago."

"Was that during the war?" All through her short life, Naima had heard French adults speak ominously of *la guerre*, some long-ago cataclysm that still seemed to haunt them.

"For Paris, it was the end of the war," Papa said. "This was where one of the last battles to liberate the city took place. Right here, where we stand. The German army—the Nazis—invaded Paris in 1940. For four long years, the Nazis controlled us. Finally, in August of 1944, the people of Paris rose up against the oppressors. For six days, ordinary people fought the Nazis with any weapons they could find. Guns they had hidden. Kitchen knives. Even cobblestones that they tore from the streets to hurl at the enemy. At the same time, two great armies, the French and the American, were racing across France, coming to chase away the Nazis. There was much gunfire, explosions of grenades in the streets. Nowhere was the fighting more violent than here in the Place Saint-Michel. Come, I show you something."

Papa took Naima by the hand and led her to the side of the fountain. He squatted and pointed to various small holes in the stone. "Those are bullet marks," he said.

Naima gasped. *"Oh là là."*

"Yes," Papa continued, "many brave Parisians died on this spot. Many of them were members of the Resistance, that is to say, the secret forces who had spied against the Nazis during the occupation. And many were also Communists. Do you know what that means?"

"No, Papa."

"It is a political organization, an ideology. Communists have done some very bad things in the world but the Communists in Paris during the war were among the bravest people, willing to fight and to die for freedom. Do you know who General LeClerc was?"

"I don't think so."

"He was a courageous French soldier. And he led the French army into Paris during this battle. The streets here were filled with French army tanks. The French soldiers killed the last of the Nazis who had not already fled. And it is very appropriate that victory was won on this spot. Do you know why?"

"No, Papa."

"Because Saint-Michel is the patron saint of France. He is the angel who protects our country."

Naima was awestruck by all that her papa had told her. She looked up at the statue of the archangel. *"Merci, Saint-Michel."*

Papa laughed lightly. He pulled Naima close to him, kissed her cheek and stroked her curly hair. "I was here then, you know."

"You were?"

"Yes, we lived very close to here, on the rue Hautefeuille."

"Did you fight in the battle?"

"Oh, I wanted to. But I was only ten years old. My mother wouldn't let me out of the house."

"And your father?"

"He died before the war, back when we lived in Bretagne. It was after my father died that we moved to Paris. Anyway, my mother finally let me out just as the battle ended. It was extraordinary. Where only a few hours before there had been horrific bloodshed, now the streets were filled with people cheering. The Americans had arrived and huge caravans of tanks and jeeps, decorated with the stars and bars of the U.S. flag, came rolling down our streets. And I will never forget, a row of trucks filled with black United States soldiers. I had never before seen such big groups of brown-skinned men. One of the soldiers reached down and lifted me up onto the truck. They were so nice to me, those black American soldiers. I rode through the streets with them, cheering and waving a little American flag. Such wonderful men. They gave me chocolate candy and chewing gum, treats I had not had in four years." Papa was smiling but Naima could see tears glimmering in his eyes. "During the next days I was a sort of errand boy for a whole platoon of black soldiers. They taught me the first English I ever learned and I translated things for them. They were so kind to this fatherless little French boy. I met many white American soldiers, also, but they were not so nice. They were not cruel but they just did not have the humanity, the warmth and open-heartedness of the black soldiers." Loïc Rose looked down at his amber-toned daughter, smiling sweetly as a single tear rolled down his cheek. "I have loved black Americans ever since."

And from that day forward, Naima loved the Place Saint-Michel.

Monday, August 27, 2001. New York City. Naima Rose was showing off. Not grandiosely but in a smooth and subtle way. Really, she was just being herself. But she could tell that her colleagues were astounded.

It was one of those airless, sweltering American summer days. There was a break in the filming as the director paced about the set, grumbling to herself. The production had sealed off a block of Charles Street for the day's shoot. With its redbrick townhouses and tree-lined quaintness, this part of Greenwich Village was one of the few New York neighborhoods that reminded Naima of Europe, though it evoked London or Amsterdam more than it did her home-town. Naima leaned against a big white trailer, trying to be as inconspicuous as possible. As third assistant director, her job consisted mainly of taking orders from the first and second assistant directors and bossing around the members of the on-set life-form just beneath hers, the production assistants. Naima knew she should feel lucky. She had a pretty good gig for a twenty-three-year-old smack in the middle of her graduate film school studies. This production was at the high end of low-budget independent cinema. Everyone told Naima that even if she didn't learn all that much on the set, the job would "look great" on her résumé. While the crew buzzed about the set trying to look busy as the director attempted to figure out how she wanted to shoot the next scene, Naima hoped no one was going to ask her to do anything. She was hot and tired and grumpy. This was the first time in her life she had spent the entire month of August working.

Naima was just starting to fantasize about lying on the beach in Brittany when the second assistant director came up to her, accompanied by a woman who looked a bit like the actress Juliette Binoche. Naima knew it was not Binoche but she was dead certain that the woman was French. The second A.D. introduced Naima to her friend, Isabelle. "She's visiting from Paris."

"Bonjour," Naima said.

And from the way Naima uttered that one word, Isabelle knew she'd met a compatriot. *"Bonjour, chère amie!"* she said excitedly.

A small crowd of crew members gathered around Naima and Isabelle as they prattled away in rapid-fire French, discussing their different Paris neighborhoods and the places Isabelle should visit during her stay in New York. Out of the corner of her eye, Naima could see the astonishment in her colleagues' faces. That was when she began to show off, speaking even faster with Isabelle, laughing more knowingly, gesturing more extravagantly. Naima recognized the looks she was getting. After living in the United States for five years, she knew that younger Americans were often surprised to hear a white peer speak perfect French. When they heard a black peer do it, they were downright shocked.

Naima was really flaunting her fluency when she noticed that the director, Saskia Gruber, had joined the crowd of onlookers. Saskia was a pale and intense, spiky-haired *auteur* whose first feature, a lesbian coming-of-age story, had been an audience favorite at the Sundance Film Festival and a moderate box-office hit. There was a lot riding on the film she was shooting now, her second feature, a lesbian romantic comedy. "Less edgy than my first film," Saskia often said, "but, you know, still kinda quirky." The fact that she had a deal with Miramax and was considered a talent to watch made Saskia extremely nervous, and her anxiety had spread to most of the cast and crew. She agonized constantly over "sending the right message" with the film. Though Saskia was enough of a feminist to have hired a predominately female crew, she was enough of an arrogant jerk to treat most of her sisters in arms with a rudeness bordering on contempt. During the three weeks of shooting, Saskia had hardly said a word to Naima, except to bark the occasional command at her when the first or second A.D. was not nearby to receive her orders. Now, as the second A.D. escorted her guest Isabelle to the trailer where the lead actresses were getting made up, Saskia Gruber approached Naima, looking at once bewildered and impressed. "Wow," the director said, "your French is incredible. Where did you learn to speak like that?"

"At home," Naima replied in her perfectly flat American accent.

"Where are you from?" Saskia asked before quickly blurting out, "No wait, let me guess!"

As Saskia squinted at the third A.D., seeming to concentrate on her bronze skin and short, tightly coiled, light brown dreadlocks, Naima felt she could read her boss's mind, hear her saying to herself, *And I thought Naima, or whatever her name is, was just a regular African American.*

Finally, after several seconds of scrutiny, Saskia said, "You're from . . . Haiti!"

"Nope," Naima said.

Saskia seemed startled that she had guessed wrong. "Um . . . okay . . . Martinique?"

"Nope."

Now Saskia looked completely stumped. "Tunisia?"

"Actually," Naima said, "I'm from France."

An electronic bleat was heard and everyone in the vicinity reached for their cell phones. Naima was surprised to find that she was the one receiving the call. "Yes?"

"Hello, my sweetie?" her father's voice asked. There was a good deal of static on the line, and a faint echo.

"Papa?"

"I tried you at home," Loïc said, in his softly accented English, "and spoke to Darvin. He gave me the number of your portable."

Naima suddenly felt as if she were about to faint. The crew members who, a moment earlier, had been gathered around her, fairly gawking, had now dispersed. Naima slumped against the trailer to keep from falling down. She was certain that her mother had died. Why else would Papa be calling her, out of the blue, like this? It had been weeks since they'd spoken. "What happened?"

"I'm afraid I have some bad news," Loïc said in that politely measured, "brace yourself" tone of his that Naima had come to detest.

"*Quoi?*" she snapped.

"Your mother is in the hospital."

"*Mon Dieu.*"

"She had a car accident this afternoon."

"In Douarnenez?"

"Um, no," Loïc said, sounding extremely uncomfortable. Naima could practically hear him squirming. "We returned early from Brittany. Maman had a wreck on the Boulevard Saint-Germain. We're not sure how serious are her injuries. But I think she needs you at her side."

Naima was still slumped against the trailer, struggling to stay on her feet. "Is Maman going to live?" she whispered.

"I'm sorry, Naima, but we don't have much time. Your mother needs you here. Can you catch a flight to Paris tonight?"

"Huh?" Naima reflexively looked at her watch: four o'clock. That meant that in Paris it was already ten at night. "I don't know. Yes, I can try."

"I've made a reservation for you on a seven o'clock flight out of JFK. Can you make that?"

The static on the line grew louder. Naima wasn't sure she had understood. "You made me a reservation?"

"Yes. Listen, Naima, this is a bad connection. Go to your apartment and I'll call you there. I can give you all the flight details. I'll meet you at Charles de Gaulle tomorrow morning."

"Wait a minute," Naima said, finally getting a grip. "I want to talk with Maman."

"I'm very sorry," Loïc said, sounding pained again. "Maman is still unconscious."

Naima felt tears sting her eyes. "Shit."

"Just go home and pack your bags."

"Okay. I'll do that. I will. *Merci, Papa.*"

"*Bon courage*, my sweetie."

Four

MARVA DIDN'T KNOW WHAT she was dreaming and what she was remembering, drifting in and out of a drugged half-sleep, unsure of
what had really happened in the past day or so and what she had only
imagined. Was she really alone in a hospital bed, the sky dark outside
her window? Or was she in some other bed, with her husband, or her
lover, beside her?

She saw herself standing on the beach with Loïc in Brittany,
looking out at the Baie des Trépassés, the Bay of the Dead, where so
many shipwrecks had occurred over the centuries. This was where
they had found Loïc's father, his body twisted across jagged black
rocks. She suddenly saw Loïc's body twisted there, too, the waves
crashing over him. She let go a scream and everything went black for

a moment, then she opened her eyes wide and found she had only
been screaming in her nightmare. She heard a single car pass outside
the hospital window. Her mouth was closed and dry. Yes, this was
now, she had had an accident, in the car. A crash. A tree. A scream.
An airbag in her face.

Voices in French:

"Do you think she suffered a concussion?"

"Difficult to say. A woman her age . . ."

"It might only be shock, a state of . . ."

"Shock to the system. A woman her age."

"She was delirious before—"

Faces hover above her. Bright white lights. The faces of strangers.

"Call Naima," Marva says, or tries to say. "My daughter."

"Give her the injection," a gruff unfamiliar voice replies.

Suddenly she sees the face of Loïc, floating—sadly, silently—
above her.

"Hassan," she says, or tries to say, to Loïc. "Forgive me, my love,
but we have to save Hassan."

"One hundred milligrams," the gruff voice says.

Loïc's sad, silent face hovers above her.

Marva did not know if her eyes were open or closed, if she was
really seeing or only dreaming that the door of her hospital room was
slowly opening, the fierce white light from the corridor slitting the
darkness, then seeping through it. A silhouette in the beam of light.
Yes, this is how Marva has heard it happens. The corridor of light.
She realized she was about to die. As the white light grew brighter
and the shadowy figure approached, memories flooded her mind. But
it was not Marva's whole life that flashed before her eyes. Only the
small part of it that had contained Hassan.

The third of July. To think that Marva had been annoyed with herself for having let Charisse Bray talk her into catering an event.
Marva hadn't done anything like it in ten years; she was too old for

such grueling gigs. But somehow Charisse, way back in April, had cajoled her into feeding the folks at WORTHEE's upcoming Independence Day party. To think that Marva had actually been looking for a way to wriggle out of the commitment. But after a month of flagrant flirting with Hassan, ever since that night in June when Jeremy Hairston tried to bust the new sous-chef for messing with the sacred fried chicken recipe, Marva was tickled to have to spend so much time in the kitchen . . . supervising, as it were.

She had been in and out of there all night that third of July, checking on how things were going with Benoît and Hassan, exchanging long looks, little wisecracks and sly smiles with her number-two cook. Jeremy had gone back to Arkansas, as he did every year, for most of the month of July. But Marva wasn't complaining about having to fill in for her manager this summer. That night Marva insisted that Benoît go home at the usual hour. She would stay up late, overseeing Hassan as he finished preparing for the WORTHEE feast the next afternoon. After closing time, as soon as they were alone in the kitchen, Marva and Hassan went at it: With a mutual passion that surprised them both, they started experimenting crazily with soul food hors d'oeuvres: cumin in cornbread; curry in honey-fried chicken wings; barbecued baby back ribs, simmered, tajine style, in a prune and plum sauce. They were out of control . . . and loving it! They held up, each to the nose of the other, marinated morsels of raw meat. *Get a whiff of this.* They licked spices from each other's fingers. *Taste that!* They tenderly wiped the sweat from each other's brow. *Mmmmmmm.*

Marva was the one who pounced, grabbing Hassan by the back of his head and kissing him full and lush on the mouth. Decades sizzled away, melting down like a wad of butter in a hot frying pan. Sex had suddenly stopped being the loving, gentle thing she had known it to be with Loïc over the past twenty years and exploded into the grinding, frenzied dance she remembered from so long ago. Though she had been the aggressor, Hassan responded with the same force, the same hunger. Marva pushed Hassan backward onto the huge butcher-block table, climbed on top of him, wetter than she had been in years, tearing at his pants while he pulled her panties down her wildly wriggling thighs. They came together, bodies entwined, as sauces boiled over and oils popped and splattered on the stovetop.

They rearranged their clothes, finished cooking all the dishes for the Fourth of July party, then retired to the small bedroom upstairs, right next door to Marva's office. While Hassan undressed, Marva called Loïc, got the answering machine. She was not surprised. At 4 A.M. Loïc would have been fast asleep. She left a message saying she had worked late and would spend the rest of the night at the restaurant, as she occasionally did in July, when Jeremy was not around and she had to assume his managerial duties. She told Loïc she would see him tomorrow night, told him she loved him, hung up the phone, stripped off her clothes, then plunged into the bed with her naked employee, sighing, then hissing, then gasping his name as they slammed their bodies against each other: *Hassan-Hassan-Hassan-Hassan-Hassan...*

WORLD ORGANIZATION FOR RESEARCH INTO TECHNOLOGY, HEALTH, EDUCATION AND THE ENVIRONMENT CELEBRATES AMERICA!

All those words crammed together looked comically awkward on the red, white and blue banner stretched high above the floor of the ballroom. Marva stood in the center of the hall, nervously twisting her right foot, as if she were crushing an imaginary cigarette butt on the marble floor. It was three thirty on the afternoon of July 4, 2001. WORTHEE cafeteria staffers were laying out Marva's concoctions on the long, white-clothed tables. Marva and Hassan were the only people from the restaurant who would be attending the party, scheduled to begin in half an hour. But where was Hassan? They had spent the whole day together, after waking up in Marva's narrow office bed. They had arrived here together in the van driven by WORTHEE staffers at three o'clock. That was when Hassan had promptly disappeared. Marva, having instructed the workers exactly where to place every dish, hurried out of the hall, anxious to find Hassan.

Eight weeks later, with the memories racing across her mind as she lay in her hospital bed, certain that death was near, Marva wondered if she had really seen this or was only imagining she had seen it because of what Inspector Lamouche had told her but, no, it was true: She had found Hassan in the corridor, intently studying a floor plan of the WORTHEE building that hung on the wall right near the public bathroom. Hassan jumped like a skittish cat when Marva, walking toward him, no more than a few feet away, called out his name.

"What are you doing?"

Hassan flashed his bashful yet naughty smile. "I was just trying to get orientated," he said. "This is a big building."

"Yeah," Marva said. She was standing face to face with Hassan now. The night before had been phenomenal. Marva knew that she would not allow it to happen again. Still, she had definitely acquired a new depth of affection for Hassan. He had gone from being a sexy hunk she wanted to fuck to being a sweet boy she wanted to cuddle and protect. His sleepy hazel eyes, his distracted air: Now that Marva knew what a fantastic lover Hassan was, these things had become dear to her. "This place used to belong to a duke or something," Marva said. She was trying to sound flippant but, with her body still buzzing from the night before, her words came out in a sexy purr: "Maybe he got his head chopped off in the Revolution."

"Maybe so," Hassan said.

"Why are you so interested in the architecture?" Staring into Hassan's eyes, Marva felt almost as if she was being hypnotized. "You wanna buy the building or something?"

"I want you to buy it for me."

"Oh, do you now?"

"Yes. But first we must inspect all of the property. Come."

Hassan took Marva by the hand, gently pulled her into the bathroom, locked the door behind them. They fucked like maniacs on the sink counter, Marva's back pressed against the wall mirror, her arms wrapped tightly around Hassan's shoulders. She bit her own hand to keep from screaming when she came. *Sex in a W.C.*, Marva thought as she slowly returned to her senses. *Haven't done that since way*, way *back in the day.*

Marva floated through the Independence Day party, suspended in a state of erotic euphoria. She would scarcely remember who she saw at the reception or what she said to anyone. But she kept stealing seductive glances at Hassan, her sweet secret lover. At home that night, Marva startled Loïc, passionately kissing and stroking him as he sat up in bed, in his pajamas, trying to read a Dominique Manotti novel. They made love for the first time in several weeks but with a fervor they had not experienced in twenty-four years, not since the night Naima was conceived.

Marva would spend many nights in the bedroom above the restaurant that July. She would always call Loïc just after closing time, always get the answering machine, always apologize for leaving him alone that night. Though he fretted about Marva working too hard, Loïc never complained. She often looked drained, he said, after nights spent at the restaurant. Marva just smiled and told him not to worry.

"And your husband, he suspects nothing?"

Marva was surprised by Hassan's question. In the three weeks they had been sleeping together, he had never asked her anything truly personal. Ordinarily, before and after making love, they talked about food. They could go on endlessly about the best way to cook anything from couscous to cassoulet. Now, all of the sudden, as they lay sweaty and sated in the narrow bed, Hassan decided to spoil the fun by asking Marva about Loïc.

"I'm married to the least-suspicious Frenchman in the world," Marva said.

"You are lucky."

She should have changed the subject right there, started talking about the sundry differences between duck and goose fat, but now that Hassan had cracked open the door to the intimate, Marva had to walk through it.

"Don't you have anyone waiting at home for you?"

"Just my cousin, Ramzi. We share an apartment."

"I can't believe you haven't got a woman in your life."

"Don't you count?"

"You know what I mean."

"A wife?"

"Or something."

Hassan chuckled. "No wife. And, at the moment, no something." He softly kissed Marva's forehead. "Just you."

Marva was flattered, but wary. Could this be true? Hassan, a gorgeous twenty-eight-year-old man, had focused all his attention on a sixty-two-year-old woman who was not only married but also his boss? Marva wondered if Hassan was, improbably, falling in love with her. Was she really going to have to explain to Hassan that, whatever warm feelings she might have for him, this was a summer fling? That, as good as the sex was between them, it was going to end, most likely the next Sunday, when Marva would leave for Brittany? She didn't want any problems with Hassan. Sooner or later, she would have to set him straight. But not tonight.

"Does that trouble you?" Hassan asked, his voice tender.

Marva ignored the question. "What does your cousin do?" she said in a chatty, casual tone.

"He works for the sanitation department."

"On a truck?"

"Yes." Hassan added, without a hint of defensiveness: "Good benefits."

"Of course. Is he married?"

"No. I doubt any woman could stand to be with him. His last

girlfriend, he alienated. He's not a very pleasant guy. Very bitter. Mad at the world. I sometimes think he would be different if he had something he loved, the way I love cooking. But he never had that. He talks about all the limits in his life. But some of these limits he puts on himself."

Marva couldn't help but feel touched by the way Hassan was opening up to her. "How long have you and Ramzi been living together?"

"We moved here from Toulouse two years ago. Neither one of us could afford a decent apartment alone, so we share. But I am getting tired of him. Such a negative guy. Now he doesn't stop ranting about his ex-girlfriend. How she wasn't a good enough Muslim to raise his future children."

"Yikes." Only then did Marva think of what she had failed to ask Hassan. "Do you have any kids?"

After a long pause, Hassan said, "You want to see them?"

As Hassan hopped eagerly from the bed, Marva clicked on the nightstand lamp. Hassan lifted his pants from the pile of clothes on the floor, rummaged in the pockets till he found his wallet. He sat beside Marva on the bed, flipping through the small snapshots. Hassan was in every photo, with his arms around a child or sometimes two and, in one picture, three children. All of the children, to some extent, resembled Hassan. But they varied wildly in age and complexion, from chubby toddler to gawky prepubescent, from pale, freckle-faced kids to one child who, while having Hassan's sleepy hazel eyes, bore a deep chocolate brown skin tone.

"Good Lord," Marva said. "How many kids have you got?"

"Seven."

Trying not to sound too shocked, Marva asked, "How many mothers?"

"Four," Hassan replied flatly.

Marva knew she wasn't paying Hassan well enough to feed seven children. "And do you support them?"

Hassan waggled his head in a way that seemed to answer "sort of." Then he fixed Marva with a grave look. "I love my kids."

"Of course you do," Marva said quickly, trying to erase any hint of disapproval from her tone. "You wanna see mine?"

Marva led Hassan into the office, flipped on the overhead light. It was a funny sensation, being naked with Hassan amid the file cabinets and the photocopier and the iron safe. Nobody, after all, was allowed in the office except Marva and Jeremy. She pointed to the array of photos on her desk, all of them featuring Naima, the sequence of framed images charting her life from newborn to beautiful young woman.

Hassan was clearly beguiled. "She has the face of an angel," he said.

"Yeah, well, don't get any ideas," Marva said. "She ain't gonna be birthin' your eighth child."

Hassan abruptly turned and walked back into the bedroom, so abruptly that Marva did not even notice he had left the office. She was dusting and adjusting the pictures on her desk when she suddenly heard Hassan's zipper. By the time she got to the bedroom door, Hassan was completely dressed, sitting on the bed, tying his sneakers. "What's the matter?" Marva asked, realizing, only now, a minute after making the comment, how harsh it had been.

"I am sorry, Marva, I must go." Hassan did not even look at her. But she could hear the hurt in his voice.

"Aw, come on, it was just a joke."

Hassan rose, put on his denim jacket. "Will you please let me out?"

Since it was after closing time, Marva had locked herself and Hassan in the restaurant. She had the only key, leading her to briefly consider refusing to let Hassan go. "You're not serious, are you?"

Hassan still would not look at her. He stood with his hands in his pockets, his jaws clenched, staring out the bedroom door into the office. "Please," he said.

Marva, still completely naked, took the key from her purse and walked downstairs into the darkened kitchen. Hassan followed her to the back door. "I really think you're overreacting," she said, turning the key in the lock.

Hassan pulled open the door, as if he could not get away from
Marva fast enough. "Good night," he said, disappearing into the alley that led to the rue Véron.

Marva felt like shit as she relocked the back door. Alone in the
bed, with the smell of Hassan lingering in the sheets, remembering
the pain in her lover's face, Marva started to cry. She knew she had a
sharp tongue, and that she could be one wicked witch sometimes. But
she couldn't help it. And that—the helplessness—was what really
made her weep.

For three days, Marva refused to apologize. She played it casual with
Hassan, greeting him breezily, trying to make small talk. Hassan,
meanwhile, moped around the kitchen, barely speaking, wearing a
childish frown. Marva was torn between guilt over wounding Hassan
and annoyance at his sulking. Had Marva really said anything so in-
sulting? *She* didn't tell Hassan to go out and have seven illegitimate
children by four different women. Was it *her* fault if he was a dead-
beat dad? Could she be blamed for cracking a joke that reflected her
distaste for his lifestyle and her desire to protect her daughter?
Where the fuck did Hassan get off playing the injured victim?

For three nights they parted ways at closing time. And while
Marva would arrive home feeling ticked off at Hassan, she would lay
awake, beside her sleeping husband, cursing herself for having hurt
her lover, crying over her own unconscious cruelty, praying that Hassan would find it in his heart to forgive her.

Saturday, August 4 was to be her last night at the restaurant.
Sunday morning, Jeremy would return from vacation and that afternoon, Marva and Loïc would take off for a month in Brittany. Before
their blowup Tuesday night, Marva had hoped to have one final
after-hours frolic with Hassan. She knew that Benoît would be leaving work early Saturday night to catch a flight to Guadeloupe. And
she wanted to end this affair before nosy Jeremy came back. But the
way Hassan had behaved over her one little joke led Marva to decide

that their fling had already flung. Too bad it would have to end on this sad note. Maybe, when she returned from Brittany, Marva would fire Hassan. Meaning that she would never again touch his naked body. Never again taste his salty tongue in her mouth, feel his powerful movements inside her, gasp his name. . . .

Finally, at midnight, Marva cracked.

She caught him alone in the kitchen. The waitresses, Mylène and Véronique, were in the dining room, taking last orders. "I'm sorry," Marva said, taking Hassan by the arm. "I know what I said was obnoxious and hurtful. Will you accept my apology?"

Hassan seemed taken aback. "I, er . . ."

"Please forgive me."

"It's okay."

"Tell me you forgive me."

"I forgive you."

"Stay with me tonight, Hassan. I need you."

They made love with a new sweetness and tenderness that night. As early morning sunlight slowly filled the small bedroom above the kitchen, Marva and Hassan were still awake, cooing and cuddling.

"I really am sorry, you know."

"You don't have to keep saying that," Hassan said. "It was nothing, really."

"No, it was terrible of me. And it happened just as we were really getting to know each other."

"Yes. Maybe."

"I want to know more about you, Hassan."

"Yes. But right now, I'm getting very sleepy."

"You were born in Toulouse?"

"Yes. You saw my papers when you hired me."

"But your parents emigrated from Algeria."

"Uh-huh."

"Were they Berber or Arab?"

"What difference does it make?" Hassan yawned.

"Do you consider yourself Berber or Arab?"

"Both," Hassan said, "and neither."

To Marva, that perfectly logical yet perfectly ambiguous answer proved that Hassan was, above all else, a Frenchman. "And what about Islam?" she asked.

"What about it?"

"How do you feel about Islam?"

"It's nice," Hassan said groggily.

"It's what?"

"It's very nice," Hassan said. Then he started to snore.

Weeks later, when Marva lay in her hospital bed, seeing the fierce white light of death, the shadowy figure of some being from the Other Side approaching to guide her into the next realm, she would remember the last words she'd heard Hassan say and think that surely these were not the religious views of a radical Muslim terrorist. If that was what he was accused of being.

Not that it mattered anymore. Nothing mattered now, in this space suffused with light, the silhouette growing ever closer, the features of the face slowly becoming clearer. And now Marva was sure that this was not a dream but also that she was not dying. Yes, this was Hassan Mekachera standing in the hospital room, in the dead of night, come to steal her away.

Five

FLYING HIGH ABOVE THE ocean, staring out at the black night, Naima Rose was thoroughly pissed off. It had taken several hours for her fear about her mother's accident to harden into a cold rage. Whatever distress she had felt before boarding the plane was gone. Naima was so angry she couldn't even sleep. She knew if she didn't get at least a few hours of shut-eye, she'd be a jet-lagged zombie by the end of her first day in Paris. But her rage kept her wide awake, her mind spinning with suspicion. Marva had pulled some pretty wacky stunts before, with Loïc as her enabling accomplice, but this time they'd both gone too damn far.

On the movie set that afternoon, hearing Papa's ominous tone, Naima had feared for Maman's life. After racing home, overwrought,

Naima learned from her boyfriend, Darvin, that Loïc had already called with the flight information and more news on Marva's condition. Apparently, she had suffered only a mild concussion. Naima was still freaked out, though, weeping with worry. It was only after her plane was aloft that Naima began to consider a perverse possibility: that Marva really hadn't been hurt that badly at all. Fuming in her cramped economy-class seat, Naima was certain that her parents were trying to get back at her. This hyped-up crisis was Naima's punishment for not coming to Brittany. It had been the first time she'd spent the entire summer away from home, and Marva and Loïc, probably unconsciously, were staging this melodrama just so they could get to see their daughter in August. They never imagined what their foolish little game might be costing her. This was her career they were messing with! Saskia Gruber—in an astonishing display of sympathy—told Naima she could have one week away from the set. If Naima wasn't back by the next Monday, Saskia would find another third assistant director for the rest of the shoot.

Naima's stomach growled. She should have eaten the lukewarm slab of chicken smothered in gelatinous white sauce, but she had had no appetite when dinner was served. Now she was hungry and awake in the dimly lit cabin, absorbing that weird night-flight atmosphere, hearing the windy drone of the aircraft, feeling the peculiar, intimate presence of three hundred sleeping strangers. Some dumb Sandra Bullock romantic comedy flickered silently on the wall screen ten rows in front of her; the occasional flight attendant sauntered down the aisle. Naima leaned back, closed her eyes, tried to give in to sleep.

A full year had passed since Naima had seen her parents. She had celebrated Christmas 2000 with Darvin's family in New Jersey, so had not set foot in France since the previous summer. Marva and Loïc had talked about visiting New York but never got around to it. Naima was happy to have had a bit of a break from them both, especially from Marva. Maman was always stirring things up, especially with Papa. Somehow, as a couple, they seemed to need their theatrical confrontations, the screamfests and slamming doors, the tearful reconciliations that always followed the empty threats of abandon-ment. Divorce? Marva and Loïc had never even had a trial separa-tion. When she was still a child, Naima stopped taking her parents' clashes seriously. She realized early on that it was Marva who usually instigated the fights, but she could see that Loïc never hesitated to es-calate a conflict. During her adolescence, Naima decided that her parents derived some sort of erotic excitement from their spats. The explosions always ended with tender apologies and her parents disap-pearing into their bedroom for hours. Even as a teenager, Naima found this type of behavior immature. Though she loved her parents completely and everlastingly, Naima had not felt, over the past year, a single moment of homesickness.

Naima opened her eyes, saw the white-on-black closing credits of the movie scrolling up the screen, heard the quiet, rhythmic snoring of nearby passengers. She pulled the night mask from the seat pocket in front of her, strapped it on. Still couldn't quite fall asleep. She re-membered how wonderful Darvin had been when she burst into the apartment, on the brink of hysteria, having hurried home from the movie set. He had held her in his arms, reassuring her, reminding her that so far as they knew, it was only an accident that had oc-curred, not a tragedy. Naima just had to get to Paris and find out what was what. As always, calm, reliable Darvin had been there for her. It was Darvin who packed Naima's suitcase while she lay on the bed, weeping, still fearing the worst. Darvin called for the taxi, rode with Naima to the airport, made sure she got to the gate in time, kissed her tenderly when she was still bumbling about in a daze. "If I don't hear from you in twenty-four hours I'm gonna call your par-ents' number, okay?"

"Okay," Naima had muttered.

Darvin waved to her as she plodded down the ramp, boarding pass in hand. He blew her a kiss and silently mouthed "I love you."

Naima was still too strung out by the news from Paris to respond. She handed her pass to the flight attendant and got on board.

Six hours later, as she leaned back in her seat, awake with the night mask covering her eyes, Naima wished it was Darvin sitting beside her instead of the chubby blond American woman with the blue, white and red I ♥ PARIS baseball cap. Over the past three years, she had come to depend on her boyfriend as a sort of interpreter of her turbulent emotions. Darvin explained Naima to herself. She had wanted to suggest that he come with her to Paris. But Papa had purchased only one ticket and finding another seat on the same flight, at the peak of tourist season, would have been difficult and expensive. Besides, Darvin had to stay in New York this week. He was expecting to hear, any day now, if he'd get any of the corporate jobs he'd applied for. Though Naima never understood exactly what Darvin specialized in, she was certain he'd land a good position somewhere. There had to be plenty of firms eager to hire someone who had just been awarded a Ph.D. in statistical analysis from Columbia. Especially if that someone was, like Darvin, biracial.

But even if Darvin had been free, he might not have wanted to accompany Naima. The one trip to France they had taken together, during the Christmas holiday in 1999, had been no fun at all. Naima blamed her mother. It was obvious that she felt Darvin wasn't good enough for Naima. Not because of his background but simply because Marva didn't find him sufficiently entertaining. Darvin lacked that personal pizzazz Marva cherished. He was a kind and decent, extremely intelligent young man who loved her daughter dearly. But because he wasn't witty and garrulous, Marva wrote him off. One night at dinner, as Darvin, in his shy, halting way, tried to explain what his dissertation was about, Marva yawned loudly, capaciously, and said, "My God, I'm so bored I think I'm going to faint."

Naima had never forgiven her mother for that. Nor for the fact that Marva often referred to Darvin as "Darvon," pronouncing his name as if it were the same as the sleep-inducing painkiller. Naima had never talked to Marva about her attitude toward Darvin. Theatrical confrontations weren't Naima's style. Instead, she smoldered silently. And took a defiant pleasure in knowing that her mother's disdain for Darvin only made her love him more. Darvin hadn't joined Naima on her last trip to France in the summer of 2000. Naima insisted he remain in the States. She wanted to protect him from Marva's withering sarcasm—and from her brazen hypocrisy. How dare Marva consider Darvin too ordinary, too dull, for Naima. Hadn't Marva forced her own mate to abandon his artistic ambitions and become a conventional bourgeois gentleman? Loïc was working as an assistant manager at a hotel when Marva met him, but his dream had been to become a photographer. Marva used to brag about how she had refused to marry Loïc unless he enrolled in law school. How did the wife of a tax attorney have the gall to consider a statistician boring? Of course, Loïc had the sort of glib social charm that Marva admired, the easy grace that Darvin lacked. Naima was pleased that her father had been friendly to Darvin and seemed to genuinely like him. As for Marva, she was just going to have to get used to Darvin Littlefield and learn to treat him with the respect he deserved. Because it seemed more and more likely that, someday soon, he would be her son-in-law.

Naima pulled off her night mask. It was no use trying to sleep. Through the small window, she could see the sky already lightening. She remembered the time she baffled Darvin by using a common French expression to describe her mother. She tried to explain how it conveyed Marva's greatness and her awfulness, the magnitude of her personality, the quality that made her as lovable as she was maddening. In French, to call someone a *monstre sacré* was a kind of compliment. In Darvin's scrupulous, straightforward American sensibility, the term was incomprehensible: How could a monster ever be sacred?

Naima spotted her father in the crowd as soon as she stepped off the plane. She saw his bright blue eyes anxiously scanning the stream of passengers. With his silvery hair and deep suntan, Loïc Rose was a strikingly handsome man. But one of the qualities Naima adored about her father was that he didn't seem to realize it. There was something rumpled and vulnerable, touchingly imperfect, about

Loïc's masculine beauty. When he finally saw his daughter in the crowd, he broke into a joyously goofy grin. Naima momentarily forgot her anger as she threw her arms around Loïc and basked in a long, sweet embrace, in the primal familiarity she never realized she had missed. She was nearly as tall as Loïc and savored the feeling of his cheek against hers and the scent of her father that was always the same. Papa must have used the same aftershave for all of Naima's life. Once again, Naima felt like crying but she was determined not to. She wanted to show Loïc that she was strong and that she wasn't going to put up with any neurotic family nonsense. When they finally broke from their hug, Naima stared hard at her father and asked, "What's up with Maman?"

"Good news," Loïc said. "She suffered only from a state of shock."

"Is that all?" Naima scowled.

Loïc seemed startled by her reaction. "Yes. It seems she'll be released from the hospital later today. Or maybe tomorrow."

"Well, then, Papa, I'm not going to stay very long if that's the case."

Loïc flashed a pained frown. "Your movie shoot?"

"Yes, Papa. It's an important job for me and I need to get back to it."

"Of course," Loïc said, in his most dejected tone. "We won't keep you here any longer than necessary. But, come, let's go see Maman."

As she rode with Loïc down the terminal's long, steeply tilted moving walkways, Naima was already feeling the dreamy fog of jet lag. It was 8 A.M. in Paris, but her body was still on New York time. Her wristwatch still read two o'clock. And, though the sun was shining through the glass walls of Charles de Gaulle airport, all Naima really wanted to do was go to bed. Loïc carried her suitcase as they walked through the sliding doors and headed for the parking lot. "You look fantastic, my sweetie."

"*Merci, Papa.*"

Naima could have returned the compliment but she wanted her father to know that her annoyance was not going to be neutralized with polite, mutual flattery. Loïc placed Naima's suitcase in the trunk of his familiar dark blue Peugeot. As they drove along the highway, Naima was struck by how small the cars seemed. In the year since she had last visited France, Naima had grown accustomed to the massive sports utility vehicles that dominated the American roadways. The compact cars zipping down the French highway, including Papa's Peugeot, seemed toylike by comparison. A strange sensation passed through her, the feeling that she was now looking at her home country through the eyes of a foreigner.

"I am sorry for the unpleasant circumstances," Loïc said, a bit tentatively, as if he had been reluctant to break the delicate silence in the car. "All the same, it is very good to see you, my sweetie."

Resist it though she might, Naima could feel her irritation melting. "It's always good to see you, Papa. And Maman, too."

Loïc's smile returned. "Maman is in the Hôpital Decoust. But let's make a brief stop before we go there. I'd like to show you something."

Naima had never imagined that the fountain on the Place Saint-Michel could sparkle. She had never before seen the statues actually clean, the bronze figures of Michael the archangel, Satan and the dragons of hell all shiny and bright, with nary a speck of the grime that had encrusted them for decades. Naima had never even known that the four columns framing the fountain were made of pink marble. But here they were, in all their polished glory, sunlight glinting off the smooth stone pillars. Naima had stopped being afraid of the statues on the Place Saint-Michel sixteen years ago. But it had never occurred to her that the whole fountain could be so pristinely beautiful.

"Wow" was all Naima could say at first.

"They did a good job cleaning it up, *n'est-ce pas?*" Loïc said.

Naima and her father stood side by side, listening to the whoosh of the jets of water shooting out of the gaping jaws of the startlingly immaculate bronze dragons and splashing into the spotless stone fountain. She was relieved to see that at least the bullet marks remained as they were.

"*C'est très beau.*"

"Do you remember when I first told you about the *Libération?*"

"Of course I do, Papa."

"August 1944," Loïc continued, in spite of Naima's memory. "The brave Parisians rising up against the Nazi oppressors, the French and American armed forces pouring into the Place Saint-Michel."

"The black soldiers who befriended the fatherless little French boy and gave him gum and chocolate," Naima said, smiling and stroking her father's arm.

Loïc seemed lost in memory. "There was another battle at Saint-Michel. One in which I was an active participant. I don't think I've ever told you about the seventeenth of October, 1961."

The date sounded familiar to Naima, but not because of Loïc. "No."

"On that night, more than two hundred Algerians were murdered by the French police. A great many of them between this spot and"—Loïc turned and pointed toward the bridge behind them that stretched across the Seine—"the Pont Saint-Michel. It was toward the climax of the Algerian war for independence. Didn't you learn about this in school?"

"They mentioned it a couple of times."

"It was one of the darkest, bloodiest incidents in modern French history. The Algerians were unarmed, demonstrating peacefully. But the cops were out of control. They shot people, beat them to death, threw wounded people into the Seine to drown. A total massacre. There's never even been an accurate count of the dead but, like I say, it was at least a couple hundred. Then there were the people who were savagely beaten but somehow managed to survive. . . . I was one of them."

"You were?"

"I was marching with the Algerians that night. I was very engaged politically at the time. An impassioned Communist. I never told you, did I?"

"Fuck, no!" Now that Loïc was telling her, Naima could hardly get her mind around it. Papa, the bourgeois tax attorney, had been a left-wing radical?

"My real crime, since I was white and not North African, was carrying a camera. I was filming the protest. That was unforgivable. I don't know what happened to my camera and film after the cops beat me senseless."

Naima was flabbergasted. "I had no idea," she murmured. Growing up, she had always forgiven Loïc for being a right-of-center Gaullist when everybody else in their sphere was Socialist. Charles de Gaulle had, after all, been one of the shining lights of Loïc's childhood. But, in recent years, Naima had grown more and more frustrated with her father's increasingly conservative views. Last summer, in Brittany, when he had sounded skeptical about liberal immigration policies, Naima accused Loïc of sympathizing with Jean-Marie Le Pen, the right-wing bigot who headed France's extremist National Front party.

"I was jailed for three days," Loïc continued. "And given no medical attention for my wounds. Finally, somebody arranged for me to get out. That was the end of my political activism. You really never heard about any of this?"

"No. Never. Not from you. Not from Maman, either."

"Well, all this happened about a year before Marva arrived in Paris."

Naima looked up at the statue of Saint-Michel. Even sparkling clean, his expression was impassive, inscrutable. "Bizarre," Naima said.

"How well do you really know your mother and father?"

Naima, hurt by the question, pretended not to have heard it. She just stared up at the statue, listening to the whoosh and splash of the water in the fountain. "Let's go see Maman," she finally said.

. . .

"C'est impossible," the squinch-eyed, needle-nosed nurse at the front desk said.

Even when Naima had lived in France, this was probably the expression she had most despised. But after five years in America, she found it unbearable. In France, whether it was a head waiter telling you he wouldn't give you a table or a potential love interest canceling your big date or a plumber telling you he couldn't fix your leaky pipe, the Frenchman would not first say, "Sorry, we're all booked" or "You're really not my type" or "I'm too incompetent to solve your problem." No: the Frenchman would give, as his primary excuse, a profession of total defeat, as if you were asking him to defy the law of gravity: "It's impossible."

"What do you mean," Naima said, "that it's impossible to visit Madame Dobbs?" She and her father were standing in the lobby of the Decoust Hospital, one of Paris's finest.

The nurse looked at her chart a second time. "Madame Dobbs checked out at one o'clock this morning."

"*Marva* Dobbs?" Loïc asked.

"Yes. Marva Dobbs."

"You let a sick woman check herself out of the hospital in the middle of the night—alone?"

The nurse raised her pointy chin and addressed Loïc sternly. "If a patient is capable of signing herself out, we must allow her to do so. And Madame Dobbs was not alone."

"Well, this patient happens to be my wife," Loïc snarled.

The nurse looked embarrassed. "I am sorry, sir."

"Who was with her?" Naima asked, feeling suddenly helpless and confused.

"I cannot say. I was not the nurse on duty."

"Well, who *was* on duty?" Loïc asked through clenched teeth.

"I must speak with my colleague," the nurse said, maintaining her frosty, bureaucratic tone. She turned and disappeared into an office behind the desk. Within seconds, she reemerged, accompanied by a plump, frizzy-haired co-worker.

"Were you the nurse on duty when Madame Dobbs signed out?" Naima asked.

"No, but I took over from the night nurse. Before she went home she told me that Madame Dobbs had a visitor after midnight."

"You allow that, visitors after midnight?"

"Under special circumstances, yes," the plump nurse said, sounding only slightly less chilly than her sharp-featured colleague. "The night nurse said that this gentleman was very persuasive. He returned to the desk with Madame Dobbs. The patient was dressed and perfectly in control of herself. The two of them left together."

"And you don't have a name for this man?"

The nurse showed Naima and Loïc a chart filled with scribbled names. She pointed to a signature at the bottom of the page: It was an illegible scrawl. "I can't read this," Loïc said.

"Neither can we," said the plump nurse. "But my colleague on duty said it was a young, Arab-looking man."

Now Loïc looked as if he'd been kicked in the stomach, had all the wind knocked out of him.

Naima, bewildered, fought the sudden urge to cry. "Where is she, your colleague?"

"We told you, she has gone home for the day."

"But can't we talk to her?"

The two nurses behind the desk exchanged incredulous looks, then turned back to Naima and Loïc and said, in shrill unison: *"C'est impossible."*

Six

"NO COPS," LOÏC SAID. "We must keep this within the family."

Naima and her father sat across from each other in the breakfast nook of their kitchen. Half an hour after learning that Marva had disappeared from her hospital room, Loïc was doing a bad job of pretending that nothing was wrong.

"Papa, I don't understand." Even after a cup of powerful espresso, Naima still felt the floaty light-headedness of jet lag coming on strong. "What if Maman was kidnapped? Don't you think we should at least contact the police?"

"I assure you she was not kidnapped, my sweetie. I will explain everything."

"You've been saying that since we left the hospital, yet you don't explain."

"*Du calme,* my sweetie. Please, eat your breakfast."

Naima tucked in to the meal Loïc had prepared for her, one of her favorite childhood snacks: a crêpe with banana slices, soaked in Nutella chocolate sauce. It was good to finally get something in her stomach. "Okay, Papa," she said, between bites, "I'm eating. Now will you please tell me what the hell is going on?"

Loïc flashed a crooked smile. "Remember when you were a little girl and would come home from the Jardin du Luxembourg with all your scrapes and bruises? You were quite the tomboy. And always you would demand that I make you a banana Nutella crêpe. Do you remember?"

"Yes, Papa, but right now I'd really like to talk about Maman."

"Is it good, the crêpe?"

"Papa, please! Why is it always so hard to get information out of you? It's like you're always withholding—"

"Your mother has taken a lover."

For a long time, Naima and Loïc were silent. Even as she absorbed the revelation, Naima realized she was not as surprised as she perhaps should have been. She had never suspected either of her parents of infidelity, yet infidelity did not seem out of character for either of them. Marva, especially, was a shameless flirt. What Naima mainly felt was pity for her father, who continued to smile, now sadly, painfully, at her. "Oh, Papa." Naima reached across the table and took his hand in hers. "I am so sorry."

Loïc shrugged. "These sorts of things happened more often before you were born. It's been a long time. Anyway, I don't think any harm has come to her. I suspect she will walk in the door any minute now."

"Is that who came to the hospital last night? Maman's..." Naima paused, finding she could not use the same frank word her father had used to describe the man. "Maman's ... friend?"

"Yes, I believe that was him."

"He's Arab? Do you know him?"

Loïc grimaced. "Really, Naima, I think the rest of it you should discuss with your mother when she comes home."

Naima decided not to press Loïc any more. "*D'accord*, Papa. So what are you going to do? Just wait here for her?"

"Actually, my sweetie, I am going to Lyon. This afternoon. I have business to attend to down there."

"Business? In August?"

Naima was relieved to hear her father laugh lightly. "Yes, my sweetie. Not all of my clients are French. And even some of the French have started working like the Americans."

"Is that why you and Maman came back from Brittany early?"

Loïc hesitated a moment, then said, "Exactly."

Naima wasn't sure she believed him. "Okay. What should I tell Maman when she shows up?"

"Tell her I will be back tomorrow. If she cares."

Naima felt like crying again, but again she blocked the tears. "Oh, Papa," she sighed sympathetically.

While Loïc disappeared into his study to prepare for his business trip, Naima wandered woozily into her family's living room. Dust motes floated in the shafts of sunlight streaming through the seven-foot-high windows. She felt strangely alienated from the familiar surroundings: the couches and armchairs draped in African fabrics, the Persian rugs and towering bookshelves. She remembered the first time she'd ever been made to recognize her family's wealth, and to feel ashamed of it. One of her closest childhood playmates had been a girl named Sylvie, the daughter of one of her parents' house-keepers, a Haitian woman named Louise. Naima and Sylvie, born just a few weeks apart, had spent endless hours in each other's company in this spacious apartment on the Left Bank, in Louise's one-bedroom flat in the predominately black and Arab neighborhood of Barbès and in the kitchen, dining room and upstairs office of Marva's restaurant in Montmartre. Suddenly, one day when they were both twelve years old, Sylvie decided that she and Naima could no longer hang out together.

"Why not?" Naima asked.

"You're just too rich," Sylvie said.

Though Naima and Sylvie would cross paths fairly often over the next several years, they would never be close again. Eleven years after Sylvie abruptly ended their friendship, Naima still felt wounded by that curt condemnation: *You're just too rich.*

The telephone on the fireplace mantel rang. "Papa?" Naima called out. No response. She knew that if Loïc was ensconced in his study, way down at the end of the apartment's long corridor, he probably had not heard her. And, since there were at least three different phone numbers connected to this apartment, Naima couldn't be sure if Loïc even knew that someone was trying to get in touch. She picked up the phone on the second ring. *"Allô?"*

"Naima! Ça va, mon chou?"

The sound of Jeremy Hairston's voice over the telephone immediately calmed Naima's frazzled nerves. She had always liked Marva's swishy assistant. During a few short stretches over the past several years, when Naima had filled in as a waitress at the Soul Food Kitchen, Jeremy had been her real boss. So far as Naima could tell, he was the one actually running the joint. And the two of them enjoyed poking affectionate if acerbic fun at Marva's dining-room-diva routine.

"Frankly, *mon chou,*" Naima said, addressing Jeremy by the nickname they used for each other, a common French term of endearment that meant "my cabbage" in English, "I've been better."

"I hear ya," Jeremy said. "When did you get into town?"

"Just this morning."

"So have you seen your moms?"

"Non, mon chou. Get this: Marva checked out of the hospital in the middle of the night, accompanied by a, quote, Arab-looking, unquote, man."

"Oh, dear."

"What the hell is going on here?"

"Your moms didn't ever tell you? I mean, before the accident."

"She most definitely did not."

"Then we need to talk! Can you come by the restaurant? Before the lunch crowd arrives?"

"I wish I could but jet lag is puttin' the zap on my head."

"Yeah, I know what that's like. Listen, you get a few hours' sleep, then come by between the lunch and dinner seatings. That way we can be alone. It would be good if you could get here by six. Then we'd have at least an hour to talk before the hungry hordes start arriving. I'll give you the lowdown then."

"You can't tell me now?"

"I'd rather we talk in person."

"That serious, huh?"

"Uh-huh."

"Okay, *mon chou,* I'll see you around six."

"Au revoir, mon chou."

At 1 P.M. Paris time, Naima lay on her bed, knocked flat by a leaden fatigue. The long shower that she'd hoped would invigorate her had only added to the narcotic sense of disoriented exhaustion. She had been awake for nearly thirty hours now, traversed an ocean and been subjected to a series of emotional jolts. Sprawled across the narrow mattress of her childhood and adolescence, dressed in her boyfriend's cotton pajamas, her skin moist and her bones aching, Naima struggled to keep her eyes open. She knew she had to call Darvin. Otherwise, he would be worried. Or worse yet, phone in a couple of hours from now, jarring her awake. Naima lifted the telephone receiver, punched in the number; heard her own voice on the answering machine in New York.

"Darvin," she said after the beep, "are you there? It's me.... No? ... Now where would you be at this hour? It's about 7 A.M. your time. I thought you would still be asleep. Or at least at home, work-

ing on your paper about . . . well, you know, your statistics paper. Oh
well. I'm at my parents' and I'm about to crash. Give me a call if you
wake up in the next ten or fifteen minutes. Otherwise, I'll call you
back when I wake up. Okay? Bye, Darvy."

After hanging up, Naima began to worry, unreasonably, about
Darvin. Had something happened to him? Had he suddenly run off
with a secret lover? Darvin was her rock. She missed him already. After less than five hours in Paris, she longed to be back in New York, in
the small one-bedroom apartment she and Darvin shared on East
Sixth Street, smack in the middle of a famous row of Indian restaurants. Naima already missed the aromas of tandoori, mughli and
curry sauce that pervaded the air on her block. East Sixth Street
could hardly be more different from the Boulevard Saint-Germain.

"Do you ever get homesick?" Marva had asked her daughter on
her last visit to Paris.

"Oh, sure," Naima said.

Maman, immediately seeing the truth, chuckled and said, "But
not really."

Naima wished that her old playmate Sylvie, the one who had
told her she was "just too rich," could understand that Marva and
Loïc's money meant nothing to her. She wished Sylvie could see her
these days, in her cramped little apartment on East Sixth Street.
Maybe, if she could, they might be friends again. The telephone rang
and Naima hurried to answer it before Loïc, who had still not left for
his Lyon business trip, picked up in another room of the apartment.
Even though Naima was sure it was Darvin calling, she could not
stop herself from saying, *"Allô?"*

There was a pause on the other end of the line, then Darvin's
voice, asking uncertainly, "Naima?"

"Hi, Darvy."

"Whoa. I didn't even recognize you."

"I'm in France, Darvy."

"And obviously very tired. Now that I know it's you, I can tell
you've got your sleepy voice on."

Naima yawned. "You miss me?"

"Of course I do, baby. What's going on there?"

"Where were you?" Naima asked, ignoring Darvin's question.

"I could hardly sleep last night. Guess I was too worried about you. At six, I decided to go out for a run. I just got back."

"You weren't with some ho, were you?"

"Naima, please, who do you think you're talking to here?"

"It was jes' a joke." Naima heard that she was beginning to slur her words.

"What's goin' on with your folks?"

"Oh, a lotta weird shit. Did you ever feel like your parents were total strangers to you?"

"Yeah," Darvin said. "All the time."

"Well, I never did. Not till today."

"Naima, it sounds like you're about to pass out. Maybe we should talk later."

"Okay, okay. Mistra Know-It-All. But tell me, did you hear from any of those companies yet?"

"Not yet. It's still pretty early here, baby."

"Oh, yeah. Don't worry, Darvy. You're gonna get a great job. I jes' know it."

"Thank you, baby."

"You're gonna make a shitload a money, and then all your friends are gonna say, 'You're jes' too rich' and then they'll all hate you."

"Naima, baby, you go to sleep now, okay? What is it, one fifteen there?"

"I dunno."

"I'll call you later, okay? Late tonight, your time."

"Okay."

"I love you, Naima."

"Love you, Darvy."

Naima was slipping into unconsciousness even as she hung up the phone.

Seven

THE DISTINGUISHED ELDERLY BLACK man, sitting in the brassy afternoon sunshine beside the enormous stone fountain in the Jardin du
Luxembourg, dressed in a black beret, open-collared black shirt and
charcoal gray suit, casually tossing bread crumbs to the ducks and
seagulls that glided across the glassy surface of the water, was the picture of lordly elegance. Long-limbed and dark-skinned, with a trim
gray moustache and heavy-lidded brown eyes brimming with a wary
intelligence, the old man might have been a diplomat or perhaps
even the former president of an African nation, someone who had led
the struggle to transform a French colony into an independent if
fragile democracy, then decided to retire in, of all places, France.

A white-haired white woman, walking a chocolate brown dachshund, stopped beside the regal gentleman. They exchanged a few pleasantries. The Frenchwoman spoke of how the authorities in this sprawling park always allowed her to break the ban on dogs. They knew that her pet was clean and well trained. A family of eavesdropping American tourists had no idea what the woman was saying, but they heard the old man respond in impeccable French. The woman walked off, the plump little sausage of a dog trundling beside her at the end of its leash. The tourists approached the old man, somewhat tentatively. "Hello there," the father said in an accent as wide and flat as the Kansas plains. "Can you help us out? We seem to be a little bit lost."

The elegant black man looked the tourists up and down, the mom and the pop, the daughter and son, all of them pink and fleshy, all of them dressed in baseball caps, T-shirts and shorts. For a fleeting moment, he considered giving them some assistance, then said: *"Excusez-moi. Je ne parle pas un mot d'anglais."*

The father looked baffled, then embarrassed. "Oh, um, sorry," he said. He and his family hurried off, waddling across the pale, sandy ground.

The old man smiled thinly, in grim self-satisfaction, knowing that the pudgy tourists would now never guess the truth: that this elderly black fellow in the beret who had claimed not to speak a word of English was, if anything, even more American than they were. He tossed more bread crumbs to the waterfowl. Here was Cleavon Semple on the afternoon of Tuesday, August 28, 2001—an Ohio native who, at the age of seventy-nine, had grown snugly into his foreign disguise, hiding in plain sight, seen but not known, living in a deeper exile than most people could ever imagine.

Cleavon spotted Harvey Oldcorn striding in his direction, as unmistakably American as the befuddled family of tourists. Even after forty years in Europe, good ole Harvey looked exactly like the dapper, country-clubbing Yalie he was. No amount of international refinement could obscure his origins. Blue-eyed and ruddy, with snowy strands of hair styled in a comb-over across his balding pate, dressed in a blue blazer with gold buttons, khaki pants, Brooks Brothers shirt and a polka-dot necktie, Harvey Oldcorn had that ludicrously confident American bounce in his gait. He had worked in U.S. embassies in a dozen countries but always wound up back in Paris. He spoke French fluently but, unlike Cleavon, with a choppy, clunking, instantly recognizable accent. Harvey was a merry, backslapping, gin-and-tonic-swilling anachronism, a living relic of a bygone era: the glory days of the Ivy League spy.

"Bon-jer, mon-sir," Harvey Oldcorn said, holding out his hand.

"Don't *'monsieur'* me," Cleavon growled, wincing at both Harvey's jarring accent and his bone-crushing handshake.

"I always respect my elders," Harvey said, taking a seat beside Cleavon on one of the green metal chairs that surrounded the fountain. Harvey was right on time: 2 P.M. sharp. It had been at least a dozen years since Cleavon had seen Harvey, but he remembered his perfect punctuality. Cleavon had not wanted this rendezvous. He would have been content to live out the rest of his days without ever seeing good ole Harvey again. But Cleavon could tell from Oldcorn's voice on his telephone two hours earlier that he had no choice.

"So what do you want from me, Harvey?" Cleavon said, continuing to toss bread crumbs to the ducks and gulls, not even looking at the man sitting beside him.

Oldcorn chuckled. "For Pete's sake, Cleavon, we don't see each other in God knows how long and that's all you have to say? No common niceties. No 'So how's the wife, Harvey?' "

"So how's the wife?"

"She's dead. But thanks for asking."

Cleavon, unmoved, said nothing. He had never been bothered by awkward silences and he let this one linger until Harvey could not stand it anymore.

"So how long have you been back in Paris?"

"A few months."

"How long were you in Toulouse?"

"Twenty-three years."

Harvey whistled. "That long, huh? Lovely city, Toulouse. All that pink brick architecture. *La ville rose*, isn't that what they call it? Why did you leave?"

"All my friends there got old and died," Cleavon grumbled.

"Oh yeah? And you think your friends in Paris are gonna live forever? You think *you* will?"

"So much for the niceties, Harvey. Now what the fuck do you want from me?"

Harvey let go a forlorn sigh, as if Cleavon had hurt his feelings. "You're aware that the WORTHEE building was attacked Sunday night."

"That joint shoulda been blown up long ago."

"Really? What do you know about it?"

Cleavon turned to look directly at Harvey. The aged preppy was staring hard at Cleavon, his swimming pool–blue eyes sparkling with suspicion. "Only what I read in the papers and see on TV," Cleavon said. "What? You think I did it? I'm retired. And besides, explosions and such were your *métier*, not mine."

Harvey continued to stare evenly at Cleavon. "So what do you make of it?"

Cleavon looked away, returning his gaze to the birds in the fountain. "Whoever did it, if they really wanted to cause serious damage, wouldn't have set off such a relatively small explosion. And certainly not at four in the morning. Why the hell do you care, anyway? You always said it was a pinko propaganda machine."

"Yes, but it served some useful purposes."

"What, did you bastards in the Authority co-opt WORTHEE?"

"Cleavon, as I am sure you are well aware, the Authority was disbanded back in 1992."

"So what's your scam these days, Harvey?"

"I'm in the private sector. Carmichael Associates. Investments, geopolitical consulting, human security issues. I run the Paris office."

"No longer serving your country, then?"

"Oh, I do what I can. And I've gotten some feelers from some old friends in the new administration."

"Ah, yes, you were pals with Poppy, weren't ya? Boola boola and shit."

"Anyway, we were talking about WORTHEE. The director of the organization got blown up outside the building the other night."

"I thought it was some unlucky passerby."

"It was Webster Janes."

"Web? He was still there?"

"So you really didn't know." Harvey smiled faintly, obviously relieved. "He's in critical condition. Burns over ninety percent of his body. It hasn't been announced yet. They're still trying to track down the nearest family members. But he won't live long. The question I'm asking is this: What if the WORTHEE bombing was just practice—a dry run?"

"For what?"

"A bigger target. Like . . . maybe . . . the U.S. embassy."

"Aw, come on, man. Who the fuck's gonna try that? The Red Brigade? What are you, nostalgic?"

"Sure, go ahead and sneer. We've got new enemies today, Cleavon. Don't you remember the metro bombings back in '95? How many innocent people died at the hands of those terrorists?"

"The French cops caught those guys."

"Of course. But now we've got *new* guys to contend with. Crazy fucking Islamics who hate America and everything she stands for. Open your eyes, Cleavon. This world is full of swarthy bastards who will stop at nothing to destroy our way of life, who hate democracy, capitalism, and the whole Judeo-Christian tradition."

"Sounds like you're talking about the Commies again."

"The vermin I'm talking about make the Commies look like John Birchers. These are people with no fucking respect for human life. Not even their own! Like those goddamned suicide bombers in Israel. You better wake up to the new threat that's before us, Cleavon."

"I'm too happy napping, thank you. I told you, Harvey, I'm re-tired."

Another uncomfortable silence. Cleavon tossed the last of his crumbs into the water, glanced at his watch, hoping Harvey would take the hint.

"So when you lived in Toulouse," Oldcorn said, "did you have any Muslim, Arab or North African friends?"

"Of course," Cleavon replied. "It's only white Americans I ever shunned."

"Uh-huh. And did you ever know a fellow by the name of Ramzi Mekachera—a garbage collector?"

"No."

"How about Hassan Mekachera, a cook?"

"No."

"Hmmph." Harvey snorted, sounding unconvinced.

"What do you want with them?"

"Interpol thinks they might have ties to al Qaeda."

"Who's he?"

"You shittin' me?"

Cleavon tilted his head and saw Harvey staring incredulously at him. He honestly had not recognized the name. "Al *who?*"

"Al Qaeda!" Harvey snapped. "Arabic for 'the Base.' Jesus Christ, Cleavon. It's the most dangerous terrorist organization in the world today. Osama bin Laden. That name ring a bell?"

"Vaguely."

"Kenya. Tanzania. He blew up two U.S. embassies in Africa back in '98."

"Al Qaeda?"

"Bin Laden. He runs al Qaeda. What the fuck, Cleavon, have you got Alzheimer's already?"

Cleavon shrugged. "I figured the CIA was behind those bomb-ings."

"Oh, that's cute, that's real cute."

"You forgetting your history, Harvey? This is Africa we're talking about."

"Yeah, right. Well, times have changed, Cleavon, that's what I'm trying to tell you. Whose side are you on anyway?"

"Ah, yes, that's always the question, isn't it?"

"You're goddamned right it is!"

Harvey took a deep breath, tried to hold on to his composure lest people stare at him and Cleavon or, worse yet, eavesdrop on their conversation. Cleavon discreetly surveyed the scene around the fountain: the little boys using long, thin poles to push their model sailboats across the water, the trim young joggers in gym shorts and expensive sneakers kicking up clouds of sandy earth, the groups of camera-toting tourists wandering aimlessly, gawking at the alabaster statues and tall potted palm trees. As always, Cleavon was determined not to be the one to break the silence.

"So," Harvey finally said, "obviously you're not up on current events. How do you spend your days? Writing your memoirs?"

Cleavon's body went rigid. He felt that sparking sensation he'd always experienced in the presence of danger: something like little firecrackers popping in his brain. He'd had the same feeling at noon, when he heard Harvey Oldcorn's voice on the phone and wondered not how the son of a bitch had acquired his unlisted number but why he had bothered to use it. "What?" Cleavon rasped.

"You're banging away on that old IBM Selectric all day long," Harvey said. "You always break for lunch at one café or another, always between twelve thirty and one thirty. Then it's back to work in your two-room apartment on the rue de Latran. Sorry, by the way, to have interrupted your routine today. And, of course, you didn't return to Paris a few months ago, Cleavon. You've been back in town for three years now."

Cleavon looked up and squinted into the sun, biting the insides of his cheeks, saying nothing, a thousand tiny explosions searing his mind.

"And it wasn't your dying old friends that drove you out of Toulouse, was it?" Harvey continued, in a needling voice. "It was problems with some young friends. Like the little Tunisian girl you were screwing. Her father didn't like it when you got mad and slapped the piss out of her one day. You had to hightail it outta Toulouse before he shish-kabobbed your ass. Women have always spelled trouble for Cleavon Semple. Am I right or am I right? Though you seem to have a nice arrangement these days, boffing the concierge in your building. What's her name again . . . Madame . . . Ficelle?"

He could have murdered Harvey at that moment without the slightest concern for the consequences. If Cleavon had been carrying his pistol that afternoon, he'd have blasted the smug, smirking ofay right there, shot him dead in the middle of the Luxembourg Garden.

"Don't get me wrong, Cleavon. I'm not passing judgment. I actually admire you. Getting it up at your age without the benefit of Viagra. Impressive. As is your writerly discipline. You don't go out much, do you? Except for those regular dinners at Archie Dukes's place. With your . . . *bruthas*." Harvey pronounced the last word with a coarse, pseudo-black accent.

All at once, with no apparent provocation, the ducks and seagulls in the fountain took flight, wings flapping noisily, a sudden spray of water sprinkling Cleavon and Harvey. The firecrackers had stopped popping in Cleavon's brain. His fear and rage had been overwhelmed by an ancient sorrow. "Why do I merit so much of your attention?"

"You're a fascinating man," Harvey said, sounding not entirely sarcastic. "A traitor without a cause."

"I'm going now," Cleavon said wearily.

"Not yet, mon-sir."

"Then I'm asking you for the last time, Harvey: What the fuck do you—"

"I would like to hire your services, Cleavon."

"And if I say no?"

"You won't. I'll pay you double your last fee."

"Did you account for twelve years of inflation?"

"I've brought half for you. We can discuss the second and final payment after completion of the assignment."

"Comme d'habitude."

Harvey handed Cleavon the manila envelope. Cleavon felt the heft of the paper brick as he slipped it into his jacket.

"Have you been to eat at Marva Dobbs's restaurant lately?"

The mere mention of the Soul Food Kitchen set off, as it always did, a jumbled swirl of memories, of blurred faces and echoing laughter, of the smell of barbecue sauce and crackling chicken grease. But Cleavon did not reveal this sentimentality to Harvey. "You oughta know," he growled. "You act like you know everything else about me."

"Marva is missing."

Now Cleavon could not conceal his concern. "Missing?"

"She might just have run off with her lover. Who knows? Maybe her husband had her killed. Loïc has always been a wild card in this business of ours. But maybe you should go by the restaurant. Ask around. Find out what you can."

"Loïc," Cleavon muttered. In his mind's eye he saw the scrawny little ragamuffin on the Boulevard Saint-Michel, in August 1944, racing up to the truck, flinging himself into the air, into Cleavon's arms.

"You ever hear of string theory, Cleavon? It's one of those trendy scientific notions. You know, physics. About how all these seemingly disconnected things are ultimately tied together. Everything is connected. Particles. All through the universe. Inextricably strung up with one another. But, of course, you and I knew that a long time ago, didn't we?"

Cleavon rose from his green metal chair. "Good-bye."

"I'll be in touch."

Cleavon looked down at good ole Harvey, saw in that swollen, booze-reddened, thinly white-haired, beady blue-eyed head, the faint, lingering traces of the impish, likable young American he'd met four decades earlier.

"Just one question," Cleavon said. "How do you sleep at night?"

Harvey shrugged. "Xanax."

Cleavon took a circuitous route home, playing the role of the old man on a leisurely stroll, making sure no one was following him or staking out his building on the rue de Latran. Cleavon's was a quiet and secluded block, not far from the heart of the Latin Quarter. Even if he had been under surveillance recently, Cleavon knew that, as of now, he would be able to roam as he pleased. He had been hired. Oldcorn would make sure that he would be free to do his work. With no material witnesses.

Cleavon didn't wait for the elevator. He bounded up the four flights of spiral staircase with the sprightly grace of an aging Bill "Bojangles" Robinson, burst into his apartment and double-locked the door behind him. Standing over his desk, he ripped open the manila envelope, quickly counted the five hundred 1000-franc notes. Only after thumbing the wad did Cleavon notice the slip of white paper that had fallen from the envelope and landed on the keyboard of his typewriter. Small and thin as a message from a fortune cookie. There were two words typed on the paper, the name of the person Harvey Oldcorn was paying Cleavon to assassinate: LOÏC ROSE.

Eight

NAIMA AWOKE WITH NO idea of where she was. Her eyes still closed, she reached over to touch Darvin, who always slept on her left. Her arm abruptly slammed into a wall. Naima was so startled she jumped up in the bed, opening her eyes, seeing slits of sunlight coming through the shutters. Then she spotted Babar in the shadows, propped in a blue high chair. The elephant king's yellow crown was filthy and one of his ears had been chewed down to a ragged gray clump. That was when Naima realized she was in her childhood bedroom. She turned on the bedside lamp, fumbled for her wristwatch. Eleven o'clock. It took Naima a moment to remember that her watch was still on New York time. So it must have been five in Paris, Tuesday afternoon. Even after a four-hour nap, she still felt groggy. "God-damned jet lag," she muttered as she stumbled to the bathroom.

Fifteen minutes later, having dressed again, Naima figured she would have just enough time to make it to her six o'clock rendezvous with Jeremy at Marva's Soul Food Kitchen. Naima assumed that Loïc had already left for Lyon and that Marva had not yet returned home, but as she walked down the long hallway of her parents' apartment, she had the distinct feeling that she was not alone. "Papa?" she called out.

"No," a deep male voice answered. "It's me."

At first, Naima did not recognize the tall black man standing in the center of the living room. The shaved head threw her off. So much so that she gasped when, in the next second, she realized who the man was. "Juvenal!"

"How are you, Naima?"

They both stood frozen in place, Naima at the threshold, Juvenal in the middle of the room. It had been five years since they had last seen each other and Naima suddenly felt as if she had been plunged backward in time, becoming once again the teenager who was so desperately in love with Juvenal Kamuhanda. He was still a beautiful man with his smooth, dark skin and aquiline features. But he had changed in small, startling ways. Instead of one of his usual colorful dashikis, he wore a gray button-down business shirt. He had the same penetrating stare but Naima saw fine creases around those dark, deep-set eyes. And then there was his perfectly bald head. Yes, Juvenal had aged. Naima, still somewhat stunned, did a quick mental calculation and realized that Juvenal was, in fact, quite old now. He would have turned forty this year. Naima heard herself say, in a smallish voice, "You cut off your dreadlocks."

Juvenal smiled. "Oh, yes, they've been gone for quite some time now. I'm sorry to take you by surprise like this. Your father let me in a couple of hours ago."

"Where is he?"

"He left for Lyon. He said you knew."

"Yes. Right. Of course."

Juvenal strode across the room, bent over and kissed Naima once on each cheek. "Are you all right?"

"I'm okay, I guess," Naima said, recovering from the shock of seeing Juvenal, her consciousness returning from the girlish past to her current twenty-three-year-old self.

"I had lunch at your mother's restaurant today. Jeremy told me what had happened. I called here this afternoon and spoke with Loïc, asked if I could come over, try to help in any way. So, er, here I am."

"Thanks. That's very kind of you." Now that she had fully returned to her senses, Naima recalled her icy rage, that freezing little rock of resentment that, some three or four years ago, had taken the place of her love for Juvenal. Naima crossed her arms and pursed her lips. "Starting to be considerate of others in your old age?"

Juvenal smirked and shook his head. "I was going to tell you that you are more beautiful than ever."

"*Et patati, et patata,*" Naima said, the French version of "yadda-yadda-yadda."

"Were you on your way to see Jeremy? I have my motorcycle. I could give you a lift to the restaurant."

"Don't you have a job to go to?"

"I don't need to be back at the gallery until seven. Come now, Naima, don't be such a hard American woman. We had a lovely story together."

"So what do you want?"

"I am here as a friend to your family. Please let me help."

Naima eyed Juvenal suspiciously. "Okay, I'll accept your offer of a ride. But first I want to go to a café and get a cup of coffee."

"Very well. I know the perfect place."

Every June 21, France celebrates the summer solstice with an ebullient ritual known as the Fête de la Musique. All over the country, musicians—professional and amateur—of all ages, cultures and inclinations take to the streets and play their hearts out. During the Fête de la Musique, the center of Paris is jam-packed with people, wandering from one corner to another, taking in the plethora of sounds: the jazz quintets, the classical violinists, the gypsies playing accordions, the heavy-metal rockers, the rappers with turntables, the opera singers, the gospel choirs, the Indian sitar players and Hare Krishna chanters, the folk guitarists, conga and bongo beaters, Dixieland bands, techno DJs, Brazilian ensembles, a cappella doo-wop quartets, lute-strumming medievalists, and brass and drum orchestras. In Paris, the sun sets around ten thirty on this longest day of the year. And the party continues all through the shortest night, right up until the dawn of June 22.

The evening of the Fête de la Musique in 1995, Marva and Loïc were hosting a party at their country house in Normandy, leaving their daughter alone in Paris. Naima had scheduled a rendezvous with some girlfriends near the Place de la République, where James Brown was giving a concert, but she never made it. Juvenal Kamuhanda phoned the apartment at six o'clock, casually asked Naima if she'd like to check out some music with him. He was standing right in front of Naima's building, calling from his portable.

Naima had gotten to know Juvenal a bit at the restaurant, during the brief stints when she had filled in as a waitress over the past year. Plenty of customers had flirted with her. But those older men seemed either to be doing it in a joking, blatantly harmless way or in such a slimy manner that there was no chance Naima would ever have found one of them attractive. Juvenal, however, a weekly diner at Marva's place, was the only man who seemed to flirt with Naima seriously, almost as an equal. He didn't make naughty innuendos or bluntly invite her out on a date. He talked to her as if she were a mature woman—which, at sixteen, she believed she was—actually asking her questions about her studies and career plans, seeming to truly listen to her replies, staring at her with that dark and scrutinizing intensity in his eyes, subtly conveying that he found her attractive, wordlessly asking if the attraction was mutual. Yet this was never quite provocative, partly because Juvenal almost always had some dazzling twenty-something woman sitting across the table from him. And Naima couldn't help but notice that Juvenal rarely came into Marva's with the same date twice.

So it was with a mix of innocent curiosity and flattered disbelief that Naima met Juvenal out on the Boulevard Saint-Germain. However serious his flirting had been, it was always just flirting. But seeing Juvenal standing there, in his vibrant dashiki, with his sexy dreads and stripping-you-down gaze, Naima stopped thinking of him as a distant older guy, a friend of her parents. They really were equals now. After all, she had just turned seventeen.

Juvenal and Naima explored the Left Bank that night, listening to countless musicians, talking easily about the styles and sounds they liked or disliked. They ate crêpes and ice-cream cones. Naima forgot all about the James Brown concert. At one point, as they sat on a bench overlooking the Seine, a lone saxophonist playing a mournful tune nearby, Juvenal spoke of his anguish over the horrific genocide that had taken place in his native country, Rwanda, the previous year. He had left his homeland with his parents when he was a little boy. But he knew of people, friends and family, who had been slaughtered in the bloodbath of Hutu against Tutsi. He wanted to go back to Rwanda but cursed himself for not yet having the courage to face the excruciating aftermath. Naima gently took Juvenal's hand in hers, wanting, almost painfully, to console him. Juvenal smiled sadly at her and said, "Wanna dance?"

A rambling crew of African drummers had taken over the Place Saint-Michel. All around the musicians was a swirling horde of revelers, of all ages and hues, moving their bodies with orgiastic abandon in the ten o'clock dusk. Naima and Juvenal were among the people who were actually dancing in the fountain, gyrating wildly as the drumbeat rose in a spiraling, seemingly endless crescendo, their feet kicking in the bubbling pool, their bodies wet from sweat and from the jets of water shooting out of the gaping jaws of the bronze dragons. Squeezed and jostled by the roiling crowd, their bodies

pressed against each other, Naima and Juvenal kissed for the first
time in the fountain, under the grimy, impassive gaze of the
archangel Michael, wielding his sword in one hand, pointing to
heaven with the other. Their clothing soaked, they walked back up
the Boulevard Saint-Germain. They kissed again on Naima's
doorstep. She invited him upstairs. They made love in her narrow
bed. Naima did not tell Juvenal it was her first time. He left at dawn,
hours before Naima's parents would return from the countryside.

Six summers later, sitting at the Café Le Départ, across from the
cleaned and sparkling Fontaine Saint-Michel, Naima assumed that
Juvenal had picked this spot out of a piquant sense of nostalgia. She
was sure that Juvenal was silently cherishing, as she was, the memory
of the Fête de la Musique, 1995.

Riding to the café on the back of Juvenal's motorcycle, Naima
had tried not to cling to him as she used to six summers ago. Still, she
felt a tingling intimacy, the stirring of erotic memory, from the necessary contact, wrapping her arms around Juvenal's midsection as he
guided the moto expertly through the brisk traffic on the boulevard,
then down the twisting, narrow streets of the Latin Quarter. Sitting
at a small sidewalk table, Naima sipping a *café crème*, Juvenal nursing a tall glass of orange juice, they exchanged long, silent looks, as if
they needed time to simply take each other in. Naima was old
enough now to match Juvenal's appraising gaze. She wondered if he
was having trouble absorbing her new maturity, adjusting to the fact
that, though still young, she was a woman of some experience now:
an Ivy League graduate, a budding filmmaker, a New Yorker, someone who had not only had her heart broken more than once but who
had broken one or two hearts herself. Certainly Naima was finding it
a bit difficult to adjust to this altered Juvenal. The funky, youthful
painter and sculptor who loved arranging shows for his fellow artists
had evolved into a prosperous-looking, distinctly middle-aged gallery

owner. Juvenal's shaving his head struck Naima as the final step in his transformation from bohemian to businessman.

Over the past several years, Marva had often mentioned Juvenal's burgeoning success to her daughter. Naima sometimes wondered if Marva knew that she and Juvenal had been lovers. But, in the end, she always ruled out that possibility. Naima had never told her mother anything. And Juvenal would have been too worried about harming his friendship with Marva to reveal the secret. Six summers after the affair, Naima still found Juvenal, even in his new bourgeois incarnation, powerfully attractive. But now she regarded him with a cool eye. There was no way Naima could lose her heart over this man today. Besides, at forty, Juvenal Kamuhanda was not quite as handsome as twenty-nine-year-old Darvin Littlefield.

"So," Juvenal finally said, "the American way seems to suit you."

Naima was instantly annoyed. "What do you mean?"

"Don't get defensive."

"If I feel I'm being attacked, I defend myself."

"No one is attacking you, Naima. I am only saying that you seem to be doing well. Marva tells me you are happy."

"Does that disappoint you?"

"Bon sang," Juvenal said with a heavy, exasperated laugh. "I am trying to pay you a compliment. Okay, let me start again. How do you like your life in America?"

"Enormously."

"Voilà."

"It's just that I know you don't like the States, Juvenal. Didn't you live there for a little while?"

"Five years. New York, Chicago, Los Angeles. Back in the eighties. And, yes, you are right. I hate that damn country."

"To each his own."

"The extraordinary hypocrisy of the place. All those forever smiling faces. Smiling as they grind you into the dirt. And the segregation!"

"There are laws on the books against it in America. Unlike here."

"Oh, yes, legal segregation there may be a thing of the past but what you have now is more insidious, more poisonous. It is *chosen* segregation. Black with black and white with white. The whites all say there is no racism but they stick to their own kind. The blacks complain all the time about racism but they stick to their own kind as much as the whites do. This American obsession with race, it is bred in their bones. It is an apartheid of the mind."

"You had some bad experiences. That isn't the case for everybody."

"Not for you, no, of course not. You can always pass."

Naima's eyes narrowed and her voice rose several decibels: "Say *what?*"

Juvenal kept a straight face. "For American, I mean. You are half-American, after all. You can pass for . . . all American."

"I'd like to go now."

"Yes, of course, just let me finish my orange juice, please."

Naima was furious that Juvenal had tried to insult her over her biracial background—she knew damn well he had been implying that she could pass for white in America—but she also felt a certain spiteful pride. She could sense that Juvenal was somehow threatened by her. And she liked that.

Juvenal downed the last of his orange juice. He called over the waiter and paid the bill. Then he gave Naima a tender look and said, "You know what I always think of at this café? The summer of nineteen ninety-five."

"Me, too," Naima almost said, but didn't. She continued to stare at Juvenal, leaning ever so slightly toward him, expectantly, waiting to hear his remembrance of the night she gave up her virginity to him.

"The metro bombing," Juvenal said, turning away from Naima and staring out at the Boulevard Saint-Michel. "I was on my moto. The evening rush hour. I had just come across that bridge. Don't even remember where I was going. The ground shook. I went skidding off my bike. Thought it was an earthquake. Then we saw the people running up, coming above ground, screaming and gagging from the smoke. They turned this café into an emergency hospital. Do you remember?"

"Of course," Naima said. It had been the first of a series of terrorist attacks in Paris that summer, orchestrated by Algerian radicals. The war for independence had ended thirty-three years earlier but, that summer, Islamic militants who wanted to overthrow the ruling Algerian government decided to attack France for its support of that government. There would be eight bombings in six weeks before the French authorities tracked down the terrorists, shooting the ringleader dead in the middle of the street.

"*Quelle horreur,*" Juvenal said. "I saw the dead, covered in blood. I saw people who had lost arms and legs, crying out in agony. I tried to help. But soon the *pompiers* and the police arrived and they pushed me and the others away. It was for the better. They were professionals, they knew what to do. But still, to this day, I feel guilty. I wish I could have done more to help more people."

Naima could not tell Juvenal that she was untroubled by the bombs that summer. What tormented her back in July of '95 was the fact that Juvenal seemed to lose interest, stopped returning her calls, failed to show up for appointments after their third night together. He never gave any reason. It was as if Naima was supposed to understand that this was the way adult relationships worked. So she kept her anguish to herself. She spent August in Brittany with her parents and aunts and uncles and cousins. No one noticed that Naima was eating only one meal a day and crying herself to sleep every night. How could she tell Juvenal now that she had been devastated by their silly little affair while he had been preoccupied with his own heroism in the face of death and destruction?

"Don't be so hard on yourself," Naima said, sounding more gruff than sympathetic.

"You know, somebody tried to blow up the WORTHEE building the other night. A car bomb."

That bit of news hardly registered with Naima. "Let's go. Jeremy must be wondering why I haven't shown up yet."

. . .

Naima clung tightly to Juvenal as they drove up to the Eighteenth Arrondissement, climbing the rue des Martyrs into the northern reaches of Paris. They stopped at the corner of rue Germain Pilon and the sublimely seedy Boulevard de Clichy, the main artery of the Pigalle district, with its neon signs and porn palaces, dark bars and that ever-popular tourist attraction, the Moulin Rouge. Naima hopped off the motorcycle. She took off the crash helmet Juvenal had lent her, put it into the squarish black plastic carrying case attached to the back of the seat. Juvenal, still perched on the moto, raised the visor of his helmet.

"Thanks for the lift," Naima said, standing on the sidewalk.

"I want to apologize," Juvenal said, "for being so disagreeable at the café."

"It was nothing. I was pretty *désagréable* myself."

"Yes, but you are under a lot of stress right now, not knowing where your mother is. I am sorry." Juvenal placed his hand on Naima's cheek. There was nothing sexual in his touch. Naima was warmed by the pure human kindness of the gesture. "I gave you the number of my portable. Please call me tonight."

"I'll try," Naima said.

As Juvenal tore off down the boulevard, Naima climbed the narrow rue Germain Pilon, crossing a sort of border as she headed north, the sleaze of Pigalle giving way to the quaintness of Montmartre. Dreary, side-alley nightclubs and tattoo dens dissolved into white-stoned early-twentieth-century mansions with well-tended gardens behind black wrought-iron gates. Naima was already half an hour late for her meeting with Jeremy Hairston. She turned left, looking forward to seeing the familiar façade of the Soul Food Kitchen among all the other establishments—Japanese, Togolese, Italian, Brazilian and plain old French—that formed a funky restaurant row down the rue Véron.

Instead, she was greeted by the sight of two patrol cars, an ambulance, a police van and a gathering crowd of cops and onlookers in front of her mother's restaurant. She jostled her way through the buzzing little mob, walking right up to the four uniformed cops who stood in the doorway.

"Excuse me," Naima said in as authoritative a tone as she could muster, "but I need to enter this restaurant. My mother is the owner and I would like to know what's happening here. So please don't tell me that it's impossible."

The cops cast bemused glances at each other. "Okay," one of them said, "we won't tell you."

Just as he and his colleagues broke into contemptuous laughter, the door of the restaurant swung open. Seeing the short, oily-looking man in the dark green suit step into the doorway, the cops abruptly shut up. The moon-faced Frenchman smiled at Naima as if they were old friends. "Ah, yes, ze daughter!" he said in English. He held out his hand, Naima shook it. "I am Inspector Lamouche. Would you like to enter?"

"Yes, please."

"You do not remember me," Lamouche said over his shoulder as he led Naima through the restaurant's dining room. About a dozen men, half of them in plain clothes, half of them uniformed cops, milled about the space. "I have eaten here many time."

"Uh-huh."

"But perhaps you will recognize zis person here," Lamouche said, stopping at the threshold of the kitchen. "Maybe you can give us an identification of ze body."

Jeremy Hairston lay on his stomach, in the center of the kitchen floor, his arms spread, his head twisted toward the door. His right cheek was pressed against the beige floor tiles. His left eye was wide open, staring gruesomely. A large butcher knife, only half its blade visible, was sticking out of the center of his back. Blood had plastered his black shirt to his torso.

Naima stood in the kitchen doorway, her hands raised to her mouth. Since stepping on the plane in New York the night before, she had held on to her composure, refusing to cry. But at the sight of Jeremy, all of her self-control exploded in a torrent of sobs.

PART 2

Le Père

Nine

DRIVING THROUGH GOLDEN WHEAT fields in the Normandy country-side, early in the evening of Tuesday, August 28, 2001, Loïc Rose was surprised by how easy it had been for him to decide to commit suicide. There was an implacable logic about his decision. If life was, as he had sometimes wished to believe, a game, then he was on the brink of losing. Whatever desperation, whatever anguish—if not downright terror—Loïc felt at this moment, the decision to kill himself was similar to a chess player's decision to resign when it was clear that his opponent would checkmate him in the next move. Loïc had never been a very good chess player, though he knew when he was cornered, beaten. His resignation from the game of life would come in the form of a bullet to his brain.

But first he had to get his gun, the only one he'd ever owned, the .38 caliber revolver he kept hidden in the bottom drawer of a dusty old armoire in the cellar of what Marva called their "weekend getaway" house near Gisors, just an hour and a half's drive from Paris. Guiding his blue Peugeot along the winding country roads, Loïc was not sure where exactly he would shoot himself. Inside the Normandy house? Or inside his car? Maybe he should return to Paris and do the deed under a bridge on the Seine? The only location he had ruled out was his apartment on the Boulevard Saint-Germain. The likelihood of Naima finding his corpse was too terrible even to contemplate. The fact of his suicide would be damaging enough for his daughter. Loïc knew that all too well. Erwan Rose had, after all, taken his own life, passing on to his son the bleakest of legacies.

Loïc could only hope that Naima would forgive him, as he had forgiven his father. Loïc and Naima had had a beautiful last moment together. Loïc had not yet decided that morning, when he had made a banana and Nutella crêpe for his daughter, that he would kill himself. He hoped that Naima would remember how happy he had been to see her. He hoped she would remember that he had not expressed any anger toward Marva. Naima had worried, after Marva's disappearance from the Hôpital Decoust, that maybe her mother had been kidnapped. Loïc told her it wasn't so. What he did not explain was that Marva had, in fact, chosen to flee. To flee, and maybe even to die, with Hassan Mekachera.

There was so much Naima was going to have to sort out. He hoped that if the tangled truth of this whole catastrophe was ever revealed, Naima would realize that Loïc's suicide had been a choice calculated to save the lives of others. A little more than an hour earlier, when Loïc had entered Marva's restaurant through the back entrance—the door that opened into the kitchen—and discovered Jeremy Hairston on the floor with a knife in his back, he knew he would have to sacrifice himself to stop the killing. Would Naima ever understand this?

Loïc knew that Naima would never view his suicide the way he did: as an inevitable endgame. And yet Loïc could not help but feel a grudging admiration for his adversary: Harvey Oldcorn. The American had played a masterful game these past two or three months. Loïc could still not figure out how many moves ahead Oldcorn had seen. Did Harvey have a precise and detailed strategy mapped out back in early June, that night he and Loïc had had dinner together at Marva's restaurant? Or had Harvey simply improvised the whole scheme, executing his moves on the fly, taking brilliant advantage of the mistakes made by his opponent? Pluralize that, Loïc thought: *Opponents* was more accurate. Harvey Oldcorn was like a grand master going up against several other players at once—and vanquishing them all.

"What America needs," Harvey Oldcorn told Loïc Rose in June 2001, "is a new Pearl Harbor."

They were dining at the Soul Food Kitchen. Marva was home in bed that night, resting after the removal of a cyst the day before. She said she felt fine and had wanted to come in to work but Loïc had talked her out of it. He was afraid that if Marva saw Oldcorn, who was back in Paris after a nine-year absence, she wouldn't be able to resist zinging some nasty little wisecrack his way. Marva had never liked Harvey. Loïc wasn't particularly fond of the jolly, jowly Oldcorn, either. In fact, he had been putting off this meeting for weeks. Harvey Oldocrn was one of those Americans who always wanted something from you.

"It's ridiculous," Harvey said between mouthfuls of catfish. "Greatest superpower in the history of civilization and we behave like a timid, helpless giant."

"Isn't that going to change now?" Loïc asked, adding wryly, "What with the Restoration in Washington."

"Sure, the grown-ups are back in charge, but it's going to take a while to undo the damage wrought by the Arkansas pigfucker. The American people have been encouraged to think that this is a safe world. Even when our own interests are attacked. What happened when terrorists blew up two of our embassies in Africa? Nothing! Last year a U.S. naval vessel was hit by suicide bombers in fucking Yemen, in broad daylight. A bunch of our sailors murdered by Islamist terrorists. Does America respond? Of course not! Even with the new crew in Washington—and there are some damn good men on this team, people who understand what power is all about—it doesn't matter one jot when the population has grown weak and complacent. We finally have the right leadership in place. Now the entire nation needs to be shaken out of its torpor."

The restaurant was buzzing and Loïc was relieved that customers at nearby tables were too caught up in their own conversations to eavesdrop on Harvey's tirade. Oldcorn wasn't raising his voice but he spoke with a humorless intensity that Loïc found somewhat embarrassing. Back in the old days, the American was always cheery, no matter how dark the business at hand. When had Harvey turned so grim?

"Okay, so the lazy American Colossus is sleeping," Loïc said, trying to strike a lighthearted, levelheaded note. "You don't seriously believe he needs another Date That Shall Live in Infamy to be roused."

Oldcorn didn't crack the smile that Loïc had hoped for. "I'm dead serious," he said. "And so are a lot of other people."

According to Harvey Oldcorn, the sainted Franklin Delano Roosevelt, every Frenchman's favorite U.S. president, had known that the Japanese were going to attack the American naval base in Hawaii on December 7, 1941. But he allowed it to happen because he knew this was the only way to galvanize the country into joining the war against fascism. This was a theory Loïc had heard before—and had always dismissed.

"FDR *knew*," Harvey stated solemnly. "I know he knew. He recognized that Americans would have to die before the country could live up to its responsibility. Its destiny." Harvey prattled about America's enemies in the Third World: Iraq, Iran, Syria, Libya. "Countries," he pointed out, "with precious natural resources." He rambled on about America's need to seize this moment in history, to assert its power. Loïc began to feel sickened when Oldcorn spoke of the need for total war, perpetual war. Perpetual war, Harvey said, would be good for the world economy. It was also the key to building a successful empire. "You Europeans, you Romans and British and French and Germans, you've had your imperial moments and blown them all. Now it's our turn to show you sons of bitches how to make it work."

"But only after the new Pearl Harbor."

"*Exactement.*"

Loïc would have been troubled if Harvey had struck him as a man with a tenuous grip on sanity. But Oldcorn seemed totally sane. That was what really frightened Loïc.

A loud crash came from the kitchen, startling some of the diners, hardly registering with most. "Damn it!" Jeremy Hairston nearly shouted. Loïc spotted him near the center of the dining room, in the process of seating a handsome couple. Jeremy twirled around and went striding furiously toward the kitchen. Loïc had noticed that Jeremy, in Marva's absence, had been skittish and irritable all evening. Loïc knew Jeremy was a highly competent manager but lots of things were going wrong that night in early June: orders mixed up, seatings delayed, side dishes forgotten. Loïc had tried not to pay too much attention. He wanted to seem more like an ordinary customer than a 50 percent owner of the restaurant. It also occurred to Loïc that maybe his very presence, in Marva's absence, was making Jeremy nervous. Many times during his dinner with Harvey Oldcorn, Loïc had heard Jeremy snap at the two waitresses.

Oldcorn continued his tirade, babbling now about all the faults of European immigration policies. He spoke of the need to crack

down on cells of Islamist terrorists living in cities like London and
Amsterdam, Hamburg and Milan, Madrid and Paris. Back in the
1960s, when Western European economies were booming, these
cities welcomed Muslims from North Africa and elsewhere. They
provided cheap labor. But now, in leaner times, these immigrants and
their children were a burden on their adopted homelands, according
to Harvey Oldcorn. What's more, he complained, many of them had
refused to integrate, to learn the language and assume the customs of
whatever European country they were living in. Now, all over Western Europe, one saw these young Muslims who were bitter, often un-
employed, many of them turning to crime, others even to terrorism.

"Good Lord, Harvey, my daughter accuses me of being a Gaullist
right-winger. But you sound as bad as Le Pen himself. Are you sure
you don't have some French blood in you?"

Harvey didn't even look at Loïc. He was staring past him, at
someone beyond the Frenchman's shoulder. "Take him, for instance," Harvey said.

Loïc turned around and saw, at the entrance to the kitchen, Jeremy and a young cook. Loïc couldn't hear much through the buzz of
the crowd but it was clear Jeremy was balling the kid out. "I told
you," Loïc heard Jeremy fume, barely audible over the din of the diners, "I done told you already!"

"Who's that?" Harvey asked.

"Jeremy?"

"No, not him, the cook."

"A new hire. I forget his name. I don't get involved much in the
day-to-day business here anymore."

"You see," Harvey said, still not raising his voice but sounding
consumed with anger, "that's what I'm talking about. Young kid, Algerian, Moroccan, whatever, hired for a menial job. You're his damn
employer and you don't know anything about him, if he has a prison
record, if he's a drug dealer, a rapist, a terrorist. You have no idea."

"Now get your ass back in the damn kitchen," Loïc heard Jeremy
snarl. The young cook, a handsome if sullen-looking kid, turned and

walked away from Jeremy without saying a word. Loïc spun back around in his chair, returning his full attention to Harvey, not wanting Jeremy to know he had seen the little confrontation.

"Actually," Loïc said, "I think his name is Hassan. Hassan . . . something. And if Marva hired him then I know one thing for certain. No matter where he's from or what he might be guilty of, he must be one hell of a cook."

Harvey scowled and said, "Hmmph."

Nearly three months later, driving up to the black wrought-iron gate of his Normandy property, Loïc remembered how he had fought with Marva over the purchase of this country house. Breton to the core, Loïc thought that Marva should be happy to spend all of their holidays in the far northwest of France, far from Paris. But Marva had insisted on having a "weekend getaway" relatively close to the city. Loïc knew that his wife also desired a place that would be truly hers, in no way connected to her husband's family in Brittany. As usual, Marva had won the argument. Twenty years later, Loïc had still never felt as at home in the Normandy house as Marva—and now Naima—did. If he shot himself there, with the gun he kept hidden in the armoire in the cellar, would it seem like some sort of hostile statement against his wife and daughter?

Only as Loïc pressed the button on the remote control and watched the gate swing slowly open did he wonder if perhaps Marva and Hassan were hiding out in the Normandy house. Hearing the tires of his car crunch along the gravel driveway, he wondered what would happen to Hassan and Marva once they were captured by the authorities. Hassan would most likely be killed on sight. Would Marva? Would poor Naima be left an orphan?

As Loïc turned his key in the front-door lock, he almost hoped he would find Marva and Hassan hiding in the house. Maybe, together, the three of them could work out a way to beat Harvey Oldcorn at his sick and malevolent game.

"Hello?" Loïc called out as he entered the darkened foyer.

The place seemed deserted. He descended the stairs to the cellar. Working his way through twenty years' worth of family junk that had been dumped below ground, Loïc approached the rotting, cob-webbed armoire. He squatted and pulled open the bottom drawer, searched through the jumble of spools and needles and yarn that had concealed the .38 caliber revolver for two decades. He groped through the mess, ripped the drawer out of its slot and turned it up-side down, spilling its contents onto the cement floor.

The gun was gone.

Ten

NAIMA STARED STRAIGHT AHEAD, at Marva's Wall of Fame, trying to concentrate on the array of photos directly in front of her. The pictures were all in black and white, most of them taken before Naima was born. Marva was in every one of them, smiling victoriously as she stood beside the likes of Ray Charles, Aretha Franklin, Jean-Paul Belmondo, Toni Morrison, Jeanne Moreau, James Baldwin and a couple dozen other prominent personages of the era. It was a stunning display of star power but one Naima had hardly ever paid any attention to.

But this Tuesday evening, Naima sat rigidly in her chair, just one foot in front of the Wall of Fame, focusing on the pictures in order to blot out the commotion behind her. She could hear cops and medics coming in and out of the restaurant. She cringed at the squeak of a stretcher being wheeled across the dining-room floor and into the kitchen. To keep from bursting into tears again, she concentrated hard on the photo of a hugely pregnant Marva beaming beside an uncharacteristically animated François Mitterrand, just three years before he would become president of the Republic. Endless minutes later, Naima heard the squeak of the wheels again. Part of her wanted to turn around, to force herself to look at Jeremy Hairston's body on the stretcher. But she knew she couldn't take it. Suddenly, she felt two clammy hands on her shoulders. She knew it was Inspector Lamouche, trying to console her. She didn't know whether to appreciate the gesture or to tell this oily stranger not to touch her.

"Okay, we are alone now," Lamouche said.

Naima turned her chair around and saw a group of uniformed cops filing out of the restaurant. She heard the two-tone whine of sirens out on the street. Lamouche sat down in a chair beside her. "Zis is a terrible tragedy. Ze meat delivery mens found Monsieur Hairston at five o'clock. We believe he was stabbed an hour before, while ze restaurant was closed to ze public. Zere was no sign of a forced break-in. Nozing was stolen. Ze safe in ze office upstairs seems untouched. All zis make us believe zat Monsieur Hairston knew his killer. Ze knife is being checked for fingerprints."

"This doesn't make any sense," Naima said, choking back a sudden sob. "He was such a nice man. Everybody loved Jeremy. Why would anyone want to kill him?"

"Maybe because he know too many zings."

Naima took a deep breath, tried to steel herself again. "What do you mean?"

The corners of Lamouche's mouth curled in a cryptic little smile. "I am *au courant, mademoiselle.* I know zat your mohzer leave her hospital in ze middle of ze night. Have you no news of her?"

"No. None."

"We have tried to locate your fahzer, wiz no success."

"He left for a business trip in Lyon."

"*Ah bon?* Did he go by car or by train?"

"I have no idea. He said he'd be back tomorrow."

"Hmm. And you are sure he tell you ze truze?"

Naima felt her anger flaring up again. "Listen, Inspector, I'm not going to answer any more questions until I talk to a lawyer."

Lamouche sighed. "*Mademoiselle,* zis is not America. You have no automatic right to a lawyer if I arrest you."

"Are you arresting me?"

"Not if you cooperate. Do not make zis hard, *mademoiselle.* We have reason to believe zat your mohzer may have been kidnapped. Let us best use ze time we have in zis investigation before ze press jump all over ze story and ze *scandale* hit. If you please."

Scandale. The word flashed across Naima's mind like a neon sign.

Lamouche reached into a battered black satchel on the floor, pulled out a thick folder and started flipping through it.

Naima had no idea what the cop was reading, nor did she care. She kept seeing Jeremy Hairston, sprawled across the kitchen floor. She remembered what the nurses at the Hôpital Decoust had told her about Marva leaving with an "Arab-looking" young man, remembered her father's sad face as he told her Marva was having an affair, brooded over what Lamouche had said about Marva being "kidnapped." Then that word flashed across her mind again: *scandale.*

Back in America, millions of people were currently enthralled by the disappearance of a young congressional intern named Chandra Levy. She had been having an affair with her boss, Representative Gary Condit. All summer long, camera crews staked out Condit's apartment building, chased the politician down the street, demanding to know if he'd killed Chandra Levy. TV and radio talk shows featured sundry crime experts, prosecutors, psychiatrists and "profilers" speculating on whether Condit had murdered the girl himself or hired someone else to do her in, then dispose of the body.

Every day on the movie set somebody wanted to discuss the Condit case with Naima. She was amazed by the mass fascination, the sheer breadth of public obsession. Of course, the same thing happened in France, but never on the same scale as in America. Scandals were more slow-burning in France, the press more discreet, the public less hungry for daily details. Still, the appetite was there. And while Naima was often oblivious to the fact that her mother was something of a French celebrity, staring at the Wall of Fame had served as a potent reminder of Marva's notoriety. The events of the past twenty-four hours, capped by Jeremy's murder, would make irresistible scandal fodder. Naima felt sickened by the thought of camera crews outside her family's building. She was finding it hard enough to adapt to this new surreality of abduction and killing. A media maelstrom was something she felt totally unprepared for.

Inspector Lamouche's piercing whistle snapped Naima out of her gloomy reverie. She thought she recognized the tune the cop was tootling absentmindedly as he flipped through the folder in his lap. She couldn't help but stare at Lamouche as he whistled away. She began to think she'd guessed the song wrong, mistaken it for something else. But, no, she really was listening to a French cop whistle "California Girls." Lamouche abruptly stopped whistling when he noticed Naima's stare. He smiled sheepishly. "You like ze Beesh Boys?"

"No."

Lamouche looked disappointed. "Oh well."

"You know," Naima said, the cop's accent starting to grate on her nerves, "we can speak in French if you like."

"No, no. Iz good for me to practice my English. *Donc* . . . you know zat ze Wurzee building was attacked ze ozer night."

"So I heard." Naima wondered if Lamouche was trying to make conversation before asking her more questions about Marva. She wanted to ask what the hell WORTHEE had to do with her mother but she decided, instead, to be polite. "Has anyone claimed responsibility?" Naima asked, her natural curiosity perking up.

"Not yet. We suppose Islamic militants."

"But why WORTHEE?"

"Zat is a very good question! Wurzee is famous as a nonpolitical research institute, iz true. But over ze years ze mission of ze institute change somewhat. Wurzee has been involved in some very sensitive projects for ze U.S. government. Counterterrorism, zat sort of zing. One fear is zat zis attack was only ze first. Striking at—how do you say?—a soft target might have been a practice for somezing more ambitious. More sensational and deadly."

"Okay," Naima said, her patience exhausted, "but what does any of this have to do with Marva and Jeremy?"

She detected a flicker of triumph in Lamouche's creepy little smile. "Has your mohzer ever mentioned a Hassan Mekachera to you?"

"No."

"He was a cook at zis restaurant since early May."

"I haven't been home since last summer."

"We have reason to believe zat Hassan Mekachera's job was just a cover for his true vocation: terrorist."

"You don't think . . . ?"

"I'm afraid so. Hassan Mekachera has been missing since Friday. We zink zat he and an accomplice planned and executed zis attack. His accomplice is in police custody but Hassan is still at large. And we zink he kidnap your mohzer last night."

"Why?"

"Zey had, perhaps, a very special relationship," Lamouche said with a smarmy leer.

Naima tried to contain her temper. It was bad enough that Marva had been having an affair with an employee, far worse that the employee might have been a terrorist. But Naima was not about to tolerate Lamouche's smirking over it. "Answer my fucking question," she snarled.

Lamouche's face went dead. When he spoke again it was in a solemn monotone. "Hassan is a desperate man. He's been running for his life for thirty-six hours. He must have learned Madame Dobbs was in ze hospital. Let us say he abducted her, forced her to take him to zis restaurant to get cash out of ze safe or somezing. Who knows what? Zey come between lunch and dinner, expecting no one here.

But zey encounter Jeremy. Let us say zere is a scuffle in ze kitchen and Hassan stabs your friend in ze back. Hassan zen takes off wiz Marva, his hostage. We suspect he's planning to use her for some kind of ransom."

"*Mon Dieu.*" Naima was stunned by what Lamouche had told her but she struggled to hold on to her composure, to think coolly, logically.

There was a knock at the front door. A uniformed cop poked his head in, said Lamouche was needed outside. Naima could hear a buzzing crowd on the rue Véron.

"One moment, please," the inspector said to Naima.

As soon as Lamouche stepped outside, Naima raced up the spiral staircase near the kitchen and entered Marva's office. She turned on a small desk lamp, sat down in front of the computer and booted it up. A list of files appeared on the screen. She clicked on the file marked STAFF. A message flashed: ENTER PASSWORD.

"*Merde,*" Naima hissed. She decided to take a guess and typed in N-A-I-M-A. The file popped open. She clicked on the name "Hassan Mekachera" and a photo of a cute, sleepy-eyed North African guy appeared, with a list of relevant information beneath it. Naima had just enough time to print out the fact sheet and stuff it in her back pocket before she heard Lamouche reenter downstairs.

"*Mademoiselle?*"

The cop eyed Naima suspiciously as she descended the staircase. "Sorry," she said. "I just wanted to take a look at my mother's office."

"*Ah bon?*" Lamouche said coldly. "Zis whole place is still considered a crime scene, *mademoiselle.*"

Naima ignored the remark. "Can I please go home now?" she asked in a weary voice. "I'm just overwhelmed by all this. I have a headache and I need to lie down."

"Very well." Lamouche handed her a business card. "Please call me if you get any news of your mohzer or fahzer. Come: We exit by ze back door."

Walking quickly through the kitchen, Naima glanced at the police-drawn outline of Jeremy's body on the tiles. Lamouche led her out the kitchen door and into the back alley.

"I want a refund!" the angry black tourist shouted.

Naima and Lamouche had just emerged from the alley onto the rue Véron. She saw two police cars, several uniformed cops and a cluster of about a dozen African Americans gathered outside Marva's Soul Food Kitchen. Naima hovered on the edge of the crowd as a seriocomic chant rose up: "Refund! Refund! Refund! Refund!"

A hefty woman wearing a billowing, kente-patterned dress and an elaborate braided hairdo stood before the group, her back nearly pressed against the door of the restaurant. Naima recognized Charisse Bray from her waitressing days. She was the ethnocentric tour guide with the booming voice and abominable French. She was smiling but looked unnerved as the crowd chanted at her.

"Refund! Refund! Refund!"

Charisse held up her hands to quiet the tourists. "I'm sorry everybody but there's nothing I can do. We'll have to eat dinner somewhere else tonight. The police have sealed the entrance. This is a crime scene."

The chant died down but was replaced by puzzled muttering. "Say what?" somebody asked.

"There was a murder here this afternoon," Charisse said, her voice quavering.

"Not Marva!" one of the tourists gasped.

"No, not Marva," Charisse said, her eyes welling with tears. "Somebody else."

As the crowd tittered and Charisse promised to make up for this thwarted dinner date somehow, Naima started to walk away. Lamouche grasped her by the arm. "Can I offer a ride home, *mademoiselle*?"

"No, thank you," Naima said, as meekly as she could manage, trying to hide her eagerness to escape the cop and to avoid being recognized by Charisse. "I'll take the metro. I'd like to be alone with my thoughts."

Maximilien-François-Marie-Isidore de Robespierre, the vicious tyrant who presided over the Reign of Terror during the French Revolution, did not have a street named after him in Paris. Yet he was too important a figure in France's history to go completely unacknowledged, however bloody his brief rule had been. So the name of Robespierre was geographically marginalized, placed just outside the Paris city limits. The mile-long rue Robespierre cut a north-south swath through two small cities immediately east of Paris, Bagnolet and Montreuil. In Montreuil, the man who, as commissioner of public safety, sent untold numbers of citizens to the guillotine before he himself was beheaded by popular demand, even had a metro stop with his name on it. Naima emerged from the subway station at the corner of the rue Robespierre and the rue de Paris and stepped into a France the dear, decapitated dictator could never have imagined.

There was nary a white face on Montreuil's rue de Paris. Naima was among first- or second- or third-generation Frenchmen and Frenchwomen whose roots stretched south to Africa, west to the Caribbean, east to Turkey and Lebanon. She walked past an outdoor grocery shop whose stands overflowed with ripe green plaintains, fuzzy brown coconuts, long fat purple sweet potatoes and tubular, thick-skinned rootstocks like yams and manioc. She walked past men in ankle-length robes and sandals, mothers in veils pushing little kids in strollers and groups of young guys working on their thug attitudes. Naima was always intrigued by the way American street styles gradually worked their way over to France. Going back and forth between the two nations of her citizenship, she had seen the one-way migration (mainly via video) of popular gestures and facial expressions, of backward baseball caps, do-rags and baggy, low-riding pants. These days it seemed the American penchant for flaunting huge, ferocious dogs had definitely been adopted by French wannabe hood-

lums. The disconcerting difference between, say, New York and Montreuil was that in the French town, the Dobermans, Rottweilers and
German shepherds were permitted to trot beside their masters unleashed.

It was eight in the evening but the August sun was still shining
brightly. Turning onto Hassan Mekachera's street, rue Etienne Marcel, Naima was greeted by rows of boarded-up condemned buildings
and houses that seemed to have been only partly demolished, as if the
crews wielding the wrecking balls had suddenly lost interest in their
destruction and decided to leave remnants of brick façades—
shuttered windows and chained doors intact—to stand in ghostly
vigil over the block, surrounded by rubble. Naima approached one of
the few complete, seemingly inhabited structures on this stretch of
Etienne Marcel. She noticed a panel of buttons beside the front door.
There was no name in the slot beside the button for the Mekachera
residence, *Appartement* 13. Instead of ringing the buzzer, Naima
pushed against the front door and, not surprisingly, found that the
automatic lock did not function. She entered the gritty lobby,
climbed the stairs to the second floor. She rang the doorbell of *Appartement* 13 but heard no sound. She waited a while, then knocked
three times. No answer. She decided nobody was there but knocked
three more times anyway, nearly yelping in fright when the door
suddenly swung open.

"*Quoi?*" barked the young woman standing in the doorway under the harsh light of the bare bulb hanging from the ceiling inside
the apartment. She was a tall, almost gangly, unmistakably French
woman, with reddish blond hair parted in the middle, darkening at
the roots and tied back in a short ponytail. Long-necked, with a
prominent nose, a smattering of freckles on her cheeks, and smallish
brown eyes, she had a vaguely giraffelike quality. Yet she was, in a
quirky, self-possessed way, quite pretty. She wore a purple tank top
and tattered blue jeans sporting multicolored paint stains. Making a
quick, clinical social judgment, Naima decided that the woman in
the doorway was a bohemian with a monied background. An unlit

cigarette dangled from the woman's lips and, in the crook of her right arm, she held an olive-toned infant with a sweet, sleepy-eyed expression Naima recognized instantly.

"I'm looking for Hassan Mekachera," Naima said, in French, of course.

The woman smirked, the cigarette tilting upward between her lips. "Don't tell me," she said. "You're a very close friend of his."

"Actually, I've never met the man. But I think he's kidnapped my mother."

The woman's smirk turned into a sympathetic, knowing frown. She seemed sorry for her brusque attitude and made a touchingly French peace offering: "Would you like a glass of wine?"

"Yes. Thank you."

Naima entered the short, narrow hallway of *Appartement* 13, closed the creaky door behind her. The woman switched the baby to her left arm, held out her right hand. "Marie-Christine Pinchot."

"Naima Rose."

"Not Dobbs?"

"Dobbs is my mother's maiden name."

"This is Xavier." The baby squealed a merry greeting and waved at Naima.

"How old is he?"

"One year and three days. Come."

Naima followed Marie-Christine into a spartan room that was decorated in a familiar young-bachelor-on-a-miniscule-budget style. A futon in the corner, a battered dresser with drawer handles missing, a bare table with two flimsy-looking wooden chairs. There was a compact stereo set placed between the two tall windows in the room. The radio was tuned to a jazz station, Charles Mingus's "Good-bye Pork Pie Hat" playing softly. In the center of the room was a small-screen television propped up on a plastic milk crate, tuned to the French all-news channel, the volume turned all the way down. A square-jawed female newscaster spoke earnestly, soundlessly, into the camera. Marie-Christine placed Xavier on the floor and he crawled rapidly across the threadbare brown rug toward a cluster of toy cars and trucks in front of the TV. Only then did Naima notice, lying beside a closed door (did it lead to a closet? A second room?), an open black suitcase, articles of clothing spilling out onto the floor.

"Just a moment," Marie-Christine said. She turned and headed back down the short hallway. Naima heard kitchen noises, the opening and closing of a refrigerator door, the clatter of dishes and glasses being rummaged through in a sink, a blast of tap water. She walked over to the single, squat bookcase in the room. Its three shelves were filled entirely with cookbooks.

"Gaaaaah!" Xavier squealed.

Naima turned and saw the little boy sitting on the rug, grinning and waving a tiny police car at her. "Well, hello, young man."

Then Naima noticed, just behind Xavier, that the image on the television had changed. The screen was filled with the charred façade of the WORTHEE building. The camera panned to the smoking, mangled remains of a car and the word LUNDI (Monday) appeared in a corner of the screen. Xavier twisted around to see what Naima was looking at. "Gheeeg," he said to the television. Next thing she knew, Naima was staring at her mother. Marva was walking in slow-motion down a red carpet, her back to the camera, in a sequined dress. As Marva turned to face the paparazzi, Naima saw palm trees swaying in the background. This must have been a clip from one of the Cannes Film Festivals, an opening- or closing-night ceremony, maybe three or four years ago. Marva smiled winningly as flashbulbs exploded in her face. She was absolutely radiant, Naima's mother, glamorous as an ageless movie goddess, acknowledging the paparazzi, her hand slicing the air in an ethereal, decelerated wave.

Mesmerized by the image, Naima didn't even think to turn up the sound on the television. The title on the screen read: MARVA DOBBS (ARCHIVES). There was no mention of the man beside Marva, walking just a few steps ahead of her along the red carpet. The silver-haired gent in the tuxedo did not turn to face the cameras. But Naima naturally recognized him, even from behind. And she couldn't help but smile at her father's loosey-goosey, arm-swinging gait, endearingly comical as it was, even in slow motion.

"Bizarre, isn't it?" Marie-Christine said, returning to the room with two wineglasses and a perspiring bottle of rosé in her hands, a trail of smoke unfurling from the cigarette that still dangled between her lips.

"Papa!" Xavier shrieked.

Now Naima saw the black-and-white ID card photo filling the television screen. The title in the corner read: HASSAN MEKACHERA. Yep, it was him all right, with that heavy-lidded, unconsciously seductive look in his eyes. Marie-Christine quickly grabbed the remote control from atop the bookcase, snapped off the TV.

"Guh?" Xavier inquired.

"Play with your cars," Marie-Christine growled at Xavier who, after a brief, befuddled pause, resumed that activity. She then plopped down on the futon, poured two glasses of pink wine and handed one to her guest.

Naima sat in one of the wobbly chairs, took a sip of her wine. It tasted like refrigerated cough syrup. She drank it down anyway. It was a sweaty, sticky August evening and she was thirsty. Marie-Christine refilled her glass. "So, do you live here?"

"Not at all," Marie-Christine replied, pulling an ashtray from a nearby windowsill. "We came up from Marseille this morning. But Hassan gave me keys to this place a long time ago."

"So you live in Marseille?"

"Yes." Marie-Christine took a big gulp of wine. "I was hoping, when I heard your knock, that you were a reporter."

"Why?"

"Because we need to get the truth out! The media is broadcasting the idea that Hassan is some kind of a terrorist. You yourself said he kidnapped your mother!"

"Isn't that so?"

"It's impossible!" Marie-Christine exploded. For once, Naima didn't mind hearing a French person utter those words. "Probably he was trying to save her!"

"Save her from what?"

"Not what. Who." Marie-Christine angrily stubbed out her cigarette in the ashtray. "Probably the same people who are trying to frame him for this bombing."

"You aren't making any sense," Naima snapped.

Marie-Christine gave her a dagger-eyed stare. "Hassan was fucking your mother. I guess you know that."

Naima cast a glance at Xavier, who was crashing cars into each other on the rug, then returned Marie-Christine's nasty look. "Seems he fucked you worse."

Marie-Christine leaned back on the futon, a wry smile creeping across her face. It was as if she was recognizing that she couldn't mess with Naima. Glad we've got that issue out of the way, Naima thought.

"I have never asked anything of Hassan," Marie-Christine said, sounding at once defensive and boastful. "He is a free man. And I am free also. I chose to have this baby. And I am very happy that I did. So, as a matter of fact, is Hassan."

"Right. You and Xavier live in Marseille. But Hassan lives in Paris. Does he ever even get to see your child?"

"He comes down south fairly often. For instance, he was with us in Marseille just this past weekend."

Marie-Christine had to know Naima would be shocked to hear this news, but Naima tried not to show it. "Oh really?"

"Yes. Really."

"*Maman!*" Xavier shouted. He threw one of his cars against the wall, then started making gurgling noises.

Marie-Christine smiled. "He's hungry." She turned to Naima. "Why don't you stay and have dinner with us? I'm making spaghetti bolognese."

"I don't know," Naima said, still not sure what to make of this
woman. "Maybe I should go."

"No. Please stay. I'll tell you everything I know."

The first thing Naima needed to understand, according to Marie-
Christine, was that Hassan was a genius. Temperamental, yes. Im-
petuous? Of course! In love with life, in love with love but, above all,
in love with cuisine. That was what drew him to Marva. She was a
master. "She is at the summit of her art and she doesn't even know it,"
Hassan had told Marie-Christine in Marseille last Sunday afternoon.
Marie-Christine told him that, despite his age difference with Marva,
he did not have a mother complex; he had a *master* complex. Marie-
Christine could see how two romantic artists could tumble into a tem-
pestuous affair. In that way, Marva and Hassan were no different from
George Sand and Alfred de Musset, Jean-Paul Sartre and Simone de
Beauvoir, Yves Montand and Simone Signoret. Hassan was in awe of
Marva. He wanted to learn all that he could from her. But, Marie-
Christine insisted, as a chef, Hassan already had his own poetry.

How Naima, the half-French half-American girl, loved listening
to the French talk about food—especially about food as art. She had
never tasted Hassan's cooking, so she couldn't judge Marva's youthful
apprentice. But Naima knew her mother was a genius. And she knew
that her mother also knew she was a genius. But Marva would probably never admit such a thing. As imperious and moody as she was,
she wore her culinary gift lightly. In her particularly American way,
she shrugged it off. "It's just home cookin'," she liked to say. Of
course, Marva took her work seriously. But to talk about it as art
would have struck her as pretentious. Still, Naima's mother had chosen to live in Paris, where others were eager to describe her as an
artist while she could adopt a pose of ineffable cool about her talent.
As usual, Marva wanted it both ways—the best of the American and
the French modes. And, more often than not, she got it.

"I am not a genius," Marie-Christine said. She was a painter of landscapes and wanted to let Naima know that she made a decent living at it, selling scenic tableaux to tourists in the South of France. She met Hassan at a party in Marseille three years ago. He was there visiting friends. Hassan lived in Toulouse and, for a year, he and Marie-Christine had a casual, sporadic relationship, hopping on trains, hanging out for rhapsodic weekends in each other's cities. She knew Hassan had other lovers. Why wouldn't he? He was a beautiful, twenty-five-year-old bachelor. Marie-Christine was ten years older and no longer had the desire for many affairs. She devoted much of that passionate energy to her painting.

Marie-Christine was happy for Hassan when he told her he was moving to Paris to work in a fancy hotel restaurant. She was less thrilled that Hassan's cousin Ramzi would be sharing an apartment with him. She had met Ramzi in Toulouse and always found him to be a bit bizarre, too sullen and intense. All the same, she figured she and Hassan would continue their sporadic rhapsodic affair. Soon after her first weekend visit with Hassan in Paris, Marie-Christine became pregnant. He endorsed her decision to keep the baby. But Marie-Christine stated, once again, "I have never asked anything of Hassan."

"Did you love him?" Naima asked.

"Of course. And I love him still."

"Fweeeeee!" Xavier screamed exultantly as he tossed a few chopped-up spaghetti strands into the air. He was sitting in a high chair that Hassan had bought for his visits to Paris, bolognese sauce smeared all over his chubby cheeks and smiling lips. Xavier, tired of having his mother feed him, and ignoring the plastic spoon she had given him, reached into his spaghetti, scooped up a fistful and stuffed it happily into his mouth.

Naima and Marie-Christine were each finishing second helpings and polishing off the bottle of chilled Côtes du Rhône that had followed the rosé. It was almost ten o'clock. Naima could see, through the tall, open windows, the dusk gathering over the wreckage of Hassan's street. She still felt a bit guarded with Marie-Christine but somehow she couldn't help admiring the painter's flinty independence.

"In his way," Marie-Christine said, "Hassan is a very good father. Even though he lives in another city, he spends more—what is it the Americans say?—more quality time with Xavier than a lot of bourgeois fathers who live in the same house every day with their children."

"Papa!" Xavier squawked, seemingly in agreement.

Hassan eventually grew restless working at the fancy hotel restaurant, Marie-Christine explained. The head chef there was suffocating his genius. As soon as he heard there was an opening at Marva's Soul Food Kitchen, he applied for the job. He seemed happy there, at least during the first three months, from May through July. Marie-Christine said she did not learn of Hassan's affair with Marva until this past weekend but she could tell, in phone conversations throughout the month of August, that something had gone wrong at the restaurant. Marie-Christine attributed it to creative differences between Hassan and the manager who was running the place while Marva was on vacation.

"Jeremy Hairston," Naima said. "Someone stabbed him to death today."

Marie-Christine lowered her eyes. "Yes, I know. I saw it on the news."

For a long time, both women were silent. Xavier continued to fist-feed himself. Naima heard a group of teenaged boys laughing as they walked down the rue Etienne Marcel, a French rap song blasting from the boom box they toted.

"Continue," Naima said after the noise from the street died down.

"Hassan clashed with Jeremy, it's true. But there was no violence in Hassan's anger. Jeremy just rubbed him the wrong way. Hassan became very agitated, distracted. I told him countless times to remember to call to wish Xavier a happy birthday. But he kept forgetting what the date was. That is not like Hassan. After all, he was with me in Marseille last year, the night Xavier was born. It was the stress at work that was making him grumpy and forgetful. Finally, we spoke last Thursday morning and I told him again not to forget to call and he asked me again what day it was and I said, 'It's Saturday, you narcissistic asshole, and if you forget to call I'll never forgive you and Xavier will never forgive you!' "

"Like Xavier would even know what day it was?"

Marie-Christine shrugged. "I know. I went a bit far. But then, the next day, Friday morning, Hassan showed up in Marseille. He said he was fed up with Jeremy. Last Thursday night, some customers complained about the strange flavors creeping into their favorite dishes. Jeremy stormed into the kitchen and told Hassan, 'This ain't no Algerian restaurant, boy!' Hassan started yelling back at Jeremy, then stomped out of the place. Friday he told me he had quit his job and was going to move back south, either to Toulouse or to Marseille, wherever he could find good work. Xavier was, as always, thrilled to see his papa. We celebrated his birthday as a family. Then, on Sunday, Hassan told me his whole story with Marva. I told him he should go back to Paris, meet with her at the *rentrée* before he decided to quit. He had clearly fallen in love with your mother. I knew that he had to fall out of love before he could leave Paris definitively. But Hassan, sometimes he does not know his own heart." For a moment, Marie-Christine looked as if she were about to cry. But she quickly composed herself. "As I told you, he is sometimes a strange man."

"But not a murderer?"

Marie-Christine startled Naima with an abrupt shriek of a laugh. "My God, no! And not a terrorist or a kidnapper, either. Really, the accusation would be funny if this situation weren't so dangerously fucked up."

They drank some more wine. Xavier yawned and stretched in his high chair, let out a squeaky little fart. Naima's eyes fell on the closed door. "And what about Ramzi?"

Marie-Christine lit a cigarette, her hand trembling slightly. "The police locked his door after they arrested him."

"Arrested? When?"

"Monday morning. You didn't know? Ramzi and Hassan are accused of doing the bombing together. Somebody, a woman from the neighborhood, called me in Marseille—my God, was it just yesterday morning? She woke us up, actually, at eight o'clock. She said nobody could find Hassan. People had called him on his cell phone but his service had been canceled because he'd neglected to pay his last bill. I didn't tell the woman, Madame Zebouni, that Hassan was with me. It was she who first told me that the WORTHEE building had been attacked. The cops raided this apartment at dawn, two hours after the bombing. They expected Hassan to be here, too. They threw Ramzi in prison. No one has heard anything from him since. But, of course, they're allowed to hold him for seventy-two hours without a single charge."

"And why was Ramzi a suspect?"

Marie-Christine started blinking rapidly, fighting back tears.

"*Maman!*" Xavier whined. He was twisting and writhing, trying to get out of his high chair.

"Let me put him to bed," Marie-Christine said, getting a grip on her emotions again. "Then we'll talk more. I have a cold bottle of limoncello."

"That sounds nice but first you've got to tell me—is there a reason to think that Ramzi is a terrorist?"

Marie-Christine threw up her hands and gave what Naima considered a classically French answer, both eminently sensible and utterly inscrutable: "It depends on what you mean by a reason!"

Eleven

HOW CAN YOU WRITE your autobiography when you are afraid of the truth? Or was it that Cleavon Semple had forgotten what was true? When first told, a lie is always harder to remember than the truth. Once you embrace the lie, commit to it, live it, the lie may supersede the truth but can never quite obliterate it. Cleavon, sitting in front of his electric typewriter, would often find himself writing a version of something that had happened and, seeing the words on paper, realize that he was transcribing a lie he had told to others, or to himself, so many times that only in the transcription did he remember the truth. But once the truth came back to him, Cleavon would realize he could never allow it to be published. So he invariably stuck with the lie. He wondered if this was the case with all memoirists.

Cleavon much preferred writing novels. But none of the seven he had produced over the past fifty years had ever been able to find a publisher. He liked to think that perhaps his novels would be discovered after his death. At seventy-nine, however, he was getting sick of fantasies of posthumous acclaim. He wanted recognition right now, damn it. He kept hearing that black memoirs were popular back in the States. It was a hot genre. So Cleavon had resolved to write the story of his life. The story of a black Ohio farmboy who grew up to be a war hero and an international adventurer. A man of action, a man of letters, a man of the world.

It would be more than a mere autobiography. It would also be a history of African Americans in Paris in the second half of the twentieth century. After all, Cleavon had rubbed elbows with such luminaries as Richard Wright and Josephine Baker, James Baldwin and Sidney Bechet, Beauford Delaney, Ollie Harrington, Marva Dobbs and Chester Himes. He had wonderful anecdotes he could share about these famous black expatriates. He just couldn't mention that he had informed on every one of them.

Nor could Cleavon mention all the "legal criminality," to use an old friend's expression, that he had practiced. He could not mention the things he had stolen, the money he had extorted, the reputations he had helped destroy, the men—and the woman—he had murdered.

No, Cleavon could not dare publish such revelations. Still he was determined to write his autobiography. It would be, out of necessity, a lie. He would just have to *sell* it as the truth.

Cleavon's phone rang but he didn't answer it. He had a heavy old black model with a jangling rattle of a ring. It was rare that anybody phoned Cleavon. But at noon that Tuesday, he'd received his unpleasant surprise call from Harvey Oldcorn. Since Cleavon returned from his meeting with good ole Harvey in the Jardin du Luxembourg, his phone had rung on three different occasions. Three calls in less than four hours. That was more than Cleavon usually received in a month. He had answered none of them. Having regretted picking up the receiver at noon, Cleavon simply gritted his teeth and endured the jangling rattle, counting the loud, shrill rings. After five, the caller hung up.

Was it Loïc Rose trying to reach him? That would have been Harvey's logic. He knew that Loïc was in trouble, that Loïc would seek Cleavon's help, giving Cleavon the chance to get close to Loïc, close enough to put a bullet in the Frenchman's brain. Harvey had to know this was the cruelest, sickest assignment Cleavon could get. But he knew that Cleavon could not refuse it. He had never refused one before. And now he was already hired. He had taken the money. He knew the rules. There was no backing out of this job.

Hell, Cleavon hadn't seen Loïc, or Marva, in sixteen years. He avoided the Soul Food Kitchen. He preferred the gauzy, fragrant memory of the place to the current reality. He had sometimes thought it might be nice to see Marva again. He did not feel that way about Loïc. Their friendship had evaporated long ago. If Loïc was suddenly trying to contact him, the matter must have been grave indeed. Something connected to the WORTHEE bombing? Since returning from his meeting with Oldcorn, Cleavon had assiduously avoided watching the television, reading the newspaper or listening to the radio. He pretended it was an ordinary day and he, the disciplined writer, was simply putting in the requisite hours at his desk. Refusing to answer the phone would not nullify his assignment. It would just extend the pretense a little longer.

Cleavon leaned forward in his chair and squinted at the lies on the page. Was it foolish of him to want to leave this testament? He had fathered no children. At least, none he was willing to acknowledge. There were no offspring to pass his story on to. It was only natural, then, that he would wish to leave some record of his journey on this earth. Especially if there were people who would spread lies about him. Why shouldn't he offer his own lies about himself, in counterpoint?

Cleavon needed a drink. He rose from the desk, walked over to the armoire. The Green Fairy twinkled amid the clutter of bottles and glasses on the middle shelf. Cleavon poured the absinthe into a small, fluted glass. Was this shit still contraband? He couldn't remember. He took a sip of the emerald liqueur, felt the slow-motion kick in the head. Was this why his memory was playing tricks on him, because of the Green Fairy? Or was it just that he was a lyin' old man?

"You're a traitor without a cause."

Wasn't that what Harvey Oldcorn had said to him this afternoon in the Jardin du Luxembourg? Is that what all those ofays in "the Authority" thought of Cleavon Semple? When it was *Cleavon* who had been betrayed—again and again and again. And what was that shit about having no cause? Cleavon had fought for the white American way and been betrayed by white America. He'd defended France and been betrayed by the French. He'd stuck up for black folks his whole damn life and had them, his own people, betray him, time after time after time. And what about the Arabs? How much had he sacrificed for their cause, only to be betrayed? Hell, they were even more duplicitous than niggers. But Arabs were just niggers by another name when you got right down to it, weren't they?

Cleavon plopped back down in front of the typewriter. His fingers attacked the keyboard almost involuntarily, as if jerked by some spasm. He heard the sudden metallic clank of the machine as he rapidly, violently slammed out the sentence. Then his hands dropped to his sides. Cleavon stared, in numb astonishment, at the words that had leapt from his fingertips onto the page.

I want to die.

He stared at the four words as if they had been typed by someone else and he had just stumbled upon them by accident. He felt a sickening jolt of recognition. He knew these were the truest words he might ever have written. He shut off the typewriter, ripped the page from the machine. Cleavon carried the piece of paper into the kitchen. He turned on one of the stove burners, held the page above the flames. As the page ignited, he dropped it into the sink, watched it burn down to a little pile of smelly ash.

The phone rang again. That jangling rattle. Cleavon walked over to the desk, picked up his glass of absinthe, then practically collapsed on the couch. The telephone shrieked. If it wasn't Harvey or Loïc calling, he was sure it was some other old acquaintance he'd hoped would remain forgot. Why didn't they just leave him the fuck alone, these spooks of the past?

Spooks. Sipping his emerald liqueur, Cleavon smiled at the word's triple meaning: ghosts, spies, and niggers. Cleavon Semple mused that he was all three: the ultimate spook. He slumped into the couch, suddenly realizing how drunk he already was. How drunk . . . and how spooky. The ghostly nigger spy. In his solitude. How he longed to be held. Or, at least, have his dick sucked. But there was no chance of that happening until Madame Ficelle returned from her holiday Sunday morning. Cleavon hadn't realized how much he would miss her this August, his horny forty-year-old concierge. With her mop of curly auburn hair turning gray, her bovine brown eyes and vapid smile, her squishy, succulent flesh, that short, round body that teetered on the line between pleasingly plump and repulsively fat. Cleavon could do anything to her and she loved it. Did that mean she was in love with him? Was he in love with her? No matter. She fucked like a beast and, for this seventy-nine-year-old spook, that was enough.

The phone continued to scream. Cleavon had lost count of the rattles. Had it been ten? Fifteen? It had to be Loïc calling. Cleavon was sure of it now. Loïc was in a crisis. A crisis that required his being killed.

Cleavon downed the last drop of absinthe in the fluted glass. No, he realized, the Green Fairy did not blunt your memory. If anything, it gave certain memories a hypnotic power. Like the memory of that ragged little skeleton of a French boy, with his dirty face and blazing blue eyes, running up to the truck and leaping into Cleavon's arms. August 1944. Fifty-seven years later, Cleavon's memory of that time was almost tactile.

Cleavon sprang from the couch, suddenly seized by the writing compulsion. He rushed over to the desk, clicked on the typewriter, heard its electric hum, rolled a fresh page through the carriage. He was determined to write the truth. At least, what he remembered of it.

Tuesday, August 28, 2001. Paris. 7:00 P.M.

What can I say about Loïc Rose? I'd like to say he was like a son to me but, never having been a father, I don't know what the hell that means. Let's say he was like a nephew, my little white nephew. French white, that is, which can never be confused with American white. In America that little white boy would never have looked up to me the way he did. In America you have these Huck-and-Jim relations where the black man, anyway you look at it, is inferior, even to some dumb-ass barefoot redneck kid. But Loïc, at a certain time in his life, revered me.

I am writing now of this city, this neighborhood, more than half a century ago. I remember Loïc's mother, Micheline, the seamstress. First white tail I ever had. Popular girl. I guess it was in her blood. The womenfolk in Micheline's hometown in Brittany even had a song written for them: "Les Filles de Camaret." One verse lingers in my mind:

Mon mari s'en est allé à la peche en Espagne,
Il m'a laissé sans le sou,
Mais avec mon petit trou,
J'en gagne.

For you non-French speakers, the lines go something like this:

My husband has gone fishing in Spain,
He left me without a cent,
But with this little hole of mine,
I'll earn something yet.

So Micheline was, I suppose, just a typical girl from Camaret. Somehow, her husband didn't know about the local tradition, even though he was a Breton and a fisherman himself. I don't remember the name of Loïc's father. All I know is when he came home from a long fishing excursion and learned his wife had been screwing half the men in town, he couldn't handle it. He went out in a rowboat, by himself, in the middle of a storm, in the middle of the night. They found his body smashed up on some rocks. Loïc was four or five years old at the time. Everybody told him his father had died in a shipwreck. Which, in a sense, was true. They just didn't tell him it had been a sort of suicide. That was something Loïc would only learn later.

When I met him he was still a happy-go-lucky street urchin. I can see him like it was yesterday, scampering up to the truck, hurling himself into the air. I can feel him in my arms, his bony little body, squirming with joy. He and Micheline had come to Paris just before the war, after the father's "shipwreck." During those heady days after the Liberation, Loïc was my loyal pint-sized mascot. I remember sitting with him and Micheline in their shabby apartment on the rue Hautefeuille, eating Micheline's potato soup, drinking cheap wine and feeling more welcome and comfortable with these French white folks than I'd ever felt with any other people anywhere, even my own. It wasn't about love. Micheline was a slut, Loïc a filthy ragamuffin. Since they didn't speak English and I didn't speak French, we could barely even communicate. Still, I just felt something, something soothing and full of ease with them. As the summer ended and my regiment and I went on to fight our way across the rest of France and into Germany, I thought I'd never see Micheline and Loïc again. I certainly never thought I would someday be in a position to betray them.

Cleavon abruptly stopped typing. He had been writing very fast, fingers dancing, lost in the metallic music of the machine, the keys slamming against the page like tiny jackhammers. So far, so honest.

Cleavon knew that if he was going to continue writing the truth, he would need another drink. But he couldn't handle any more absinthe. That would just knock him out. He rose from the desk, pulled a half-empty bottle of Scotch from the armoire, poured himself a glass, then sat back down in front of the humming machine.

The phone rang again and now Cleavon leapt from the chair in a rage, lunged for the receiver and snarled into it: "What the fuck do you want?"

"Cleavon?"

"Yeah, what?"

"Take it easy, brother. It's Archie Dukes."

Cleavon began to calm down. "Oh. Hey, Archie." He did not completely drop his guard. He remembered that Harvey Oldcorn knew he was a regular guest at Archie's Million Man Dinners. The first Saturday night of every month, except July and August, Archie opened his home to any African-American male who was living in, or even just passing through, Paris. Cleavon had known Archie Dukes for forty years. He'd always liked him but had never quite trusted him. Cleavon had informed on Archie and had always told the Authority what an upstanding American Negro he was. But Cleavon could never be sure whether or not Archie was informing on *him*, or what he was saying if he was. For instance, who had told Harvey that Cleavon was attending Archie's dinners? Had it been Archie himself?

"Are you hip to all that's goin' on?" Archie asked.

"Nigga, I don't even wanna know what the fuck you're talkin' about," Cleavon growled. "Is it you who's been callin' me all day?"

"Nope. Frankly, I didn't want to get you involved. But then, I figured, maybe you already *were* involved."

Now Cleavon was even more pissed off. "Oh, yeah, you one of them educated Negroes, ain't ya, Archie? Like to talk in riddles."

"I didn't call to upset you, brother," Archie said in a condescendingly calm tone. "I just know that you've been close to both Marva and Loïc and, given the current situation, you might want to—"

"Well, I don't!"

"Have you heard from Naima, their daughter? I—"

Cleavon slammed down the receiver, returned to his desk. The call from Archie was a bad sign; a sign that, whatever mess Harvey had gotten Cleavon mixed up in, it was even bigger than he'd assumed. Now he suspected that if he did indeed kill Loïc Rose, then he, Cleavon himself, would soon be killed. Thus, what he was writing now would be a final testament. A confession. His fingers attacked the keyboard.

Once upon a time, there was something called the Authority.

A joint body. An uneasy alliance between French and American intelligence services. Basically, it was a network of informers. Strictly unofficial. It wasn't something you could apply to join. You had to be recruited or blackmailed into it. A classic Cold War operation, I guess you would say now. At the time, you cooperated with the Authority because you thought you had no choice. And they usually paid quite well.

After I got my discharge, in late 1945, I returned to Paris to live because there was no way in hell I was going back to America. For ten years, I struggled to survive. Wrote some articles for *Esteem* magazine back when black folks in America cared to read about what black folks in Paris were up to. I worked as a cook and a moving man. I taught some English classes. And I dealt hashish—until I got busted. A serious catastrophe. I was either going to be sent to a French prison or, worse yet, deported to America. Then, a few days after my arrest, a pink, baby-faced U.S. Army captain showed up at my cell. Young Harvey Oldcorn jovially informed me that I could avoid jail or deportation if I agreed to rat on my friends and acquaintances. And I could make more money doing it than I had selling hash. What was I supposed to say: No?

And today this motherfucking Oldcorn calls me a traitor. Well, if I am, or if I was, it was good ole Harvey who made me one.

You never knew when someone from the Authority would contact you. "Don't call us, we'll call you" was the motto. And you never knew who would approach you, if it would be a Frenchman or an American, if you would be summoned for a meeting at the Prefecture de Police or the U.S. embassy. And you never knew who, French, American or African, they were going to want to know about. But you had to be ready with plenty of information. If you didn't deliver the goods, the Authority always—always—had something it could use against you.

But I was writing about Loïc Rose, wasn't I? Micheline and her boy were overjoyed to see me when I returned to Paris after the war. I don't want to make it sound like Micheline was the only woman in my life. Far from it. And I, sure as shit, wasn't her only man. Nor her only black man. Micheline had a thing for us brothers. Can you blame her? In any event, some folks at the Authority, especially young Harvey Oldcorn, were particularly, pruriently, interested in what Micheline did and which Negroes she did it with. I delivered the goods.

And I watched little Loïc grow into a bright, handsome young man. He wasn't much interested in school. Photography and women, and photographing women, that was what he was into. He worked menial hotel jobs and seemed singularly unambitious. But what he lacked in drive he made up for in charm. He was one of those easygoing Frenchmen who had no problem hanging out with black folks. Maybe it was because his mother had so many brown-skinned boyfriends. Who knows? But Loïc, in his early twenties, was a common presence at the Monaco and the Tournon and the other cafés where black expats met to drink and laugh and tell our tall tales.

Wasn't it at the Tournon that Loïc told me his mother was dying? It was just him and me that afternoon, must have been sometime in 1958. Micheline had cancer. It killed her mercifully fast, five or six weeks after she found out it was in her. And just a few days before she died she told Loïc the truth about his father. He was pretty rattled. But he rarely mentioned it to me again. Sometimes he would make an oblique reference to his father's suicide and I would utter an equally oblique word of consolation, subtly acknowledging tragedy in the way that men, and maybe black men, and maybe French men, in particular, do, giving you a glimpse of the pain inside but not blubbering about it. They certainly would not want you to feel sorry for them, and they'd let you know that they didn't feel sorry for themselves. I don't know who else Loïc shared his secret with. But it was a secret I protected. That is to say, I never breathed a word about his father's death to anyone in the Authority.

Cleavon rose slowly from his chair, bones creaking after the long crouch over the typewriter. He poured himself more Scotch, sat back down in front of the typewriter with his fresh glass of inspiration. The jangling rattle of the phone gave Cleavon a start. But he stayed in the chair as the phone continued to ring. He stared at the page, wondering how many lies he'd just written. Hardly any. Unless you counted lies of omission. The shrill alarm of the phone continued. At the ninth ring, he stomped over to the telephone and picked up the receiver in mid-rattle.

"What?"

No one replied. Cleavon heard only a ventilator-like white noise in the background. Click. Dial tone. Cleavon hung up the phone. He was trembling slightly but he didn't know if it was from drink, anger, fear or plain old age.

He slid back into the chair and resumed typing.

Would it be accurate to say that I saved Loïc Rose's life? At least once? I suppose it's not for me to judge. All I can do is try to recount what happened.

In the years just after his mother died, Loïc became rad-
icalized. I figured it was just a passing fancy. He joined the
Communist Party, started dating Jewish girls and North
Africans, carried around Mao's little red book and was always looking to provoke some sort of ideological debate. In
short, Loïc was becoming a left-wing sap, a humorless bore.
And I duly told the Authority all about it. Reassuring everyone, of course, that he was no threat to the Republic.

Then came October 17, 1961. Anyone with any sense
stayed indoors that night. But Loïc was out there, marching
with the Algerians who were protesting the imposition of a
curfew on all Muslims and North Africans. The police responded to the march by going on a bloody rampage. For
days, no one heard anything from Loïc. I feared he had
wound up like the two hundred or so Algerian protesters
who were shot or beaten to death. Or thrown into the Seine,
wounded but still alive, flailing desperately until they
drowned. Finally, a connection of mine in the Prefecture located Loïc. I went to see the poor fellow in his subterranean
jail cell. His face was puffed up and bruised. He thought his
ankle was broken but since he had not been allowed to see a
doctor, he couldn't be sure. With the French-Algerian war
still raging, the cops might have kept an alleged agitator like
Loïc in jail indefinitely. That was why I recruited him for
the Authority. He was released from prison that very day.

Loïc, at that time, was too much of an idealist to admit
that he was—wisely—trying to save his own skin. So he convinced himself that by informing on his radical friends he
was actually protecting them, helping to keep them out of
jail. Maybe there was some truth to that. Maybe Loïc was indeed saving his Commie pals just as I had saved Loïc. I think
that once the war ended in 1962, Loïc thought the Authority
would have no more use for him. He was dead wrong. He
didn't understand the nature of the beast. The beast de-

voured information, any information. And if you didn't have any to give, the beast would devour you.

That same year, Marva Dobbs came to town. Wasn't a brother in Paris—yours truly included—who didn't want a taste of her. But Marva only had eyes for Loïc, at least in that first year or so. Loïc told me he'd experienced *a coup de foudre*—the thunderbolt of love at first sight. He said he wanted to make Marva his wife. Naturally, that did not stop him from informing on her to the Authority.

Marva whipped Loïc into shape, got him to grow up. He went back to school and got a law degree, started a lucrative practice as a tax attorney. His clients were just the sort of people the Authority wanted to keep tabs on: wealthy Socialists, bourgeois revolutionaries, radicals who owned châteaux. Once Marva's Soul Food Kitchen got off the ground, I'm sure Loïc informed on the restaurant's guests—just as I did. No doubt he, unlike me, was rewarded with all sorts of little tax breaks, and under-the-table perquisites for his information. By the early 1970s, Loïc was enjoying French society's favorite *ménage à trois,* that scintillating nexus where politics, business and celebrity wrapped themselves around one another.

I recently heard a new word that has apparently entered the American lexicon; a young brother at one of Archie's dinners introduced me to it: "frenemy." A friend who is your secret enemy, or could become one. Or an enemy with whom you are forced to pretend to be friends. It occurs to me now that my life in Europe has been full of frenemies. This is largely my own fault, of course. I chose the informer's road. Who was it who said, "On the road of the informer, it is always night"?

I suppose it was in the early seventies that Loïc and I became frenemies. Still fond of each other while not knowing whether we could trust each other at all. Maybe, on some level, Loïc resented me for bringing him into the secret club. At the same time, he had to know he had benefited from membership in that club. It had paid off for him far more handsomely than it ever had for me. So perhaps I resented Loïc as well.

I knew from our mutual frenemy Harvey Oldcorn that Loïc's list of clients was getting more and more shady: Arab sheiks with property in France, Turkish arms dealers and Middle Eastern money launderers the French government either couldn't or wouldn't arrest. According to Oldcorn, Loïc and some elite French criminal lawyer had a vague sort of partnership going. Loïc kept the motherfuckers out of jail for conspiring to defraud governments and banks while Olivier Matignon kept them out of jail for conspiring to commit murder. Marva, it seems, knew nothing about her husband's double-dealings. She was too busy running the restaurant and gettin' laid. I was happy when Loïc and Marva had a kid in '78. The same year I left Paris for Toulouse. I had a going-away party at the Soul Food Kitchen. Loïc didn't even show up. Too busy over in Switzerland with one of his important clients. Or so Marva told me.

I saw Loïc one more time, on a visit to Paris in 1985. We smoked cigars and walked around the Île Saint-Louis late at night. He was stilted, almost formal with me. Wanted to tell me how successful he was. That seemed to mean a lot to him, my knowing how successful he was. His marriage was sound, Marva's business was thriving, his seven-year-old daughter was a beautiful genius. Was it my pride or my envy he wanted to provoke? He knew I was an old childless bachelor, scraping by on a meager pension and English-language-class fees in Toulouse; he knew that my usefulness as a spook had come to an end. Loïc puffed on his cigar awkwardly, like a callow teenager feigning manliness, as he continued to brag. Harvey Oldcorn, he told me, was back in Paris after an ab-

sence of many years. Back then, Oldcorn was involved in ne-
gotiating top-secret arms-for-hostages deals between the U.S.
and Iran and the various terrorists under Iran's influence.
Those deals were often cut in Paris. Loïc was glib and cyni-
cal, chuckling about the "legal criminality" he helped make
possible. I made a few allusions to the old days, the old trau-
mas. Loïc artfully deflected my references to the all-too-
painful past.

We walked to the taxi stand near the Saint-Paul church.
We shook hands and kissed each other once on each cheek.
Even after all these decades in France, it's something I do
rarely, and only with Frenchmen. After all this time, it's still
an odd sensation for me, the feel of another man's stubble
touching mine, another man's lips on my face. But exchanging *bisous* with Loïc that night, some sixteen years ago, felt
especially strained. I would call it a Judas kiss if I could figure out which one of us I considered Judas. Loïc took the first
taxi available and sped off into the night.

Cleavon stopped typing. He trudged to the bathroom, took a piss
and washed his hands. His head throbbed but not too painfully. He
was, by now, quite drunk. Good. He would have to be quite drunk if
he was going to kill Loïc Rose soon. He stretched and yawned,
walked back to the desk, sat down in front of the machine once again.
He knew that the next time the phone rang, he would answer it. In
the meantime, he would write, pick up where he had left off, tell as
much of the story of Loïc Rose as he could before he had to do the job
Harvey Oldcorn had hired him to do.

Hell, we're both too old for this bullshit. The bony little boy
who leapt into my arms would be sixty-six, sixty-seven years
old now. I never figured I'd outlive him. Maybe I'll outlive
'em all. I'm as healthy as a black man my age could be. No
high blood pressure, no prostate problems, no Parkinson's or

Alzheimer's disease. After the reckless life I've lived I've already exceeded the life expectancy of men like me by a good twenty years.

And maybe this is my curse: to outlive anyone who really knew me. To die an ancient exile, forgotten, unmourned. Except, maybe, by Madame Ficelle.

Cleavon's hands dropped to his sides. He swayed in his seat. *"Et alors?"* he said out loud, the French version of "So what?" It was still early, only about nine o'clock, not even sunset. But Cleavon, drunk and inconsolable, passed out, as he had so many nights before, slumped over his humming typewriter.

Cleavon awoke suddenly, choking on drool. He bolted upright in his chair, found himself in a darkened room. The only light came from the streetlamp outside his fourth-floor window. He was disoriented, coughing back phlegm. Then he heard the shriek of the telephone. He remembered that he had been writing. But how long had the phone been ringing? Was it the jangling rattle that had jolted him awake? The ringing stopped and Cleavon wobbled slightly in his chair. Now he heard only the low hum of the electric typewriter. The streetlamp cast a shadowy blue light in his small living room. Cleavon groped for the glass he saw glinting beside the typewriter. Took a gulp of Scotch. Things were beginning to cohere. Yes, he had been writing, writing about Loïc.

The scream of the telephone. Cleavon rose from the desk, picked up the receiver after the second ring. He said nothing, listened to the faint whir of traffic on the other end of the line. Finally, the familiar voice.

"Cleavon?"

"Yes."

"Do you know who this is?"

"Of course."

"You don't sound very happy to hear from me."

"You don't sound very happy to be calling me."

"I would like to meet with you. At the traditional place."

"When?"

"Right now."

"À tout à l'heure."

Cleavon hung up the phone. The little firecrackers started popping in his brain. He shut off the typewriter. He walked into his bedroom and opened the closet, dialed the combination on the small safe inside. He removed his pistol from the safe, screwed on its small tubular appendage. If he was going to have to kill Loïc Rose in the street, he would definitely need the silencer.

Twelve

Loïc Rose was contemplating the afterlife—contemplating, that is to say, whether such a thing as the afterlife even existed. He stood before the façade of the Notre Dame Cathedral, surrounded by a crowd of summer nighttime tourists, staring at the array of statues carved into the stone wall. He remembered how, as a child, he'd always been baffled by the statue of Saint John the Baptist, he who had christened Jesus, then lost his head because of Salome's whim. The statue of Saint John depicted him with a stub of a neck, cradling his severed head in his arms. Little Loïc had wondered if Saint John had to walk around heaven in the exact same state in which he'd left the earth, with his head chopped off.

On this sweltering August night, Loïc Rose, now an old man, reminded himself that he was a nonbeliever. He had expected to be dead by now. But the gun was missing from the armoire in the cellar of his house in Normandy. So Loïc was still alive. And he'd had to come up with an alternative plan. He reluctantly decided to contact Cleavon Semple: the last resort. It had been difficult even finding a phone booth in the center of Paris. In the age of the cell phone, the local powers had obviously decided to make more space for pedestrians. It was after having made the call, walking toward his rendezvous with Cleavon, that Loïc paused for a moment in front of Notre Dame. Gazing at Saint John, severed head in arms, he wondered about the recently murdered men he had known. Was Jeremy Hairston walking around paradise with a knife in his back? Was Webster Janes all burned up?

"Something is about to happen." That is what Webster Janes told Loïc Rose in July 2001. "Something terrible. And it's going to happen soon."

Loïc remembered that his wife had never been particularly fond of Web Janes.

"When it comes to affectations," Marva had once said, "Web is a triple-threat man. He wears suspenders, a bow tie *and* he smokes a pipe." But, of course, Loïc's wife had always seemed to have a slight bias against white American males. Perhaps Loïc shared her bias. All the same, he liked Webster Janes. Web and Harvey Oldcorn were part of the same social milieu: WASP, Ivy League, foreign service. Despite their being bitter enemies, they had an enormus amount in common, including, Loïc learned that summer, terrorism on the brain.

"Al Qaeda is going to launch a major strike against an American target," Web told Loïc. "And very soon."

Loïc had spent the second half of June and almost the whole of July examining twenty-five years' worth of Webster Janes's records:

tax returns, expense accounts, program budgets, etc. The WORTHEE director had been cooperative, if a bit chilly. Loïc figured that Web considered him a henchman of Harvey Oldcorn and Carmichael Associates. But after several meetings, and weeks of investigation, it was clear to Web that Loïc was not out to get him. Finally, the American began to open up to the Frenchman, to tell him of his grinding fear.

Since the bombing of the U.S. embassies in Kenya and Tanzania in 1998, Web Janes had become an expert on Osama bin Laden's terrorist organization. He had traveled to Saudi Arabia, Egypt, Sudan, Pakistan and Afghanistan to study the origins of al Qaeda. In the past three years, he had interviewed a dozen men associated with the group. Web Janes claimed to be interested in the "root causes" of terrorism: poverty, fundamentalism, broad geopolitical trends, the unintended consequences of globalization.

"There need not be a clash of civilizations," Web said, "unless that is what certain people desire."

Only as Loïc's audit came to a close, in the last week of July, did Webster Janes say that he had received specific information about an imminent terrorist attack. The last time Loïc had seen him, the WORTHEE director had none of his tweedy, academic aplomb. He seemed panic-striken. Loïc asked him if he had alerted important officials about his suspicion.

"Of course I have," Web practically wailed, "and I'm not the only one. But our warnings are ignored by the most powerful people, the very people who might be able to prevent this from happening. Which leads me to ponder the unponderable. That these same people—they *want* it to happen!"

And what exactly was the "it"?

"I can't tell you," Web said. "All I can say is: If I were you or a member of your family, I'd stay away from the Place de la Concorde during the month of September."

Loïc took the obvious inference: Another U.S. embassy was going to be bombed. This time, right in the heart of Paris. Such an attack, Loïc thought—with the inevitable loss of many American lives— might very well amount to a modern-day Pearl Harbor.

Harvey Oldcorn was no longer working for the U.S. government. He had quit public service in 1992, the same year the Authority was dissolved. He was now working for the private sector. A rich if shadowy outfit called Carmichael Associates: investments, geopolitical consulting, human security issues. Oldcorn ran the Paris office.

According to Oldcorn, during his dinner with Loïc at Marva's restaurant in June 2001, the new crew in Washington was reassessing all sorts of American commitments. The World Organization for Research into Technology, Health, Education and the Environment was particularly ripe for reassessment. Ostensibly a think tank, WORTHEE had been useful in gathering intelligence in Eastern Europe and Central and South America during the last decade or so of the Cold War. Back then, America had paid half of WORTHEE's annual budget. But during the 1990s, the U.S. slashed its funding to 25 percent. In June 2001, some members of the new crew in Washington thought America should drop out of WORTHEE altogether. They accused the think tank of having become an instrument of the radical Left, of supporting anti-Western regimes in Africa and the Arab world. There was a vocal group of neoconservatives, however, who thought the U.S. should continue to fund the outfit but who argued that WORTHEE should be purged and placed under different management, its mission redefined to suit the needs of the folk who had taken power at the dawn of the New American Century.

Naturally, this meant that Webster Janes would have to go.

Harvey Oldcorn called Web Janes, the career diplomat who had directed WORTHEE since its inception, "a dangerous egghead." Even back in the 1980s, when WORTHEE's staff of five hundred multinational researchers had helped gather intelligence that undermined the U.S.S.R., Web Janes had been considered by American hard-liners to be suspiciously fair-minded. Too much of a pragmatist, not enough of a true believer. Harvey made it plain to Loïc that he wanted Web Janes gone. But there was no way the WORTHEE director would voluntarily step down. No matter how much his fellow Americans distrusted him, Janes had the solid backing of WORTHEE's European membership, which provided three-quarters of the think tank's funding. So Webster Janes would have to be forced out somehow, coerced to resign, preferably in disgrace.

The U.S. had hired Carmichael Associates to do an audit of WORTHEE, so that the new administration could decide whether to keep funding it. Carmichael already had a team of analysts going through WORTHEE's records. But Harvey wanted to hire Loïc to deal specifically with projects that Web Janes had supervised directly. That was the purpose of their dinner at Marva's restaurant. For Harvey to offer Loïc the job. It was obvious that Carmichael needed a Frenchman as one of the top auditors so that the audit would not look like an all-American putsch. Loïc didn't particularly want this job but he knew that Oldcorn would lean on him—in one way or another—until it became impossible for him to say no.

Loïc also understood that Harvey would want him to find some kind of malfeasance, evidence of fraud. Loïc did not know Web Janes very well, but he knew him well enough to know that he was not a crook. Loïc had worked with enough crooks in his career to be able to smell the difference. He would perform the audit, confident that he would uncover nothing that Carmichael Associates could use against Web.

Monday, July 30, 2001. Harvey Oldcorn phoned Loïc at home that morning. Loïc had turned in his audit of the WORTHEE director's activities to Carmichael Associates the previous Friday. Harvey was obviously disappointed. Where was the dirt? Where were the actionable offenses? The smoking gun? What Loïc had delivered was more like a wet match.

"Come to my office today," Harvey said. "This may be worse than we thought."

Loïc spent much of that afternoon with Harvey, in Oldcorn's well-appointed cavern of an office. Harvey bombarded Loïc with top-secret intelligence dossiers, grainy surveillance photos, transcripts of wiretapped telephone conversations and printouts of e-mail exchanges. All of the printed material was in Arabic, a language Loïc did not understand. But all of this evidence, according to Harvey, showed that Webster Janes had gotten too close to some of his al Qaeda sources. One name came up again and again in Oldcorn's file on the WORTHEE director: Ramzi Mekachera.

The name meant nothing to Loïc. He had not seen it in any of the Janes records he had combed through over the past several weeks. But, according to Oldcorn, Ramzi Mekachera had attended an al Qaeda training camp in Afghanistan in 1997. He was currently working as a garbageman in Montreuil but was believed to be a member of a sleeper cell of Islamist terrorists. And it seemed, from the evidence Harvey waved at Loïc, that Webster Janes had grown a bit too chummy with Ramzi Mekachera. He showed Loïc more transcripts of e-mails in Arabic, blurred photos of a white man who might have been Web meeting in a shadowy café with a tan-complexioned man who might have been this Mekachera.

Loïc tried to be cagey, tried not to reveal what Web Janes had told him. "Surely," he said to Oldcorn, "you're not suggesting that the American director of WORTHEE is a terrorist."

Harvey shrugged. "Not exactly."

Oldcorn accused Janes of being naïve, of consorting with people who wanted to do him harm. Oldcorn claimed there were signs that Ramzi Mekachera had become suspicious of Web, that maybe Web had grown too knowledgeable about al Qaeda and its various plots, that maybe Ramzi wanted Web dead.

"Well," Loïc said, "wouldn't that suit your needs, too?"

Oldcorn gave him one of those blood-freezing North American stares, the same stare Loïc had seen in sepia-tinted photographs of homesteading pioneers out in the nineteenth-century frontier, those immigrants and children of immigrants from Germany, Scandinavia and the British Isles who killed anyone who stood in their way. But Oldcorn's gaze quickly softened. He affected an affronted hurt in his eyes when he said, "No matter what I might think of Web's politics, he's my countryman. And I don't want to see any fellow American put in harm's way."

"But what about that thing you said to me at the restaurant, about America needing a new Pearl Harbor?"

Oldcorn winced and shook his head. "I'm sorry, Loïc, but I don't remember what the hell you're talking about. I must have had a little too much wine that night. But to get back to the matter at hand . . ."

Oldcorn said this Ramzi Mekachera was a menace, a threat not only to American security but to the precious life of one important, if gullible, American—the director of an American-funded think tank, for heaven's sake. Harvey freely admitted that he'd expected Loïc to find some direct financial link between Ramzi and Web, a wire transfer of funds or something. Oldcorn—and other unnamed Americans who, of course, only had Web Janes's best interests at heart—feared the WORTHEE director had placed himself in danger with this likely terrorist. Harvey himself had contacted old acquaintances in French intelligence to urge them to arrest Ramzi Mekachera. Simply as a precautionary measure. But the French had demurred, saying there was not enough evidence against the garbageman who, after all, had been born and raised in France.

"Why not approach Web yourself?" Loïc asked Oldcorn. "Why don't you or one of the other concerned Americans warn him?"

Bad idea, Harvey answered. Web was too deluded to believe the warnings. He might respond by tipping off al Qaeda operatives to the surveillance they were under, thus compromising counterterrorism efforts.

"So, Harvey, what exactly is it that you would like me to do?"

"Connect some dots."

"To fabricate a trail, a money trail?"

"Something like that, yes."

Harvey insisted that he wanted to see evidence of just a few transactions between Ramzi Mekachera and one or more Saudi-related "charities" with suspicious ties to radical Islamist groups. Loïc knew of such charities. He had staggeringly wealthy clients who contributed to them. They were businessmen, diplomats, royalty. Loïc knew the codes of Swiss bank accounts which, through various financial sleights of hand, had been used to funnel, without an obvious trace, monies from reputable organizations to disreputable ones. Harvey wanted Loïc to connect dots that would link Ramzi Mekachera not to any individual but to the most disreputable of organizations. If Loïc could just connect enough dots for the French spooks to arrest Ramzi, Harvey said, he might very well save the life of Webster Janes.

Loïc asked Harvey if Web had said anything to him about an imminent al Qaeda attack on an American target in Paris.

Harvey said no. Loïc could tell he was lying.

Loïc refused to connect the dots that would cause the arrest of Ramzi Mekachera. He said there simply was not enough evidence to indicate that Ramzi was a genuine threat. Harvey was clearly peeved. But Loïc didn't care. He reminded Harvey that he would be leaving with Marva for a month-long holiday in Brittany the following Sunday. If Harvey had any other issues about the audit that he wanted to discuss, Loïc would be at his disposal until the weekend. They shook hands and Loïc went home.

At nine o'clock that evening, Harvey phoned. Loïc had been reading at his desk in his study. With a reflex at once prudent and paranoid, he pushed a button on the console in front of him, automatically taping his conversation.

"There's something I didn't tell you this afternoon," Harvey said. "Ramzi Mekachera has an accomplice. Someone who might help him hurt Web Janes. I thought you might make the connection yourself, what with the last name."

"I don't know what you're talking about, Harvey."

"Mekachera. Ramzi's accomplice is his cousin, the cook you've got working in Marva's kitchen. Hassan Mekachera."

Loïc, flabbergasted, was trying to access the memory of the young chef's face when Harvey said, "Are you still there?"

"I'm here."

"There's something else. Hassan is fucking your wife."

Cleavon was writing in his head now as he strode across the cobblestones on this sultry late summer's night, taking a somewhat indirect route from his building to the Île Saint-Louis.

I note the couples strolling hand in hand, the clusters of tourists, the accordion player on the Saint-Louis bridge, the bridge connecting the two islands in the middle of the River Seine. Though it is late, I walk like a man with someplace to go, a pressing rendezvous. In my beret and Pierre Cardin suit, I stride past the hordes at the sidewalk cafés, staring blankly and slurping their spoonfuls of Berthillon ice cream. I head for the one bank of the island that is almost always quiet, the Quai de Béthune. I see Loïc standing under a tree, beside a bench. He is dressed entirely in black. To see a Parisian dressed so funereally in the early twenty-first century is not unusual. But to see Loïc Rose in such inky garb is disconcerting. Even more unsettling is how much Loïc looks his age. He is tanned and healthy, to be sure, but his face is surprisingly gaunt and creased. He smiles, sort of wryly, when he sees me. No *bisous*. We simply shake hands.

The blazing white lights of a passing bateau-mouche interrupted Cleavon's reverie. He and Loïc were sitting side by side on the bench as the massive tour vessel chugged along the Seine. Cleavon saw Loïc squinting into the white lightstorm. With his shock of gray hair, his long, wrinkled face and the blue eyes that now seemed more haunted than lively, Loïc suddenly reminded Cleavon of Samuel Beckett, whom he had spotted several times back in the 1970s, wandering spectrally around the Fourteenth Arrondissement. Cleavon held up a hand to block out the lights of the ship, glimpsed the shadows of tourists on the huge upper deck, waving at the silhouettes on the Quai de Béthune. Across the river, the top half of the Eiffel Tower, glittering in gold lights, was visible. The bateau-mouche passed beneath the Pont de Sully. Cleavon and Loïc were once again in near darkness, the grand apartment buildings behind them silent, largely deserted, their tall windows shuttered, most of the inhabitants enjoying the last days of August far from the center of Paris. But all year round, the Quai de Béthune was dark and discreet at night. Loïc and Cleavon had met here many times in decades past, to be sure that they were talking alone.

"I know you don't have the patience for niceties," Loïc said.

"You look good," Cleavon replied.

"You're a lying old man."

Cleavon tried to suppress a smile but couldn't. He felt the pistol in its shoulder holster underneath his jacket. The leather of the holster was making him sweat and itch. "What's goin' on, Loïc?"

Cleavon was startled when Loïc let go a sudden, explosive sob. The Frenchman quickly recovered, seeming to force back tears. When he spoke it was in a voice drenched in grief. "Two good men are dead," Loïc said. "And I killed them both."

Thirteen

NAIMA WAS SMOKING AGAIN. Like most Parisians, she'd picked up the habit in high school. During her first two years at Brown, she hung around with other expatriate undergraduates—the "Eurotrash," as they were referred to by most of the student body—who staked out their corner of the smoking section in the cafeteria. Once she started dating Darvin Littlefield and hanging out with more Americans, she quit. Darvin was highly allergic to tobacco; being around smoke actually made him break out in hives. Naima had never missed the nicotine fix, confirming her theory that smoking, for her, was a purely social activity. As Americans grew increasingly intolerant of the habit during the five years Naima lived in the States, smoking became something she did only in France. In the fourteen hours since

Loïc greeted her at Charles de Gaulle Airport, Naima had not had
the urge. But sitting with Marie-Christine, their bare feet propped on
the sill of the tall open window, each of the women puffing on a
Marlboro Light, Naima felt as if smoking together was some sort of
special act of communion. Then again, after not having had a drag in
almost a year, Naima felt the nicotine hit like a blow to the head. It
took a while for the painful thud to fade and for the more pleasant
little buzz to take effect. The cigarette went well with the sweet
lemon liqueur that Naima and Marie-Christine were drinking. Feeling a bit tipsy, it occurred to Naima that this was precisely the sort of
night booze and cigarettes were made for. A little mild substance
abuse helped make the bizarre more palatable.

"So, you live in Paris?" Marie-Christine asked.

"No, New York City," Naima replied. "I'm in film school there."

"New York, New York, what a wonderful town!" Marie-
Christine sang in English. "How long you live zere?"

"Two years."

Since Naima had responded in French, Marie-Christine
switched back to their native tongue. "I have several good friends in
New York, both French and American. I would love to live there
sometime."

"Maybe you will. But now, tell me about Hassan's cousin."

"*Oh là là.*" Marie-Christine took a deep breath, then launched
into the Mekachera family history.

Ramzi was born bitter. That was what Hassan had always said.
Though he grew up in a loving family, Ramzi was sulky, uncomfortable in his own skin, locked inside his head. The one person he
showed some minimal affection for was his cousin Hassan, an only
child who became an orphan after losing his father in a car accident,
then his mother two years later (from a widow's grief, the family
said, though it was actually from breast cancer). Hassan, ten years old
at the time of his mother's death, should have been the bitter one.
But Hassan had a sunny nature. And Ramzi, five years his elder, be-

came a kindly, if dour, big brother figure. "I know he's weird," Hassan once said to Marie-Christine, "but I would do anything for my cousin."

Ramzi, who had always been awkward around women, fell suddenly, obsessively in love with a nineteen-year-old Pakistani girl who was living in Toulouse at the time. A devout Muslim, Farida had never allowed Ramzi even to kiss her. Farida's father, an engineer working in the aeronautics industry, did not approve of his daughter's friendship with a twenty-eight-year-old garbageman, especially one who had never been particularly religious. When the family moved back to Karachi, some folks speculated it was to get away from Ramzi. Not to be deterred, Ramzi also moved to Karachi, giving up his secure job and the benefits that came with working for a French sanitation department. In Karachi, Ramzi took various odd jobs, lived in a squalid rooming house, tried to see Farida as much as he could, though she often seemed to be avoiding him.

"So Ramzi was stalking this poor girl?" Naima asked.

"That certainly wasn't how he saw it," Marie-Christine said. "Sometimes he believed she was in love with him, too. He wrote letters to his family in Toulouse saying that it was just a matter of time before he would win over Farida and her father. He wrote about fate and destiny and the will of Allah. This was not a way he had spoken before going to Pakistan. Finally, after six months, the family sent Hassan to Karachi, frankly, to rescue Ramzi."

"When was that?"

"Oh, about a year before I met Hassan, in 1997. Ramzi was a wreck when Hassan found him. He was hanging out with some very scary guys—young toughs but deeply fundamentalist. Hassan would sit with them in tea shops. They were trying to recruit Ramzi to come to some fundamentalist training camp, paramilitary stuff, very creepy. The camp was in Afghanistan."

"Was Ramzi interested in that?"

"Who knows? Hassan didn't think so. They tried to recruit Hassan, too, but gave up when they realized what a wimp he is. Anyway, Hassan was in Karachi for about ten days when Ramzi suddenly vanished. Hassan spent the next two weeks trying to find him. He appealed to the police, uselessly. Hassan spent all his savings looking for Ramzi. He lost his job in Toulouse. Then, after two weeks, just as Hassan was about to give up and return to Toulouse, Ramzi reappeared."

"Where had he been—Afghanistan?"

"Ramzi never said. Hassan asked him but he would never answer. All Ramzi would say was that he had spent two weeks looking into the meaning of things and that he was now a new man. He returned to Toulouse with Hassan, got his job back, never mentioned Farida or his stay in Pakistan again."

"But you think he spent two weeks in a terrorist training camp?"

"I don't know."

"What about Hassan, could he have gone with Ramzi?"

"Naima, really, you must finally believe me. Hassan would not last two hours in any kind of training camp, let alone two weeks in Afghanistan. Please!"

"Papa," Xavier murmured. He was lying on his back on top of the futon, snoozing away.

"Already he starts to talk in his sleep," Marie-Christine said, sounding half bemused, half worried.

"So Ramzi went back to being his grouchy old self in Toulouse?"

"Exactly. A couple years later, Hassan said he was moving to Paris. Ramzi told him how expensive it was in the big city, offered to come here and share an apartment with him. He knew people who could get him a job with the Montreuil sanitation department."

"And did Ramzi seem to be involved with any—what did you call them?—creepy characters, in Montreuil?"

"No, not at all. He has a few friends, normal guys. That's why Hassan was so shocked when Madame Zebouni called us in Marseille to say that Ramzi had been arrested. Hassan said he needed to get back to Paris to help his cousin. I begged him not to go. If the cops were looking for him as well, he had to protect himself, at least get a lawyer. Hassan laughed in my face. Called me a silly little *bourgeoise*. As if any lawyer would represent him in a moment like this! Besides, he said, if the cops wanted him, they would get him whether he had a lawyer or not. All he knew was that he had to try to help Ramzi. He wasn't making much sense. He was blinded by the crisis. He hopped on the first train to Paris yesterday morning."

"Have you heard from him since then?"

Marie-Christine squinted as she took a long drag on the cigarette. She exhaled slowly, a quizzical look on her face, as if she weren't quite sure of the answer to the question. "No," she said.

Naima did not speak. If Marie-Christine was lying to her on this point, Naima wondered what else she had lied about. "So back in Marseille," she said finally, "didn't the police want to question you about Hassan?"

"I received a notice in the mail this morning, instructing me to go to police headquarters for an interrogation tomorrow."

"You mean the cops didn't actually show up at your house? Didn't they think this was an urgent matter, a fugitive, an alleged terrorist?"

"It's Marseille," Marie-Christine said with a lavish shrug. "It's August."

"So did you go see the cops?"

"Of course not. Xavier and I caught a train to Paris an hour after I got the note. I thought I could do Hassan more help up here. I don't know, I was just kind of panicked. Madame Zebouni called me last night to say that five other men from this neighborhood had been arrested as suspects in the bombing."

"Friends of Ramzi?"

"Two of the men, yes. At least, I think so. I'm not sure. Madame Zebouni was hysterical. And she made me quasi-hysterical. I told her I would come to Paris to try to help. Anyway, she called me again on my portable just a few minutes before you arrived here. She said the five men were released from jail this afternoon. Evidently, they are no longer suspects, but none of them had any news of Ramzi."

"Have you talked with any of them?"

"No. But Madame Zebouni said the men were going to have a meeting tonight to trade notes on what had happened to each of them while they were held, separately, in custody."

Now Naima was annoyed. "Why didn't you tell me this before?"

"We have been speaking of other things."

"Yes, but we could have gone to meet with those other suspects. Certainly they could give us information we don't have."

"I don't know where they were meeting. And even if I did, I'm sure men like these would not have wanted any women around."

Naima looked at her watch: It was almost eleven thirty. She stubbed out her cigarette, downed the rest of the limoncello in her glass. "Okay," she said, lowering her feet from the windowsill, reaching for her shoes. "I'm leaving."

Marie-Christine looked suddenly frightened. "But why?"

"It's late."

"Naima, you are upset with me. I can tell."

"I'm sorry but you seem to be getting a little slippery. At first, I thought I could trust you but now——"

"Please forgive me!" Marie-Christine grasped Naima's arm, as if to keep her from rising from her chair. "Do not leave, I beg you."

"Listen, Marie——"

"I lied to you before! When I said I hadn't heard from Hassan."

"I know."

"I ask you again to forgive me."

"Why did you lie?"

"I don't know. Fear. It was irrational of me. But now I will tell you the truth. Hassan called me in Marseille last night. He was in a phone booth in Paris, he said he couldn't talk very long. He had just found out that your mother was in the hospital."

"Who told him?"

"Jeremy Hairston."

"Jeremy!"

"Hassan sought him out in desperation. He wanted to get in

touch with Marva and thought she was still in Brittany. He thought that maybe, with her connections, Marva could help get Ramzi out of jail and clear both him and Hassan. Jeremy wanted to help Hassan. Even though he disliked him and was probably envious of his genius, Jeremy knew Hassan was no terrorist."

"Oh, Jeremy," Naima whispered. No wonder he had wanted to meet with Naima in person, not to say too much over the phone. Naima silently cursed herself for having been too jet-lagged to go to the Soul Food Kitchen before lunch that afternoon.

"Hassan told me he was certain that he and Ramzi were victims of a plot. He said something about an e-mail account in his name, about suspicious messages being sent over the Internet and linked to him, though he had nothing to do with them."

"What did he say about my mother?"

Marie-Christine sighed and looked at Naima with something like pity in her eyes. "He said he was going to wait until late, then go to the hospital to see Marva. He thought she might be in danger, as I mentioned before, from the same people who were trying to frame him."

"But who are these people he was talking about?"

"Well, one of them, he believed, was your father."

"What! Why?"

"Perhaps because he knew about Marva's affair with Hassan. But there might also have been other reasons, connected to your father's position."

"His position?"

"Yes, in the secret police. Or whatever it is they call themselves. You know, French intelligence."

Naima could neither speak nor move. After a long moment, she realized her mouth was hanging open, so she closed it. Marie-Christine was still staring at her with pity. When Naima finally had the wherewithal to speak, she asked, "Who told Hassan my father was in French intelligence?"

"Once again, it was Jeremy."

A telephone bleated. Xavier stirred but did not wake up. Marie-Christine searched for her cell phone amid the pile of clothes and pillows on the futon, found it and answered after the third musical bleat: *"Allô?... Oui... Bonsoir, Madame Zebouni!"*

Naima wanted to eavesdrop on Marie-Christine's conversation but she was still too stunned, lost. Her mind was swimming. Loïc a secret agent? What disoriented Naima was not solely the outrageousness of the allegation; it was also the fact that, as outrageous as the allegation was, Naima could imagine it to be true. *Papa a spy.* It was the last thing Naima wanted to believe about her father, yet she did not find it unbelievable. Loïc had always seemed to be keeping precious secrets, personal and professional. Maybe there was a reason for this that Naima would never have guessed.

Marie-Christine snapped off the phone, sat back down beside Naima. "Did you get all that? One of the wives of the men who were arrested called Madame Zebouni to find out when he'd be coming home. Evidently, the meeting is still going on."

"Where is it?"

"A place called La Guillotine."

"The theater?"

"You know it?"

"Yeah. The run-down joint on rue Robespierre. I did a theater arts workshop there, back in high school."

"Papa!" Xavier shrieked. He was suddenly wide awake, writhing and wailing on the futon. Marie-Christine raced over to her child. Naima slipped into her shoes, rose from the chair and took a few steps toward the door.

"Calm down, Xavier, calm down," Marie-Christine whispered in the ear of her screaming son. She held him in her arms, trying to pat his back. Xavier squirmed and flailed, screaming uncontrollably.

"I'm going to leave now," Naima said.

"I need to change his diaper," Marie-Christine said, trying to keep her son from wriggling out of her grasp. "Just wait a few minutes."

"Thanks but I'm really tired. I'm just going to catch the metro back to Paris."

"Waaaarrrrrgggghhhh!" Xavier screamed.

Marie-Christine managed, while maintaining her hold on Xavier, to pull a business card from her pocket and hand it to Naima.

The two women exchanged *bisous*. "I'm sure we'll meet again," Naima said.

"I hope so," Marie-Christine replied.

"Blaaaaccccchhhh!" Xavier wailed, his pudgy face contorted in anguish.

Naima quickly descended the rickety spiral staircase of the apartment building. She didn't know if she could trust Marie-Christine Pinchot. But somehow she couldn't help liking her. Naima stepped out into the thick, humid air on the rue Etienne Marcel. Naturally, she had lied when she told Marie-Christine she was going home. Naima was headed for La Guillotine.

Naima was walking her New York walk. She strode across Montreuil's Place de la Fraternité at 11:45 P.M., a nasty bop in her step as she passed the groups of wannabe hoodlums hanging out, gathered around the benches that dotted the small public square, listening to French rap on their boom boxes, smoking hash-and-tobacco joints, drinking tall cans of 8.6, the bitter, potent Bavarian beer that was the Colt .45 malt liquor of the boyz of the *banlieue*, the dodgy districts that formed a ring around Paris. She looked straight ahead, but her peripheral vision was sharp. Naima wore a faint scowl on her face. She exuded the attitude of a woman who knew where she was and where she was going. She did not pause, hesitate, turn to look around her. She knew the homeboys were checking her out but she also knew they wouldn't fuck with her. Because she was walking her New York walk, wearing her New York street face. She had the aura of a woman who might very well whip out a can of mace, start screaming hysterically, so that any cops within a ten-block radius would hear her as she sprayed the poison in the eyes of anyone who dared approach her. In the dim light of the streetlamps around the Place de la Fraternité, Naima radiated the quality that was most disturbing to young thugs: She was unafraid.

Her cell phone vibrated in her pants pocket. She pulled it out and snapped it open just as she left the square and turned onto the deserted rue Arsène Chéreau. *"Allô?"*

"Naima. It's Juvenal." She could hear a panic in her former lover's voice. "I called your house but there was no answer. Where are you?"

"Relax, Max," Naima said, using a common bit of French slang, feeling buzzed from all the drinking she'd done with Marie-Christine. "I'm in Montreuil."

"What are you doing there? Are you all right?"

"I'm fine. Just meeting with a few people."

"At this hour? Are you in the nice part of Montreuil or the other part?"

"The other part," Naima said as she arrived at the corner of the rue de Paris. She saw two or three seedy-looking cafés that were still open and a Turkish sandwich shop with a huge slab of grilled meat, the size of a fire hydrant, skewered vertically on a metal pole, spinning slowly in the window under a bluish fluorescent light. "I'm near the Robespierre metro station."

"Well, I suggest you get on the metro and come back to Paris. I heard about Jeremy. You should go home right now."

"I can't just yet. Don't worry, I can take care of myself."

"I'll come get you. I'm in the Twentieth Arrondissement, near the Alexandre Dumas metro stop. I can be where you are *tout de suite.*"

Naima crossed the rue de Paris, walked past the metro entrance, where a ragged homeless man was loitering, and headed down the rue Robespierre. "Thank you, Juvenal, but I've got to go now."

"At least make sure you catch the last metro. Service shuts down in an hour, you know."

"I know."

"Naima, are you going to tell me what's going on?"

"No," Naima said, snapping shut her cell phone and slipping it back into her pocket. She had not meant to be rude to Juvenal, but he was distracting her from her mission. After another five minutes walking down the narrow, darkened street, she arrived at the tall, double-doored entrance of La Guillotine.

There was no sign indicating that this was a theater. With its drab, graffiti-splashed façade, the building might have been one of the many garages or car repair shops in the area. If Naima remembered correctly, the building had once housed a factory of some kind. Back in 1994, when Naima had done a four-week internship at La Guillotine, she hadn't learned very much. But she had a good time hanging out with struggling actors, directors, lighting and set designers. Mostly Naima and her nominal mentors spent the days smoking cigarettes and talking about movies, books and plays that they liked.

Now, seven years later, on this sweaty, sticky August night, Naima stood in front of La Guillotine and wondered why five men of Arab and/or North African descent had chosen this place, of all the locales in the neighborhood, to discuss their recent detention by the French police. As Naima pressed a palm against one of the splintery doors, she remembered what Marie-Christine had said to her, that "men like these" would not have wanted any women at their meeting. How would they react to Naima crashing their conference? She would have to quickly explain who she was, tell them that, like each of them, she was a victim of this whole WORTHEE bombing business. She pressed hard against the door; it wouldn't budge.

She wondered if perhaps the meeting was over and the five former suspects had returned home. She knocked softly. No response. She knocked loudly. Still no answer. She slammed her shoulder against the door—three, four times, trying to force it open. Naima didn't give much thought as to whether she was being fearless or foolish. She was simply driven. And emboldened, perhaps, by all the booze and cigarettes she'd consumed. "I just want some answers," she said to herself. But at this point, there were so many questions, she couldn't even keep them all straight in her mind.

Finally, she was ready to quit. She stood on the rue Robespierre, before the impregnable entrance of La Guillotine, massaging the shoulder she had slammed too roughly against the door. That was when she sensed the presence behind her. She heard the heavy panting at about the level of her butt. Naima knew better than to make any sudden movements. She very slowly turned around and looked down at the muscular Rottweiler in its spiked iron collar. The animal looked up at her, eyes glittering in the shadows of the lonely street. The Rottweiler kept panting, not as if it were out of breath but as if the simple burden of carrying around its powerful, massive girth required strenuous effort.

Naima looked up and spotted, across the street, three young men, apparently Maghrebian, wearing warm-up suits and glowering at her. They looked like teenagers, too young, perhaps, to have been friends with Ramzi and Hassan.

"*Bonsoir,*" Naima said, barely loud enough for the guys across the street to hear.

Still glaring at her, one of the kids said something in Arabic. The Rottweiler stopped panting. Now it emitted a low, menacing growl. True, Naima the hardened New Yorker had no fear of young toughs working on their thug attitudes. But large unleashed, unmuzzled canines—especially dogs known for ripping apart small children and mutilating adults—scared the shit out of her.

Careful not to make the move too abruptly, Naima turned on her heels and started walking back up the rue Robespierre. For five agonizingly long minutes, Naima walked her sassy New York walk but, with the Rottweiler trotting a few inches behind her and the three young toughs following a few feet behind the dog, muttering in Arabic, Naima felt her fear was obvious.

"Merde!" Naima hissed when she arrived at the Robespierre station and found the metro closed, a chain-link grate blocking the entrance. She glanced at her watch. It was only a quarter past midnight—the trains were supposed to be running for another half hour. Naima turned and saw the trio of wannabe hoodlums standing by the curb. One of them practically shouted something that had to be an Arabic slur and spat on the sidewalk. The Rottweiler bared its teeth and began to snarl.

Naima was on the verge of tears. She had to get the hell out of Montreuil, right now, but there wasn't a taxi or a bus in sight.

"Naima!"

He came gliding up to the curb on his motorcycle, almost casually, as if they had made an appointment to meet here, the visor of his helmet raised so that Naima could see his face.

"Juvenal!"

The young toughs looked baffled. Even the Rottweiler seemed dismayed. It stopped snarling and, swiveling its massive head, neck muscles bulging in the spiked iron collar, turned its attention to the curb.

"What the hell is going on?" Juvenal asked.

Naima walked briskly to the curb, hopped onto the back of the moto, wrapped her arms around Juvenal's midsection. "Go!"

"You need to put on a helmet."

"There's no time for that—just go!"

At Naima's command, Juvenal revved the engine, then executed a screeching U-turn and went tearing down the rue de Paris, leaving Montreuil, zooming back to the City of Light.

Fourteen

S ITTING BESIDE CLEAVON ON a bench on the Quai de Béthune, Loïc spilled out his story in an agonized, barely linear stream, speaking in both English and French, usually switching back and forth between languages in midsentence. Cleavon tried not to press Loïc, not to rush him. He wanted to get the whole story, from the Frenchman's perspective. So he let Loïc talk, only occasionally coaxing him. If Cleavon was going to have to do the job for which he had been hired, he needed, at the very least, to know exactly why Harvey Oldcorn wanted Loïc Rose dead.

"I tell you everything I remember," Loïc said at one point. "A lot of this stuff is only starting to make sense now."

Loïc spoke of Harvey Oldcorn's obsession with terrorism, of his

obsession with Webster Janes, of Web Janes's obsession with terrorism. Loïc had done an audit of WORTHEE. Harvey wanted him to
dig up more dirt. And somehow this was all connected to a cook at
Marva's restaurant. Or, at least, Harvey wanted some terrorist activity to be connected with this cook.

Cleavon and Loïc had been sitting on this bench for an hour, on
this most tranquil of banks on this tiny island in the middle of the
Seine, in the middle of the city, when they were both suddenly
bathed in the white light of another huge tour boat. Loïc raised a
hand to cover his eyes from the glare of the bateau-mouche. Cleavon
saw the shadows of tourists on the upper deck, squealing and waving.
On the far side of the Seine, he saw the imposing mass of the Institute of the Arab World, one of the few tall, modern buildings on the
banks of the river. Loïc waited until the ship had passed beneath the
bridge, and the darkness and quiet had returned, before he continued. Then Loïc told Cleavon of the moment when Harvey had
phoned him at his home and informed him, "Hassan is fucking your
wife."

Loïc stayed awake all through the night of July 30 and the early
morning of the thirty-first, sitting behind the wheel of his blue Peugeot, parked about one block down the street from Marva's Soul Food
Kitchen, on the rue Véron. He watched the dim flickering of the
lamp in the window of the bedroom in the office above the restaurant. The faint light was only extinguished as the sky turned a pearly
predawn blue. At 8:30, Marva and her young lover emerged from the
alley next door to the restaurant, squinting in the brilliant morning
sunshine. Marva looked radiant. She beamed at Hassan. They exchanged a quick kiss, then Marva turned and disappeared up the rue
Germain Pilon. Hassan, meanwhile, strolled down the rue Véron, toward Loïc's Peugeot, a self-satisfied smirk on his boyish face. Hassan
might very well have seen Loïc behind the wheel had it not been for

the glare of the sun on the windshield. Hassan disappeared up the rue Audran. A few minutes later, Marva and Hassan reappeared on the rue Véron, returning from opposite directions, Marva merrily swinging a white plastic bag of groceries, Hassan twirling a baguette.

It was the look of rapture on Marva's face that sickened Loïc. Her obvious joy at seeing Hassan again, after a separation of roughly ten minutes, the sheer sensual pleasure that seemed to light up his wife as she and her lover approached each other and shared another brief kiss. They disappeared down the alley, arm in arm, a happy, carefree couple about to enjoy an intimate breakfast.

Feeling a sudden surge of vomit rising up his esophagus and entering his mouth, Loïc quickly flung open his car door and puked into the gutter.

Back home, he wondered why this affair of Marva's devastated him so. He had never cared about her sexual adventures back in the sixties and seventies. Maybe it was the fact that so many years had passed since Marva had last indulged in an extramarital fling. Or so Loïc thought. He had certainly been faithful since before Naima's arrival twenty-three years earlier. But, no, it was not the simple infidelity that had ripped Loïc's guts out. It was that look of rapture he'd seen on Marva's face, a look he had not seen since their earliest days together, the intoxicated radiance that resulted from the unique mixture of the deepest affection and the most naked lust. When Loïc saw Marva and Hassan together on the rue Véron that morning, he experienced a fear he had never known with her, not even in their most promiscuous, pre-Naima years. The fear that his wife had fallen in love with another man.

Marva came home for a couple of hours between the lunch and dinner seatings at the restaurant. She took a long, hot bath and puttered about the apartment, singing all the time, barely aware of her husband's moping presence, trilling "A-Tisket, A-Tasket" happily to herself. After she left to return to work, Loïc, exhausted, disoriented with hurt, went to bed. When, by eleven o'clock, he had still not been able to sleep, he drove back up to Montmartre, found the same empty parking space he'd discovered the night before.

Sitting behind the wheel, his unblinking gaze fixed on the restaurant, Loïc wondered if this was how his father had felt when he discovered that his wife was just another whore from Camaret. His father had destroyed himself. Had Erwan Rose felt the same strangeness that Loïc felt now? This angry incoherence: feeling like he knew everything there was to know but understanding absolutely nothing. Was this the raging disorientation that had led Loïc's father to take his rowboat out in a furious storm, to allow himself to be smashed and splattered upon the black rocks of the Baie des Trépassés?

Still wide awake behind the wheel, Loïc saw Hassan come whipping out of the alley at 4 A.M., scowling, walking hard and fast. Hassan glanced at the Peugeot. Loïc was sure he must have seen his silhouette in the driver's seat. Hassan quickly looked away and disappeared up the rue Audran. The faint light above the restaurant went out. Loïc stayed parked on the rue Véron till dawn. Then he drove home, showered, put on a fresh suit and tie and, at eight o'clock on the morning of Wednesday, August 1, 2001, called Harvey Oldcorn. Loïc was eager to pay a visit to the offices of Carmichael Associates. To connect some dots.

"Did you have any evidence against Hassan at all?" Cleavon asked Loïc.

"Just pieces of paper Harvey waved at me."

"How did Harvey know about Marva and Hassan?"

"French intelligence had been surveilling Ramzi Mekachera and everyone he came in contact with for weeks. Some French spook must have seen the same thing I saw when I staked out the restaurant."

"And you didn't try to confirm all this shit Harvey was telling you about Ramzi and Hassan with some of your old pals from the Authority?"

"No, it didn't even occur to me at the time. Cleavon, you must understand I was half crazed that day. I still feel half crazed. Ever since I saw Marva and Hassan together, half of my mind is functioning in a logical way. The other half is totally disoriented. I don't know how else to explain. I was in such torment. Such blinding anger. Furious that Marva would have this affair and nearly out of my mind with rage that she would have been stupid enough to have an affair with a terrorist."

"But you just said there was no real evidence that he was a terrorist."

"Harvey told me Hassan had been in Pakistan at the same time that Ramzi was in the al Qaeda training camp in Afghanistan."

"And that was enough for you?"

"Cleavon, don't you see? I *wanted* Hassan to be arrested. I wanted him out of Marva's life. That day I did not care if he was innocent or guilty. I did not care if he would be killed or rot away in a jail cell somewhere. I just wanted him away from my wife."

"So that day you fabricated links between Ramzi and Hassan and these so-called charities."

"Yes, that is what I did, there in Harvey's office. I knew, on some level, that what I was doing was wrong. The half of my mind that was lucid, the half that was manufacturing evidence, also knew that what Harvey and I were doing was criminal. That is why I wore a wire that day at Carmichael Associates."

"You what?"

"I wore a wire. I taped everything Harvey and I said. Just as I had taped our last two phone conversations."

"You deliberately incriminated yourself?"

"Yes, I suppose I did. Perhaps, like the most pathetic of criminals, I wanted to get caught. But I must also have wanted to have something to use against Harvey. Just in case."

"In case of what?"

"In case of all the shit that has happened in the last two days! All the madness that is happening right now!"

Cleavon worried that Loïc was about to become hysterical. "Okay, okay, calm down. Let's go back to the first of August. You connected the dots Harvey wanted you to connect. Then what?"

"I prepared for my vacation."

August in Brittany was hell. Loïc's rage had been replaced by a wrenching mixture of guilt and grief. Guilt over the dots he had connected and grief for the life he had loved that was now over. He knew things would never be the way they were for so many years with Marva. She passed through their holiday in a trance. She sometimes barely seemed to register Loïc's presence. He could tell she was lost in erotic reverie, daydreaming about her young lover. And not only dreaming during the day. Every other night during their vacation, he heard her in the bed beside him, murmuring in her sleep: *Hassan-Hassan-Hassan...*

Making matters worse, this was the first August since her birth that Naima wouldn't spend with her parents in Brittany. His daughter's absence only added to Loïc's sorrow, the sense that things had changed, changed irrevocably, horribly. How he missed the laughter Marva and Naima always shared together. He had never felt so alone as when he and Marva went walking along the Baie des Trépassés together, his wife absorbed in her erotic trance. Loïc stared out at the choppy waters and wondered if he should do what his father had done, wait for the next stormy night, then row out there by himself to die. Might that not be easier than facing the crisis that was to come when Marva learned that her lover had been arrested as a suspected terrorist? But Loïc felt more and more certain that, however suspicious a character Ramzi Mekachera was, Hassan was innocent. So when the inevitable arrest occurred, would Loïc tell Marva about his role in framing Hassan? How could he? It would be easier to do what his father had done. At least then Marva might grieve for Loïc almost as much as she was bound to grieve for Hassan. Walking along the Baie des Trépassés, Loïc felt the powerful urge to confess all to

Marva, right that minute. But she was strolling across the beach in a goofy daze, hardly aware of the husband beside her.

"Ain't life grand?" Marva trilled, clearly speaking only to herself.

Loïc almost burst into tears when Marva told him, on Tuesday, August 21, that she wanted to return to Paris the following Sunday, a week earlier than scheduled. She claimed that Jeremy Hairston had sent an e-mail saying they needed her at the restaurant. It had turned out to be a very busy August and with the head chef, Benoît, away on holiday, the sous-chef, Hassan, was having trouble handling the pressure. Loïc didn't believe a word of it. Marva urged Loïc to stay in Brittany for the rest of the holiday they'd planned. He politely refused to consider it. He would go back to Paris with her. "We should stay together," Loïc said. Marva could not hide the disappointment in her eyes.

The next day, Loïc called Paris to check the answering machine in his study and found a message from Webster Janes.

"I realize you're still away on holiday, Loïc. I just want you to know that I'm going to hold a press conference, here at WORTHEE, probably on September third, or at least sometime during the first week of the *rentrée*. I'm going to announce what I know about al Qaeda's plans. Harvey Oldcorn and his pals are trying to force me out of my job. But I will not go down without a fight. Anyway, you can reach me at my office if you wish to talk. I'm here pretty much twenty-four hours a day now. *Merci. Au revoir.*"

Loïc did not return Web's call.

Marva was practically giddy when she and Loïc returned to Paris on Sunday afternoon, acting more like someone who was about to depart for vacation than someone whose holiday had been cut short. Marva slept soundly that night. Loïc lay awake beside her, waiting to hear her murmur her lover's name. But all he heard was her gentle, steady breathing. Marva was still asleep when Loïc rose from the bed at 7 A.M. Wearing a bathrobe and slippers, head throbbing after his sleep-

less night, Loïc made himself a cup of coffee, then clicked on the
television and saw the blackened façade of the WORTHEE building,
the twisted, smoldering wreckage of the car that had contained the
bomb. A single, unnamed, luckless pedestrian had been critically
wounded in the blast. When Loïc heard that the bomb had exploded
at 4 A.M. he knew the victim was no ordinary passerby. It had to have
been Webster Janes, leaving his office. The bomb, Loïc surmised,
would have been set off by remote control, by someone who had been
surveilling the building from a safe distance, waiting for Web Janes
to emerge and walk by the innocuous-looking Fiat parked on the Avenue Victor Hugo. And when the newscaster said that no one had
claimed responsibility for the attack, Loïc was certain that he knew
exactly who was responsible. He raced down the corridor to his study
and phoned Harvey Oldcorn.

"You did it," Loïc snarled. "You didn't want him to live."

"Where's Hassan?" Harvey shot back.

"How the hell would I know?"

"Don't get cute with me, Frenchy. The police raided the
Mekachera apartment. They got Ramzi but Hassan's nowhere to be
found."

"Good!"

"So you did warn him, didn't you? You backstabbing, cheese-
eating weasel!"

"You can call me whatever juvenile epithets you want, Harvey
Oldcorn"—Loïc made a point of stating the name—"but you have
just attempted to assassinate a fellow American. You set up Ramzi
and Hassan Mekachera as the fall guys because you and your pals
wanted Webster Janes dead."

"You're a weak man, Loïc. You spilled your guts to Marva, didn't
you? She's the one who tipped off Hassan. Your black bitch of a wife."

Loïc was momentarily stunned into silence. Then he said, "You
know, Harvey, I am recording this conversation. Just as I recorded us
in your office on August the first. So if you—"

Harvey abruptly hung up.

Loïc returned to the kitchen and sat in the breakfast nook in his bathrobe and slippers, drinking cup after cup of coffee, feeling as if his brain had exploded, like the bombed-out Fiat. At eleven o'clock, he watched Marva—the sexiest sixty-two-year-old woman there ever was, the charismatic genius who had given him the great grace of sharing her existence with his, raising a child, constructing a beautiful life with him—gulp down a glass of orange juice for breakfast, standing in the kitchen in her sleek black pantsuit, thinking, no doubt, of her lover. Loïc once again suppressed the urge to confess. Instead, he told Marva how much he cherished her. She seemed to like hearing it. Then she left. Hours later, Loïc was still sitting in the breakfast nook, his thoughts in splinters, when an official of the emergency services called to tell him his wife had crashed her car into a tree.

The last bateau-mouche of the night chugged across the Seine, its fierce white lights flooding the Quai de Béthune. Cleavon took a long look at Loïc in the pitiless blaze, seeing no trace at all of the dirty little French boy in the ravaged face of the old Frenchman. As the boat disappeared down the river and the quai returned to its dark and silent gloom, Cleavon felt angry. Loïc had made a series of reckless blunders but the craziest was thinking he could blackmail Harvey Oldcorn and get away with it. Loïc had stayed with Marva, who was heavily sedated, at the Hôpital Decoust until ten o'clock the night before. At seven in the morning, he drove to Charles de Gaulle Airport to pick up his daughter. In between, lost in dead-of-night delusions, he had decided he would outfox the American and his cohorts. Loïc was fool enough to believe he had the upper hand. He put all his recorded conversations with Oldcorn on a single compact disk, then locked the original tapes in a safe in his study. He convinced himself that Oldcorn, terrified of having his scheme exposed, would use his influence to free Ramzi Mekachera from jail and to call off the manhunt on Hassan.

Cleavon figured if Loïc was that stupid, then maybe he actually deserved to die.

A few nasty surprises interfered with Loïc's master plan. First, he and his daughter learned that Marva had checked out of the hospital in the middle of the night. A man fitting Hassan's description had come to take her away. Loïc tried not to panic. He told his daughter he had a business meeting in Lyon. In fact, he had a rendezvous at a Masonic temple in Paris with his colleague Olivier Matignon, the slick, not to say slimy, criminal lawyer who had ties to the old Authority. Loïc had phoned Matignon at his holiday villa on the Côte d'Azur the night before. Matignon hurried back to Paris, ostensibly to help his compatriot. Loïc was certain that Olivier and other powerful figures in the French establishment would join him in sticking it to the ugly American Oldcorn. Instead, Olivier Matignon told Loïc he was a dead man. He had crossed a fatal line and no one would come to his aid. The recorded conversations on Loïc's CD were useless, Matignon said. People would say the evidence against Oldcorn was fabricated. Why would anyone believe anything Loïc had to say when he was confessing to fabricating evidence against the Mekacheras himself? Matignon also informed Loïc that Webster Janes had died from his wounds. If Oldcorn could eliminate Janes, what would stop him from getting rid of Loïc?

"There must be a way out of this for me," Loïc said.

Olivier Matignon shrugged and replied, *"C'est impossible."*

Loïc left the temple and headed for Marva's restaurant, clinging to the irrational hope that maybe Marva would be there, having escaped Hassan's clutches. Recognizing the improbability of such a scenario, Loïc hoped, at least, to be able to talk with Jeremy Hairston. Perhaps Marva had contacted him since disappearing from the hospital. Loïc entered the restaurant through the back door that opened directly into the kitchen. There he found Jeremy laid out on the floor, a butcher knife in his back.

"Jeremy's dead?" Cleavon exclaimed.

"You didn't know that?" Loïc asked suspiciously. "It's all over the news."

"I didn't know."

Loïc leaned back on the bench. When he spoke again, all of the anxiety that had fueled his telling of this tale was gone. Now he sounded utterly drained, his voice heavy with the weight of a very precise resignation, a surrender Cleavon had heard in the voices of several other men, men who knew they were about to die. "It crossed my mind that maybe you had killed Jeremy. But then I remembered that knifings weren't your style. I figure it was someone working for Oldcorn. Maybe the same specialist who set off the car bomb. He went to question Jeremy on the whereabouts of Marva and Hassan. Whether Jeremy knew anything or not, whether he talked or not, he was murdered. Sacrificed. As a signal to me."

"So is that what you meant," Cleavon asked, "when you said you had killed two good men? Webster and Jeremy?"

"Yes."

"Of course you didn't kill either of them."

"If it weren't for me, they'd both be alive. That makes me their killer."

"Don't overrate yourself," Cleavon said dryly. "You don't have the stomach to kill."

"Perhaps only to kill myself," Loïc said in the monotone of utter resignation. "After I saw Jeremy, I knew I was fucked. I drove out to our house in Normandy. I have a gun there, hidden in an armoire in the cellar. Only Marva knew of the gun, its secret location. When I opened the armoire, the gun was gone."

"Marva and Hassan weren't in the house?"

"Not at that point. Obviously, they'd come and gone. And are now armed and dangerous."

"God damn it, Loïc," Cleavon hissed.

"I know. I know what a mess I've made. It's incredible, really. The lives destroyed. And in such a short amount of time. Web and Je-

remy dead. Ramzi Mekachera in jail. They'll find Hassan and destroy his life, too. Now I can only hope that my wife will be all right.
And Naima, my daughter. If anything were to happen to her . . ."

Loïc's voice trailed off. He reached into the pocket of his black
jacket, pulled out an unlabeled CD wrapped in clear plastic, handed
it to Cleavon. "This is for you. Please make sure Harvey gets it. Then
maybe they'll let my wife and daughter live. My will, all my papers,
are in order."

Cleavon tucked the CD in his inner jacket pocket, his hand
brushing the pistol in its leather shoulder holster. He finally realized
exactly why Loïc Rose had come to him. It was for a mercy killing.

Cleavon rose from the bench, walked around and stood behind it.
He drew the gun from its holster, pointed it directly behind Loïc's
head, the mouth of the silencer inches from the nest of gray hair.
Cleavon would do the job Harvey Oldcorn had paid him to do. If he
had the strength, he might even dump Loïc's body in the Seine. This
is what Cleavon thought as he hesitated before squeezing the trigger:
"I'm doing him a favor."

PART 3

La Fille

Fifteen

NAIMA COULDN'T STOP PACING. She hurried back and forth, from one end of her parents' kitchen to the other, her heart racing.

"Why don't you sit down?" Juvenal said. He was nestled in the breakfast nook, smoking a cigarette, nursing a cup of coffee.

"I can't," Naima muttered, "I just can't. Not yet." Juvenal didn't seem to understand her nervousness, her exhilaration.

An hour had passed since Juvenal had appeared, almost magically, to rescue Naima from danger in Montreuil. Once they were safe inside her parents' apartment, Naima headed straight for the living-room telephone. She was stunned to see a double zero glowing red in the tiny window on the answering machine. It was agonizing enough that neither of her parents had phoned home, but why hadn't

Darvin called? He said he would. So why hadn't he? This wasn't like Darvy. Was he getting sick of Naima? Maybe he was seeing someone else and Naima just didn't know it. That had been the case with Marva and Loïc, hadn't it? Or maybe Darvin was just sick of Naima's family. Marva had been so rude to him. Maybe this Paris crisis was his fuck-it point—that moment, just before the breakup, when you say, "Fuck it, this relationship just isn't worth the aggravation anymore." Of course, Darvin had never given Naima any reason to think he was thinking that. But after the events of the past twenty-four hours, she was inclined to believe the worst about the people she loved. Naima started hyperventilating. She felt frightened and vulnerable. She closed all the shutters on the tall living-room windows. She wanted, in some way, to hide.

While Juvenal made a pot of coffee, and settled into the breakfast nook, Naima paced compulsively around the kitchen, spilling out the story of all that had happened since he dropped her off at the restaurant: the horror of seeing Jeremy's corpse, her interrogation by Inspector Lamouche, the long talk with Marie-Christine in Montreuil, the visit to La Guillotine, then the encounter with the young thugs and their very large dog.

"Please, Naima," Juvenal said soothingly, "sit down and have a cup of coffee."

"Coffee!" Naima snapped. "Do I really look like I need a cup of coffee right now?"

"It's decaffeinated."

"No thanks."

"How about a *digestif*, then? Doesn't your mother keep a bottle of cognac in the cupboard over there under the sink?"

"Does she?"

Juvenal rose from his seat, walked over to the cupboard he'd mentioned and pulled out a half-empty bottle of Rémy Martin VSOP. He grabbed two glasses from an upper cabinet, then gestured for Naima to join him in the breakfast nook. "Come."

Naima finally sat down, but a bit warily, wondering how Juvenal knew where Marva stashed her booze. Had Marva had an affair with Juvenal, too? The possibility that Naima had shared a lover with her mother was too yucky to contemplate. She preferred to marvel at how Juvenal had arrived to rescue her. "Isn't it amazing," Naima said, "how you just rode up on your moto at exactly that moment?"

"Not really," Juvenal said, pouring the cognac. "You told me on the phone that you were near the Robespierre metro. I drove out there, thinking that if I waited in a café, I would see you when you appeared to catch the metro home. And I thought it would be better for me to give you a ride."

Juvenal slid a glass of liqueur across the table. Naima didn't really feel like drinking but she knew the cognac would help her calm down. The buzz she'd felt after drinking with Marie-Christine had disappeared the moment the Rottweiler started growling at her. "But still, the fact that you would arrive right when I needed you. It's bizarre."

"Life is full of bizarre coincidences. Ordinarily, people just refuse to acknowledge them." He raised his glass. *"Santé."*

They clinked and sipped. Juvenal held out his pack of Camels. Naima took a cigarette, leaned across the table to let Juvenal light it for her. They sat in silence in the corner of the kitchen, drinking and smoking; savoring, Naima thought, an idiosyncratic intimacy, the shared sense of having escaped imminent danger. When they looked into each other's eyes, Naima detected something in Juvenal's gaze that she had never seen before: a sort of admiration. "What?" she asked.

"You are very brave, you know," Juvenal said.

"I'm not."

"Of course you are. Consider what you have been through in the past two days. And look at you: full of energy and determination. Your bravery shames me."

"Shames you. Now why the hell would you say that?"

"Do not take offense. Please. I mean only to say that I wish I could be as courageous as you in the same situation."

"Well, you're a man, after all," Naima said sarcastically. "*Et un africain*. You ought to be at least as ballsy as a little *riche métisse* from the Boulevard Saint-Germain. Is that what you mean?"

"Ah, Naima, how hard you've become with me. But your scorn is justified, I know." He seemed to take a deep breath and Naima, with a prickling sense of anticipation, knew a mea culpa was coming. "I owe you a profound apology for the cruel way in which I treated you years ago. The only thing I can say in my own defense is that my cruelty was not premeditated. I behaved as beastly as I did out of fear."

"Fear? Of what?"

"Of you."

"I was only seventeen years old!"

"Yes, but you were a very mature seventeen. And I was an especially immature thirty-four. But perhaps you don't realize the power you have. Your intelligence, your beauty, your belief in yourself. You had this power about you even at seventeen. More so now."

Naima felt a deep blush coming on. "I'm not aware of whatever it is you're talking about."

"Someday you will be. But I want to say again that I am very sorry to have hurt you. I hope you can forgive me." Juvenal reached across the table and took Naima's hand in his. Naima tried to keep her hand motionless as Juvenal intertwined his fingers with hers. She didn't want to show how triumphant, how flattered and suddenly lustful she felt. "Many times I have cursed myself for having been such a fool with you. Now I am forty years old and ready to be serious. To marry and to start a family."

"Juvenal, what in the world are you saying?"

"When are you going to move back to Paris?"

"I have no plans to do that."

"Surely you are not going to spend the rest of your life in America."

"I might."

Juvenal squeezed her hand tightly, stared at Naima with the dark intensity she remembered from years ago. "Please come back."

Naima gently pulled her hand away. "I'm already spoken for."

Juvenal furrowed his brow. He didn't seem familiar with the expression.

"I have a boyfriend, Juvenal. We live together. It's serious."

"Are you engaged to be married?"

"Not yet."

"Would you like to be?"

Naima let go a heavy sigh. She downed the cognac in her glass, stubbed out her cigarette in the ceramic ashtray. She felt suddenly exhausted, overwhelmed. But, at the same time, very, very horny. She had to get away from Juvenal before she did something she would regret. "I need to go to bed. You can stay here if you like."

Juvenal's eyebrows shot upward. *"Ah bon?"*

"Yes. You can sleep on the couch."

Now it was Juvenal's turn to sigh heavily. "All right."

Walking to the hallway linen closet, Naima felt a surge of guilt, realizing how close she had come to betraying her boyfriend. Yes, she was dismayed by Darvin's failure to phone but that was no excuse for her even to entertain the notion of sleeping with Juvenal. And she couldn't help but find the notion entertaining. She returned to the darkened living room with fresh sheets and pillows for her guest. She could just make out Juvenal in the shadows. With the thin light of a streetlamp sliding through the slits in the shutters, she could see that Juvenal was bare-chested. Naima dropped the sheets and pillows on the couch. She was turning to walk away when Juvenal pulled her toward him, kissed her tenderly on the mouth. Just as Naima could feel herself giving in to the kiss, she abruptly pulled away. *"Bonne nuit,"* she said.

"Sweet dreams," Juvenal replied.

Naima hurried down the hall, into her bedroom, quickly shutting the door behind her and, for good measure, locking it. She hoped that she would have no dreams at all.

. . .

Driving through the night and into the early morning, speeding north along France's A6 superhighway, Pauline Ficelle feared that her lover was dying. The bleating of her cell phone had shocked her out of a deep sleep at 2:30 A.M. When she finally located the device in a pile of clothes at the foot of the bed and saw in the tiny screen a Paris number she did not recognize, Pauline was sure someone had dialed the wrong number. The only reason she answered was to keep the insistent beeps from waking one of the other guests in her parents' home.

"*Allô?*"

"Madame Ficelle?"

She recognized the accent immediately. "Monsieur Semple! Where are you?"

"In Paris. In a phone booth."

"What is wrong? Are you all right?"

"I need your help."

"Call a hospital immediately. Is it your heart?"

"I'm fine. I just need your help for a couple of hours."

"Monsieur Semple, I am in Mulhouse."

"I know. Can you drive back to Paris? Right now."

"My niece is getting married here on Friday. I am in the wedding."

"Yes, I remember. I only need your help here this morning. You can turn right back around once we're done. You'll be back in Mulhouse before dinner."

"Will you not tell me what has happened?"

"No, I will not. Are you coming or aren't you?"

"I'll be there in six hours. Perhaps less."

"Thank you, *madame*. I will be waiting for you in my apartment. Be discreet."

Despite her lover's reassurance that he was fine, Pauline thought his problem had to be health-related. Monsieur Semple was, after all, seventy-nine years old. Though as lusty and energetic in bed as men much younger, Cleavon Semple had to be as vulnerable to the ravages of aging as anybody else. Perhaps he'd slipped in the shower and broken his hip; too proud to call an ambulance, he needed Pauline to help him get to a doctor. But why then had he called from a phone booth? He couldn't have locked himself out of his apartment if he said he would be waiting for her there. Pauline tried to empty her mind as she zipped along the almost empty highway in the dead of night.

Be discreet.

Pauline had scribbled a note to her parents, telling them there was an emergency in her building in Paris. As a dedicated concierge, she had to race back to fix the problem. She assured them she would be back in Mulhouse by Wednesday night. She knew that all her parents cared about was for her to be there for the wedding on Friday. They probably wouldn't even ask about the nature of the emergency in the building. Her folks had always been blithely incurious about Pauline's life in Paris. Few of Pauline's siblings, her aunts, uncles and cousins had ever even visited the capital more than once. They could not understand why Pauline, after the death of her husband ten years earlier, had wanted to leave Mulhouse. In fact, they couldn't understand why *anyone* would want to leave Mulhouse, a gray Alsatian city best known for its airport and textile factories, its sausages and sauerkraut.

Pauline knew that her family actually pitied her. To them, she was an overweight, childless widow, spending her life looking after the needs of a bunch of snooty Parisians who did not care at all about her. But Pauline's family would never guess how much she actually pitied *them*, how provincial and banal they all seemed to her, especially now that she had the affection of a distinguished American writer like Monsieur Semple.

Be discreet.

As the sun rose over the superhighway and the lanes began to fill with other travelers, Pauline decided that if, once she entered the building on the rue de Latran, she bumped into a tenant, she would say she had returned to Paris to pick up a wedding present she had forgotten. And if she was spotted going up to Monsieur Semple's apartment? No matter. Besides, most of the tenants would still be away on holiday.

Squinting into the sun, her grip soft on the steering wheel, Pauline smiled at the formality she and her lover of ten months still maintained. He insisted on calling her Madame Ficelle. So she continued to call him Monsieur Semple. They still addressed each other by the formal *vous,* even in bed. She laughed lightly, remembering his sweet American accent. When he pronounced his own last name it sounded like *"simple."* Of course, Cleavon was anything but Monsieur Simple. He was really Monsieur Compliqué. Only the sex between them was simple. Though Monsieur Semple had tried to make that complicated, too. He was always worried about what the neighbors might think if they suspected he and the concierge were having an affair. But Pauline knew that many of the neighbors already suspected that she and Monsieur Semple were having an affair and did not care in the least. Even after all his years in France, Monsieur Semple could not grasp the French nonchalance about sexual relations.

Maybe it was because he was twice Pauline's age. No, Pauline thought, it was probably more because he was black and she was white. Monsieur Semple seemed very preoccupied with the whole white-black difference. Maybe that was because he was old. More likely it was because he was American. Pauline had tried to read some of Monsieur Semple's manuscripts. Her English was so bad she could never make much sense of them. But she could tell that they were very much about the differences between the blacks and the whites. It was such an odd preoccupation to Pauline. She saw differences between nations, differences between religions, differences between the sexes. But, to her, a white American and a black American had more in common with each other than they had with any other people on the planet, be they European or African. It seemed so obvious. But black and white Americans were incapable of acknowledging this. She had tried to talk about it with Monsieur Semple but he had not understood. Such a shame. Still, she was sure he was a genius, even if she could not decipher all that he wrote.

It was true, what Pauline's older sister, the mother of this weekend's bride, had suggested: Monsieur Semple reminded Pauline of her dead husband, Auguste. Monsieur Semple was not a cop but he had a coplike quality about him. All the things that made cops in equal parts creepy and attractive: Cleavon and Auguste were watchful but not quite paranoid, protective but not quite loving. Auguste, like Cleavon, had been older than Pauline. Auguste, unlike Cleavon, died young, from prostate cancer, at fifty. Pauline kept his cap and uniform in the closet in her apartment on the ground floor of the building on the rue de Latran.

At 8 A.M. on the morning of Wednesday, August 29, 2001, Pauline Ficelle pulled into a parking space not far from her building. She entered her ground-floor studio, quickly rifled through the pile of mail waiting for her on the table, stacked by Delphine, the part-time substitute concierge. Out of habit, Madame Ficelle went to the courtyard and checked the large garbage bins. She could tell from the amount of trash that the building was only about one-third full. Pauline rode the elevator to the fourth floor. Though she had had only three hours' sleep the night before and had been driving for five hours straight, she was totally alert, present, ready for whatever crisis Monsieur Semple was involving her in.

Pauline tapped lightly at her lover's door. Monsieur Semple opened it, quickly grabbed Pauline by the wrist and pulled her inside his apartment. His eyes were burning red. Pauline had seen him like this before, always when he had been drinking and writing. Both in excess. "I tried to get into your studio," he said. "The door was locked."

"Of course," Pauline replied. "What did you want?"

"Your husband's uniform. I need you to lend it to me."

"Why?"

"Don't ask."

"Why not?"

"Because I don't want you to be an accomplice."

"Too late," Pauline said, adding proudly, "I already am one."

Crickets. Naima heard them chirping maniacally in a whirling crescendo, a swarm of crickets invading her dreamless sleep. She reached over for her boyfriend, her eyes still closed, and banged her hand against a wall. She bolted upright, opened her eyes and saw Babar in his high chair, with his filthy yellow crown and masticated left ear. Slits of sunlight came through the shuttered bedroom windows. Naima groped for her wristwatch on the nightstand. Eight A.M. Finally, she realized that the manic chirping was human. Dressed in her boyfriend's cotton pajamas, Naima rose from her childhood bed, stumbled over to the window and flung open the shutters.

The August morning sun was blazing. Naima saw, four flights below, three vans topped with satellite dishes. She saw the tops of the heads of thirty or more people, some of them holding cameras, some clutching microphones, all of them pressed against each other in a swirling scrum, pushing and jostling their way toward the entrance of the building. Suddenly, a man in an orange baseball cap, worn backward, looked up and pointed straight at Naima. "It's her!" he screamed, in French. "The daughter!" Naima quickly closed the shutters and windows as the chirping of the media exploded below. The *scandale* had begun.

Naima walked down the long hallway of her parents' apartment, wondering, as she yawned and scratched her dreadlocks, what her next move should be; wondering, also, if Juvenal was awake yet. "Ohmigod!" she cried as she turned and entered the foyer. There was Juvenal, wearing nothing but crimson boxer shorts. With his powerful build, bald head and ebony skin, he looked like a finely carved African sculpture as he stood motionless under the overhead light, holding open the front door. Standing there on the threshold, short-haired and cinnamon-skinned, grasping a suitcase and wearing thick-lensed glasses that only magnified the shock in his eyes, was Darvin Littlefield. "What are you doing here?" Naima blurted out.

Darvin tilted his head slightly—looking, to Naima, like a wounded, big-eyed bird—and said to his girlfriend, "Hi, honey."

Sixteen

DARVIN'S SKIN WAS ITCHING like mad. He sat in the breakfast nook, clawing furiously at the little lumps that had popped up on his forearms and hands, his neck and cheeks. He didn't say much. He just glowered at Naima as she nervously puttered about the kitchen, his gaze hurt and accusing behind the thick eyeglasses. When Naima had led Darvin into the kitchen after his excruciatingly awkward introduction to Juvenal, she saw that the ceramic ashtray on the table in the breakfast nook was heaped with cigarette butts. Evidently, Juvenal had returned to the kitchen after Naima had gone to bed and smoked up a storm. The air was stale with the smell of tobacco.

"Did you have a party?" Darvin asked, dismayed by the sight of the two-thirds empty cognac bottle and dirty glasses beside the ashtray.

"Oh, no, it was just me and Juvenal," Naima said, beginning to sweat in Darvin's pajamas, "Why don't you sit down? You must be totally jet-lagged."

As her boyfriend glared at her, Naima dumped the ashtray, cleared the bottle and glasses, put on a fresh pot of coffee, sponged clean the table, started opening and closing cupboards, forgetting what it was she was looking for, her nervous puttering accompanied by an even more nervous patter. "Wait till you hear everything I have to tell you, Darvy, you're not gonna believe it, things have been so crazy. My God, I still can't get over your being here, I hope you weren't too freaked out by the reporters downstairs though I have to say I was pretty freaked out when I saw them, too, though Lamouche had told me to get ready for the scandal but you don't know Lamouche, do you? Anyway, wait till I tell you what happened last night. Juvenal might have saved my life. Have I ever told you about Juvenal before?"

"Yes," Darvin had said as he abruptly broke out in hives. Naima knew her boyfriend was allergic to cigarette smoke. But there was no smoke in the kitchen at that moment. Just the stale stench alone was apparently enough to send Darvin into a seizure of scratching. "You've told me about him."

"Right, of course," Naima said, finding it hard to look into Darvin's agonized, oddly magnified eyes. She wasn't used to seeing him in glasses anymore. He had started wearing contact lenses soon after Naima had met him. It was striking how nerdy Darvin looked with glasses and how handsome he was without them. But he preferred to wear glasses on planes, complaining that the air in the cabins irritated and dried out his contact lenses. After more puttering, Naima placed two cups of coffee on the table and sat across from Darvin. "So, er, how was your flight?"

"Long."

"Yes, of course, right. God, Darvy, it's so weird that you're here. Why didn't you tell me you were coming?"

"Surprise," Darvin said, now scratching beneath his shirt.

"Wow, that must have been expensive. Why did you do it?"

"To be *supportive*," he said, his voice hot as he put a sarcastic-sounding spin on the adjective. "That's what you're always telling me to be, isn't it? *Supportive?*"

In the three years of their relationship, Naima and Darvin had rarely argued. Naima attributed this to her own reaction against her parents' melodramatic clashes and to Darvin's exceptionally agree-able temperament. She had always known that a cataclysmic fight about some issue or another would occur someday. And she had al-ways felt sure that their love would survive the cataclysm. She just didn't want to have to find out today.

"Darvy, I hear something in your voice I haven't heard before. So I'm just going to say this once. After I got home safe with Juvenal last night, he slept on the couch and I slept in my bedroom. Nothing at all happened between us."

Darvin glared fiercely. Naima could see the skin along his hair-line begin to rise in places. His amber-toned cheeks were already splotched with clusters of reddish bumps that looked like the bites of tiny vicious insects. "Am I supposed to believe you?"

"Yes!"

Darvin started scratching wildly at his forehead and his thin layer of fine, close-cropped hair. "I'm all fucked up right now. I'm tired and I gotta take a bath for my allergy."

"Both my parents are missing. Don't you wanna hear what's go-ing on?"

"I do, Naima. Why do you think I came all the way to Paris? Right now, though, I need to take care of these hives because you and your friend smoked a crate of cigarettes in here."

"Fine. Use the bathroom next door to my bedroom. There should be fresh towels in there."

As Darvin rose from the nook, Naima grasped his welt-covered hand. "Thank you for coming, baby. And I'm sorry about the smoke."

"Well, you know what they say." Darvin stared down at Naima, his eyes now looking cold through the thick lenses. Naima felt like a speck of a specimen being analyzed under a microscope. "Where there's smoke, there's fire."

Naima stayed in the nook after Darvin left the kitchen, drank both cups of coffee. She tried to put Juvenal and Darvin out of her mind, tried to figure out what to do to find her parents. When she finally rose and returned to the living room, she was relieved to see that Juvenal had gone, leaving the sheets and pillows neatly piled on the couch.

He had also left the shutters on the tall windows closed and the TV turned on. A weather forecast: Naima saw the familiar cartoon map of France dotted mostly by yellow sunbursts, though there were gray clouds and bolts of lightning in the southwest. Just as Naima heard an explosion of the media cricket swarm below, Juvenal Kamuhanda appeared on the television screen, exiting Naima's building, pushing his way through the gaggle of reporters thrusting microphones at him. A title in the corner of the screen read: EN DIRECT.

"*Laissez-moi passer. Merde!*"

Once Juvenal started swinging his motorcycle helmet, banging a couple of reporters on their wrists, the horde backed off. A sole cameraman made a halfhearted effort to follow Juvenal down the Boulevard Saint-Germain as he strode toward his moto. But when Juvenal twirled around and glowered at him, the cameraman scuttled back into the horde.

The image onscreen switched to a plastic-looking man standing in the gutter in front of Naima's building. "We still have no word on the whereabouts of Marva Dobbs or her husband, Loïc Rose, or their employee Hassan Mekachera," the reporter said portentously into his microphone. "Nor have we been able to confirm if Naima Rose, the daughter of Madame Dobbs and Monsieur Rose, is in the apartment upstairs."

The image changed to a plastic-looking woman sitting in a studio. "What, then, do you have to report, Gilles?"

Cut back to Gilles, looking slightly embarrassed, on the Boulevard Saint-Germain. "Er, not very much."

Cut back to the anchorwoman, looking slightly annoyed. "Thank you, Gilles. If you are just joining us this morning, we can report that two days after the bombing of the WORTHEE building, one of the prime suspects in the crime, Ramzi Mekachera, committed suicide while in police custody a little more than one hour ago."

The image switched to a grim, gray courtyard filled with modern buildings. The camera focused on a pool of blood on the asphalt ground. "The suspect had been left alone for only a few minutes when he leapt to his death from the window of an interrogation room on the sixth floor."

Cut to a black-and-white ID photo of a balding, bearded man with a heavy brow and a narrow, almost hostile gaze. "Ramzi Mekachera," the anchorwoman announced offscreen, "had links to the terrorist group al Qaeda. His cousin and suspected accomplice, Hassan Mekachera, is still missing." Hassan's ID photo filled the screen for about two seconds. Hassan looked nothing like Ramzi. But, seeing Hassan again, Naima felt he bore a resemblance to someone else, someone she knew. She just couldn't think of who it was.

Cut to the anchorwoman. "And now, back to the weather." The cartoon map of France reappeared on the screen.

Naima stood frozen in front of the TV, feeling suddenly afraid again. If Ramzi had committed suicide, maybe he really was guilty of the bombing. And if Ramzi was guilty, maybe Hassan was, too. If Ramzi was desperate enough to take his own life, what might a desperate Hassan be capable of? If he decided to kill himself, might he not choose to take his hostage, Marva, with him? Naima wondered if she should call Inspector Lamouche, tell him what she had learned from Marie-Christine Pinchot.

The telephone rang. Naima lunged to pick up the receiver, praying it would be her mother calling. *"Allô?"*

"Naima?"

"*Maman?*" Naima asked, even though she did not recognize the voice.

"No, this is a friend of your mother's. My name is Charisse Bray. Do you remember me?"

Naima's heart sank. "You're the tour guide."

Charisse chuckled softly, perhaps in response to the disappointment she heard in Naima's voice. "Yes, that's right. How are you doing?"

"I've been better."

"I hear ya. Well, as you know, I lead tours of historic African-American spots in Paris. I'd like you to join a group of us this morning."

Naima's reaction followed a trajectory from startled through baffled and straight to angry in about three seconds. "Excuse me, Ms. Bray, but you realize I have a lot of other stuff on my mind right now."

"Oh, of course." Now Charisse spoke very slowly: "But people who know your mother very well think it would be good for you."

Naima nearly swooned. She was certain Charisse was conveying a message from Marva. "Really? When is your tour?"

"We're meeting in front of Richard Wright's house at nine o'clock. I think you know where that is. I don't have to give you the address over the phone, do I?"

"No," Naima said, appreciating Charisse's caution, her obvious fear of a wiretap. "I know where it is." Naima glanced at the clock above the fireplace: 8:30. "There's one problem, though. A mob of reporters is in front of my building. I don't know how to get past them."

Now Charisse spoke even more slowly: "We're . . . sure . . . you'll . . . remember . . . the . . . way."

Naima instantly grasped Charisse's meaning. It was now beyond doubt that the tour guide had talked with Marva. "Yes, you're right. Thank you, Ms. Bray. Thank you so much!"

"See you in a little while."

"I'll be there."

Naima hurried to the bathroom. It was filled with steam. Darvin was slumped in the bathtub, chest-deep in soapy water, snoring. Naima took a quick shower in the stall beside the bathtub. She thought the streaming water might wake Darvin, but when she emerged from the shower, her boyfriend was still snoring away.

Naima went to her bedroom and threw on a black T-shirt and a pair of baggy brown cargo pants. She donned a khaki-colored logoless baseball cap and a pair of sunglasses. Then she grabbed a ring full of keys from her bedside drawer—the keys to "the way" Charisse Bray had mentioned. She stepped out of the apartment and rode the elevator down to the ground floor, walked to the rear of the lobby, then crossed a spacious courtyard. She entered the back section of her building, the entry that used to be known as the maids' quarters, seven flights of one-room apartments. She used one of the keys on the ring she'd grabbed from her bedside drawer to open a door that was practically concealed behind a narrow spiral staircase. She walked down a long, twisting corridor that connected the maids' quarters of her building to the maids' quarters of an adjoining building. She used another key to open another door, passed through a smaller, more leafy courtyard, then entered the lobby of a building whose façade was on the rue des Saints-Pères. Years earlier, Marva had befriended the concierge of the adjacent building and sweet-talked her into giving her keys to the place ("Just in case of some kind of emergency, who knows what," she'd said as she handed Naima copies for herself). Naima emerged into the sunshine on the rue des Saints-Pères, around the corner and a good ways down the street, safely out of sight of the mob on the Boulevard Saint-Germain.

L'HOMME DE LETTRES NOIR AMERICAIN RICHARD WRIGHT HABITA CET IMMEUBLE DE 1948 À 1959. So read the marble plaque beside the towering arched doorway of number 14 rue Monsieur-le-Prince in the

Sixth Arrondissement. Naima arrived at the redbrick façade at nine o'clock sharp. A crowd of about twenty African Americans had already gathered in front of the building and Naima easily slipped into the tourists' midst.

"When Richard Wright arrived in Paris in 1945, he had already published *Native Son* and *Black Boy*," Charisse Bray told the crowd. Resplendent in her flowing caftan and crown of braids, she stood with her back to the intricately, exquisitely carved wooden door. "Wright was already the most famous, critically acclaimed and commercially successful African-American author who had ever lived. He and his family moved into this building three years after their arrival."

If Charisse had noticed Naima's presence in the group, she didn't show it.

"Did Wright die here?" one of the tourists asked.

"No," Charisse replied. "He moved out the year before. He died in 1960 at the age of just fifty-two."

"Is it true he was murdered?"

"No one knows for certain. He checked into the hospital one night with gastrointestinal problems. A few hours later, he died of a heart attack. There have always been rumors about a mysterious visitor at his hospital bed. Wright was very much involved in politics at the time, the battle against colonialism in Africa. He was a fiery and eloquent leader and there were a lot of people who might have considered him a threat to their world order. He made a great many enemies. The Communists hated him. But so did the anti-Communists. Folks forget it was Richard Wright who coined the term *Black Power*."

The crowd broke into an intense discussion, several people talking at once.

"Well, hello there, young lady."

Naima turned and saw one of her parents' oldest friends leaning down toward her and smiling. "Mr. Dukes!"

"You remember me?"

Archie Dukes, a head taller than most people in the crowd, was a scholarly-looking African American with short salt-and-pepper hair and the sort of old-fashioned, black-framed eyeglasses that the film *Malcolm X* had made popular again. In fact, Naima had often thought that if Malcolm X had lived to reach his sixties, he would have looked very much like Archie Dukes.

"Of course I—"

"You know there's another very interesting historic site near here," Archie said while the crowd continued to chatter. "One of particular importance to black expatriates. Would you like me to show it to you?"

Naima knew that she had to follow Archie Dukes. She wasn't exactly sure what was going on but she realized that somehow these black elders, Archie and Charisse, had decided to come to her aid. "Okay," she said.

They discreetly separated themselves from the chattering tour group, Archie leading Naima up the rue Monsieur-le-Prince and turning left at the next corner.

"It was smart of you to wear the cap and sunglasses," Archie said as they walked down the rue Racine.

"Thank you."

"So when's the last time we saw each other?"

"It was at my parents' place in Normandy. About four or five years ago."

"Ah, yes. One of those languorous country lunches."

"Exactly."

"By the way, I don't know if anyone has ever mentioned this to you, but do you know where your name comes from?"

"Oh, yeah. My mother loved the John Coltrane song."

"Yes, but when your mother was pregnant, for some reason, she was sure she was going to have a boy. She had all these boys' names ready. I said to her, 'Marva, you better have a female name in mind. It's a fifty-fifty chance, you know.' I was sitting with her and your fa-

ther and my first wife in the restaurant. Coltrane's 'Naima' was playing on the stereo. That was the moment when Marva decided on
your name."

Naima was so moved by this little piece of family history that she
was about to start laughing and crying at the same time. "I had no
idea."

"Well, here we are," Archie Dukes said abruptly, almost as if to
preempt an emotional outpouring from Naima. "The Hôtel
Doucette."

Naima saw a tangled assemblage of scaffolding in front of her.
"Is this the hotel where my father used to be assistant manager?"

"No, they tore that place down a long time ago. That was more of
a musicians' hotel. The Doucette here was a favorite spot of black
writers, painters and, well, I guess you'd call them philosophers.
Come, let's go inside."

Archie pulled out a set of keys, led Naima beneath some low-
hanging pipes and canvas, and opened a cracked glass door. They
stepped into the darkened lobby of the hotel. Naima saw paint-
splattered white sheets covering shapeless mounds of furniture. There
were exposed walls—wood beams and dusty bricks—everywhere and
lighting fixtures hanging from the ceiling. The smell of moist plaster.

"The Hôtel Doucette had fallen into disrepair," Archie said. "So I
bought the place and I'm putting everything I've got into reviving it."

"That's great," Naima said. She started to enter the chaotic space
that was once the parlor of the hotel when Archie took her gently by
the arm. "Come this way."

He opened a heavy door at the back of the ground floor. "Go on
down," Archie whispered.

Naima did not question Archie's gentle order. She promptly descended the concrete spiral staircase, down into the *caves* of the Hôtel Doucette. Only at the bottom of the steps did she turn around and
say, "Mr. Dukes?"

She heard the shutting and locking of the heavy door above her.
Nothing else. "Archie?" she whimpered.

No reply.

Fear wrapped itself around Naima's heart and squeezed. She faced a network of underground tunnels, illuminated by dangling bare bulbs. There were rows of storage spaces in front of her, walk-in-closet-sized units, each *cave* protected by rickety wooden gates with padlocks. According to legend, heroes of the French Resistance hid out in the secret passageways beneath the grand old buildings of Paris. Naima stood at a sort of fork in the road of *caves*, three distinct mudbrick alleys leading in different directions. She could see, in the shadows, other alleys shooting off of these three alleys. For a long moment, Naima did not move, barely even breathed. She heard a distant whisper, the hushed muttering of a voice. She could not discern the gender or the language. But she heard a constant murmuring, like an incantation. She decided to follow the alley from which the murmuring emanated.

Naima crept along the filthy plastic carpet that covered the earthen floor. The murmuring grew slightly louder. Every few feet, Naima saw little white plastic bowls of rat poison—pink pellets of poison—half of them overturned, others half-empty. The murmuring was getting clearer. It sounded like Arabic. Naima reached another fork in the subterranean road. Three different mudbrick alleys shooting into darkness. The whispering grew even louder. Yes, it was someone, a man, praying.

A human figure whipped around a blind corner. Naima had just enough time to make sense of the blur of features, the fiery eyes, the two hands clutching the gun, thrusting the weapon forward.

"*Non, Maman!*" Naima screamed.

Marva froze, still clutching the revolver. It took her a moment to recognize reality. She dropped the gun. Marva and Naima flew into each other's arms, both of them bursting into tears, overwhelmed by the most elemental of all loves.

Seventeen

"No FOOL LIKE AN old fool," Marva Dobbs said with a melancholy sigh, trying to explain the inexplicable passion she'd had for Hassan during a few steamy weeks in the summer of 2001.

Naima didn't like the way her mother had characterized herself. "First of all," she replied, "you're not so old. Second of all, it seems you're not the first woman who has been a fool for Hassan. And, having seen his photo, I can't say I blame any of y'all."

Marva smiled and took Naima's hand in hers. They were sitting side by side on a musty old couch, upholstered in carpetbagger chintz. The parlor of the Hôtel Doucette, under renovation, conjured two different images in Naima's mind: the shrouded, ghostly home of Dickens's Miss Havisham and a bombed-out urban abode from any number of European cities, circa 1944. But Naima felt safe here amid the stripped walls and covered furniture, the only light in the parlor slicing through the slits in the shutters. She curled up on the couch, holding hands with Maman. A few feet away, a revolver lay on top of a sealed bucket of white paint, next to a key to the cave of the Hôtel Doucette.

"Do you really know how to use that thing?" Naima asked her mother.

"Of course," Marva said, a little too casually, a bit too eager to reassure Naima of her street-smart dangerousness. How many times had Naima heard her mother boast, in one context or another: "I'm from Bed-Stuy. Shyeeeeeeeeeet."

Naima wasn't sure how much time had passed since she'd arrived at the Hôtel Doucette and been confronted with the shock of her mother pointing a pistol in her face. Marva and Hassan had been hiding out at the deserted hotel since midnight. But they had only descended to the subterranean safety of the *caves* that morning, when they saw on television that Ramzi Mekachera had died in police custody. While Marva and Naima talked in the dusty parlor, Hassan remained underground, praying.

"Does Hassan know why his cousin committed suicide?" Naima asked.

"Suicide!" Marva nearly shouted. As if suddenly remembering she and Naima were in a secret hideout, she rasped: "Do you really believe Ramzi killed himself? Good Lord, child, did your Papa and I raise you to be gullible? Ramzi a suicide? Puh-leeeeze."

"Sorry, Maman."

Marva told Naima about how Hassan had shown up in her hospital room in the dead of night, about how scared he was. His cousin had been framed, Hassan was sure of it. And now someone was trying to frame Hassan. Marva practically sprang from her bed. Concussion, state of shock, sedation: None of that mattered. Hassan's presence, his fear, his need of her help wiped out everything else that had happened to Marva that crazy day and night. She knew she had to think fast. She and Hassan couldn't linger in that damn hospital room. She got dressed and, with a minimum of fuss from the night nurse—few people ever fussed very strenuously with Marva Dobbs—she checked out. She had made her choice. She would flee with Hassan. She would protect him.

"Please forgive me, Naima."

"What for?"

"Disappearing the way I did. For not thinking about you." Marva's eyes filled with tears. "I should have been thinking about you. But I wasn't. I didn't know Loïc had contacted you. I didn't know you were on your way to Paris. I wasn't thinking about how all this might affect you and I just want to say I'm sorry for that, my baby."

Naima squeezed Marva's hand. "Maman, it's all right. There's nothing for you to apologize for."

Marva wiped away her tears and smiled wanly. "No fool like an old fool," she said again.

After leaving the Hôpital Decoust, Marva and Hassan went to an all-night café near the Boulevard Montparnasse. Marva had deliberately left her cell phone in the hospital room, fearing the police would be able to trace her calls. From a phone booth at the café, she called a discreet limousine service.

"What do you mean by discreet?" Naima asked.

"I mean they often take rich husbands, and wives, to meet their secret lovers. The drivers keep their mouths shut."

Deciding to be ultracautious, Marva had instructed Hassan not to speak during the ninety-minute drive to her house just outside the small town of Gisors, in the Normandy countryside. While Hassan waited in the limo, Marva entered the house, went down to the cellar and took the revolver, which Naima had never known about, from its hiding place in a crumbling old armoire. She then returned to the limo and told the driver to take them to Prunella Watson's farmhouse, about five miles away.

"Pru Watson!" Naima said, smacking a palm against her forehead. Prunella was a longtime American expatriate, about Marva's age. She was some kind of academic or feminist activist or both. Naima could never remember exactly what she did for a living. But she knew that Pru had published several books, been divorced several times and had a ton of money. Marva used to call the glamorous, charismatic Prunella Watson her "white cousin." Naima couldn't believe she had not thought of calling Pru to inquire after Marva's whereabouts.

"It's just as well," Marva said. "She would have had to lie to you. And she wouldn't have liked that."

Prunella was unfazed when Marva and Hassan showed up unannounced on her doorstep at four in the morning. She led them to a huge barn on her property where they would hide out all day Tuesday. Pru, meanwhile, on Marva's instructions, tried to get hold of Olivier Matignon, a wily criminal lawyer who they hoped would defend Ramzi and Hassan. There was no answer at Matignon's Paris office, nor at his apartment, nor at his villa on the French Riviera. Pru left vague messages about "an interesting case" on each of Matignon's three answering machines but, by six o'clock Tuesday evening, none of her calls had been returned.

Pacing around Prunella's barn, which was not a home to farm animals but to piles of old furniture and rusting equipment, Marva wondered aloud about what was going through Loïc's mind. He was bound to have discovered that morning that she had checked out of the hospital in the middle of the night, accompanied by a young North African. She was considering a call to Loïc when Hassan told her about the man he had seen twice during their last week together, parked on the rue Véron in a blue Peugeot.

"That could only have been Papa," Naima said.

"*Mais oui,*" Marva replied.

"Why hadn't Hassan mentioned it before?"

"The first time he spotted him, it was just a guy sitting in a car at eight in the morning. The second time, Hassan was leaving the restaurant at 4 A.M. We'd had a fight and he went off in a huff. That time, he got a good look at the man behind the wheel. But Hassan and I barely spoke again until the last night before I left for Brittany.

We were both very . . . intense . . . and he says he forgot all about the white man in the blue Peugeot. Once Hassan finally remembered to tell me, yesterday morning, your father's behavior in Brittany made more sense."

"How was he in Brittany?"

"Strange. Very watchful and wary, as if he was carefully scrutinizing me."

Isn't he always sort of like that? Naima wanted to say. But she didn't.

"I have to admit, though," Marva continued, "I wasn't paying much attention. Too wrapped up in myself, I guess."

And aren't you always like that? Naima wanted to say. But once again, she restrained herself.

"Only when we got back to Paris did it occur to me that maybe Loïc suspected something. All the same, I didn't think he'd been staking out the restaurant, night after night, all night long." Marva was raising her voice again. "What the fuck is that?"

"Du calme, Maman."

"The jealousy, the sneakiness . . ."

"Well, Maman, you *were* cheating on Papa!"

Marva raised her chin and said, with a Faye Dunaway–like haughtiness: "I dislike the word *cheat.*"

Naima responded with an extravagant eye roll. "Anyway, let's get back to yesterday. You and Hassan are still in the barn . . ."

"When, at eight last night, Pru comes in, all red-faced and flustered. She said she'd seen Loïc in Gisors. She was in town on some errands and saw him drive by in the famous blue Peugeot."

"Did he see her?"

"She didn't think so. She said he looked totally panicked."

But Pru had far worse news. She had seen on a café TV that Jeremy Hairston had been found stabbed to death in the Soul Food Kitchen.

"That was when I lost it," Marva said. "I just lost it. I was hysterical. Thrashing around. Screamin' and cryin' and bangin' on the walls. I think I scared Hassan. But I was just so upset. I had to get it out. Pru understood. She's known me a long, long time. Once the explosion of grief was over, I could go back to thinking. To thinking ruthlessly."

Marva was now sure that Loïc and Olivier were in cahoots. That was why Matignon hadn't returned Pru's calls. Marva had wanted Olivier to help Hassan. But Loïc, crazed by jealousy, might have wanted to use Olivier to somehow hurt Hassan.

Only then, in Pru's barn Tuesday evening, did Hassan tell Marva about his conversation with Jeremy the day before. After taking the train from Marseille, Hassan had gone straight to Montreuil, where he sought out friends of his and Ramzi's. They all told him not to stick around the neighborhood, to run for his life, flee the country if he could. Instead, Hassan decided to find Marva. She was an important person, someone with connections. But Hassan thought Marva was still in Brittany and he didn't have her phone number there. He could have tried her on her portable but he had somehow managed to lose the number. So he called the restaurant and got Jeremy on the line, who told him to come by at five o'clock, during the quiet time between the lunch and dinner seatings, when the restaurant was closed to the public. Hassan was a little wary since he and Jeremy had just had a huge clash the previous Thursday, leading Hassan to storm out in the middle of a busy night of work.

But Jeremy was kind to Hassan. He gave him something to eat, told him about Marva's crash on the Boulevard Saint-Germain that afternoon, gave him her room number at the Hôpital Decoust. He also told him that Loïc might have something to do with the frame-up. Loïc, Jeremy said, was an informer for the intelligence services. "A lot of people know that," he'd added.

"Did *you* know that?" Naima asked her mother in the parlor of the Hôtel Doucette.

Marva grimaced and squirmed on the couch. "I knew ... but I didn't know."

"What does that mean?"

"Oh, baby, it's hard to explain. First of all, you have to understand what Paris was like during the Cold War. There were spies, informers all over the place. People just accepted it. If you weren't
engaged in any intense political activities—and I never was—you
didn't worry about who was rumored to be collaborating with the
CIA or the Renseignements Généraux or whoever."

"And did you hear rumors about Papa?"

"Baby, if there were rumors people didn't share them with me."

"But how could Jeremy know and you *not* know?"

"That's the second thing you have to understand, Naima. Maybe
it has something to do with the nature of marriage. Or maybe just
our marriage. You don't ask your partner questions you don't want to
know the answers to. Just as your father and I never discussed our extramarital indiscretions—and, with the exception of Hassan, mine
all occurred before you were born—there were aspects of his business that we simply never talked about."

"And yet you would have these huge arguments about leaving
the cap off the toothpaste."

Marva winced in embarrassment. "I know. All those decoy issues.
I guess we fought about the little things to avoid confronting the big
things. In any event, it didn't shock me to hear that your father had
worked with intelligence services."

"And what about you?"

"Me!"

"Did anyone ever try to recruit you as an informer?"

Marva started laughing and, after a moment, Naima joined her.
Yes, it was a bit of a ridiculous notion. "Baby, I'm just the wrong type
for that kind of gig. Loose cannons don't make for good espionage.
And I never had a political ax to grind. Me, I was friends with everybody, Right, Left and Center. I wouldn't tolerate a racist, but racists
don't tend to eat in soul food restaurants." Marva paused, then
turned serious again. "Actually, I take that back. There was something else Jeremy told Hassan. One night last June, when I was out
sick, Loïc had dinner at the restaurant with Harvey Oldcorn."

"Who's Harvey Oldcorn?"

"A known spy. And a real son of a bitch. Anyway, I don't want to get into the whole history. But certainly Loïc knows the history. And so did Jeremy." Naima could hear the anger rising in her mother's voice again. "And neither one of them said anything to me about Harvey Oldcorn being at the restaurant. I didn't even know that motherfucker was back in Paris."

"Well, from everything you've just said, it would have been out of character for Papa to tell you he'd dined with a known spy. As for Jeremy . . ."

"Yeah, he wouldn't have wanted to touch it. All the years we worked together he never said anything about what he might have heard about Loïc's spying. But he told Hassan that it troubled him to see Loïc and Harvey together."

"You don't think Papa's involved in some way with the WORTHEE bombing?"

"Oh, Naima, I haven't been able to get my mind around that." Marva paused, swallowed hard. When she spoke again her voice sounded both sorrowful and scared. "I honestly don't know what to think about your father right now. I really don't."

Naima stroked her mother's shoulder, struggled to find something comforting to say. Finally, she could only murmur, "Me neither."

Back in the barn, Prunella Watson said it was no longer safe for Marva and Hassan to stay in the vicinity of Gisors, not with Loïc lurking about. She told Marva about a call she'd gotten from Archie Dukes that afternoon. He was worried about Marva and had wanted to know if Pru had any information for him. Naturally, she'd lied and said no. But maybe Archie would be able to help. He might at least be able to provide a safe place for the night. "Are his loyalties more with you or with Loïc?" Pru asked.

"Archie's a trustworthy brother," Marva said. "Let's get a hold of him."

Pru pulled out her cell phone and punched in the number. "Hello, Archie? Pru Watson again. Listen, I've decided to have an impromptu party tonight at my place in Normandy. A bunch of old friends. I know this is rather short notice but maybe you'd like to drop by."

"I'll be there in an hour and a half," Archie replied.

"Clearly," Marva said to Naima, "a man who can take a hint."

Eighty minutes later, as night fell on Normandy, Archie pulled into Pru's driveway, behind the wheel of his battered old BMW. A clever man, Archie had thought of everything. He'd brought along a pair of large-framed, tinted, seventies-era glasses and a straight-haired reddish brown wig once worn by his dead wife, Ernestine. Covering her short, kinky hair with the wig, donning the Jackie O shades, Marva knew that somewhere Ernestine, one of the greatest friends she'd ever had, was getting a kick out of this.

Marva rode up front with Archie, perfectly comfortable in her disguise. Poor Hassan lay on the floor of the backseat, buried under a blanket and a pile of camping equipment.

"At least it was a fairly short trip," Marva said. "Archie's such a wonderful guy. He was the one who told me you were in Paris."

"How did he know?" Naima asked. With all the weird shit she'd been hearing the past two days, she was bristling with paranoia.

Marva shrugged. "I don't know. Hadn't you talked to him?"

"Not until this morning."

"Well, then, he must have been in touch with your father. Or with Jeremy. You spoke with Jeremy, didn't you?"

"Oh, yeah. Yesterday morning."

"Anyway, on the drive to Paris, Archie told me it was Webster Janes who had been killed in the WORTHEE bombing."

"Who's Webster Janes?"

"You don't know who Web Janes was?"

"No idea."

"He was the director of WORTHEE. Web Janes was the real target of the bombing. But until last night, they hadn't announced it.

The media had only said that a passerby was badly wounded. But I knew the passerby was somebody important. Lamouche had told me."

"Inspector Lamouche? I know him."

Marva was startled. "How do you know Lamouche?"

"I met him at the restaurant yesterday. I had scheduled a rendezvous with Jeremy. When I arrived, there were cops all over the place. I was the one who identified Jeremy's body."

A look of utter horror fell across Marva's face. She opened her mouth and let out a low, tormented groan. "Oh, my baby," she cried. Marva threw her arms around Naima, weeping and saying over and over again, "I'm so sorry, baby. I'm so sorry you had to go through this. I'm so sorry."

"It's okay, Maman, it's okay." Naima knew Marva needed consoling more than she did.

When Marva finally calmed down, she continued recounting her talk with Archie Dukes during the drive from Gisors to Paris. Marva believed Hassan completely when he said he and his cousin had had nothing to do with the WORTHEE bombing. But *somebody* had set off that explosion. *Somebody* had wanted Web Janes dead. And that same somebody must have been involved in Jeremy's murder.

"Well, the cops aren't interested in that somebody," Archie said. "They're going to try to pin Jeremy's murder on Hassan. The media's already saying he kidnapped you."

Marva loved Archie like a brother but he had always seemed a bit mysterious to her, in the same way that Loïc had always seemed a bit mysterious. As with Loïc, she didn't really want to know what she didn't already know about Archie. Still, she asked him: "Who do you think is behind all this?"

"I don't know, Marva. But I did get a call from Harvey Oldcorn this afternoon. He was looking for Loïc."

"Oldcorn and Loïc had dinner together two or three months ago."

Archie made an awful face, as if he'd just swallowed a dose of vile-tasting medicine. "I'm sorry to hear that," he said. "You know, I spoke with Cleavon Semple tonight. Asked him about Loïc. He sounded very agitated. In fact, he hung up on me."

Here was yet another name Naima had never heard before. "Who the hell is Cleavon Semple?"

"A very sad old black man," Marva said. "Very sad and very dangerous."

"A spy?"

"Everybody thought so."

Hassan's English was far from perfect but, lying on the floor in the back of the car, he got the gist of everything Marva and Archie had discussed. By the time they arrived at the Hôtel Doucette, Hassan had decided to turn himself in to the police. Marva and Archie pleaded with him to reconsider. Hassan agreed to sleep on it, but it was clear he had made up his mind. At eight o'clock Wednesday morning, he would go to the Préfecture de Police and throw himself on the mercy of the French justice system.

The refurbishment of the top floor of the Hôtel Doucette was already complete. Marva, Hassan and Archie slept in three separate rooms. At seven thirty Wednesday morning, Archie tapped urgently on Marva's door and on Hassan's, told them to turn on their televisions. The death of Ramzi Mekachera had just been announced.

"That was when Hassan lost it," Marva said. "Like me when I heard about Jeremy."

Marva did her best to comfort Hassan. Once he got a grip on himself, he realized that surrendering to the police was maybe not the best idea. All Hassan wanted to do at that moment was pray. Archie suggested he do it in the *caves*. He thought Marva and Hassan might both be safer hiding out below ground. They were all about to leave the top floor when Marva saw Darvin Littlefield on the TV screen, looking distressed as he forced his way past a gaggle of reporters on the Boulevard Saint-Germain.

Marva was suddenly desperate to see Naima. Marva didn't know what was going to happen in the next few hours. She herself might

be captured and thrown in jail on charges of aiding a fugitive terrorist suspect. Archie said it was too risky but Marva was adamant that
she see Naima as soon as possible. They quickly devised a plan. But it
was a plan that hung on several variables. Would Archie be able to
contact Charisse Bray? Would her tour group be gathering in the
neighborhood that morning? Would Charisse be able to get in touch
with Naima? Would Naima get the hint about how to escape her parents' apartment unseen?

When Archie left Marva and Hassan down in the *caves,* there
was still no clue as to whether the plan to get Naima there would
work. An hour later, while Hassan prayed in a nearby storage space,
Marva heard footsteps in the tunnel. She grabbed her revolver and
crept along the plastic rug. She hoped to see her daughter around the
corner but she couldn't be sure.

"Thank you for not shooting me," Naima said.

"Oh, baby, you can always trust Maman behind the trigger."

"So what are we gonna do now?"

"I think maybe Hassan has the right idea. Pray."

Naima tried not to show her dissatisfaction with her mother's answer. Marva, American to the core, had an unshakable faith in God.
Naima was typically European in her skepticism about God's very existence. "Well," she said, "I guess that could work."

They were both quiet for a long moment, then Marva said, "You
know what I feel really guilty about?"

"What?"

"Actually, I feel guilty about more things than I can count right
now but what's really eating away at me this morning is that Hassan
was on the brink of starting a whole new life. He's twenty-eight years
old and he had decided this past weekend that he was finally going to
get serious, make real commitments. After he had this fight with Jeremy at the restaurant last Thursday, he went down to Marseille and
spent three days with his youngest child and the baby's mother."

"I know," Naima said. "I've met them both."

Marva was stunned. "When?"

"Last night. In Montreuil. Marie-Christine Pinchot and little Xavier. They were staying in Hassan's apartment."

"Good Lord, Hassan has no idea. He last talked with Marie-Christine Monday evening. She was still in Marseille. He's been afraid to call her again."

"I really like her. And Xavier's adorable."

"Well, Hassan had decided he was going to quit Paris, move in with Marie-Christine and get a job in Marseille."

"You weren't disappointed to hear that?"

"Baby, I was relieved!"

"What about your relationship with him?"

"Our fling had flung. I was happy that Hassan wanted to be a full-time daddy to at least one of his kids."

Naima raised an eyebrow. "How many kids does he have?"

"Never mind. The point is he was finally getting his act together and then all this shit explodes."

"You can't blame yourself for that, Maman."

"If I'd been able to keep my hands off Hassan, he might not have been dragged into this mess."

"You don't know that for sure. Even if Ramzi was innocent, it sounds like he did have some strange stuff in his past. Paramilitary training in Afghanistan, creepy friends in Pakistan . . ."

"Ramzi was definitely innocent," Marva said, clearly annoyed. "He was as much a victim as Hassan is. And just as nobody in France wants to believe Ramzi was innocent, nobody will wanna believe Hassan, either. All the French have to do is say he's a radical Algerian Muslim and nobody will give a shit if he lives or dies. It's like Jimmy Baldwin used to say: Us black folks ain't the niggas of France. It's Hassan's people."

Marva and Naima both heard the clank of a bolt action lock. The noise came a good distance from the parlor, down the darkened corridor of the Hôtel Doucette. Marva slid across the couch, reached over and grasped the revolver from its resting place atop the paint bucket. For a few seconds, there was no sound, not even the faintest footstep, coming from the corridor outside the parlor. Naima felt as if her heart had stopped beating. Sitting motionless on the couch, she watched Marva, right beside her, smoothly turn to face the open doorway, clutching the pistol in both hands, arms straight out in front of her, extended, grip and aim rock steady.

At last, the silence was broken. "*Mar*-VAH?" a very French voice asked uncertainly.

Marva lowered the gun and called out, *"Entre, Hassan."*

Naima saw the resemblance as soon as Marva's lover crossed the threshold. The creamy coffee complexion, the height and build; the structure of the face, the fullness of the lips. Only the length of the hair and the shape of the eyes were different. The colors were the same. Naima couldn't help feeling a little bit flattered that, maybe, on some unconscious level, Marva had chosen to have an affair with someone who looked so much like her daughter's boyfriend.

"Bonjour," Hassan said, smiling shyly.

Naima rose from the couch, kissed him once on each cheek.

"I'm so glad you two got to meet," Marva said, as casually as if she were introducing two customers at her restaurant.

"You know what, Maman," Naima said, getting a good long look at Hassan, then turning to Marva, "I know how we can get Hassan someplace safe."

"You do?"

"Someplace where no one will be looking to persecute him just because of what he is." Naima felt dreamy and exhilarated, intoxicated with inspiration. "Someplace where Muslims are treated with respect."

Marva looked baffled. "Where?"

"America."

Eighteen

"NAIMA, IS THAT YOU?" Darvin asked groggily. "What are you doing?"

Standing near a table beside the window of her childhood bedroom, Naima saw Darvin sit up in bed, naked to the waist, squinting. "Hi, Darvy."

Darvin rubbed his eyes. "What time is it?"

"About eleven. How are your hives?"

"All gone." Darvin reached for the nightstand, started groping almost blindly. "Where are my glasses? I can barely see a thing."

"They're right here," Naima said in a helpful tone. In fact, many of Darvin's belongings were laid out in front of her on the table: his eyeglasses, his wristwatch, his wallet, his passport. Naima had been relieved to see that his passport photo was exactly as she had remem-

bered it. Darvin was wearing his spectacles in the picture, magnify-
ing his eyes, distorting their shape.

"I woke up in the bathtub and you were gone," Darvin said,
sounding hurt and bewildered.

Naima walked over to the bed, carrying Darvin's spectacles and a
tall glass of orange juice. "I had to run out for a while. Sorry, honey."
She sat down beside him on the edge of the bed, handed him the
glasses. "I brought you some O.J."

"Thanks, baby." Darvin put on the glasses, consumed the orange
juice in one gulp. "So where's Juvenal?" he asked, wiping his mouth
with the back of his hand.

"I have no idea, Darvy." Naima returned her boyfriend's suspicious gaze with a look of kindly solicitude. "How's your jet lag?"

"I dunno. I think it's starting to fade. What were you doing when
I woke up just now?"

"Arranging your things."

"They were already arranged."

Naima was getting impatient, waiting for the drugs to take effect. "So did you hear from any of those statistical research companies you applied to?"

"Nothing yet," Darvin said, suddenly breaking into a huge yawn.

"I'm sure you're gonna get a great job, Darvy."

"Did you say you went out?"

"Yeah, I had to run some errands."

"How'd you get past the reporters?"

"Oh, never you mind."

"What's going on?"

"What do you mean?"

"You sheem shtane," Darvin said, slurring his words.

"Why don't you get some more sleep?"

Darvin was already slumping down in the bed. "I'm not sheepy."

Naima gently removed his eyeglasses. "Sweet dreams, baby."

"Ergumbrula," Darvin muttered, then commenced snoring.

Naima quickly started gathering some articles of Darvin's clothing, stuffing them in the black leather overnight bag. The single piece of carry-on luggage was right where Marva had said it would be, in her bedroom closet. Just as the items from Marva's bathroom were exactly where she'd said they would be: the electric razor, the scissors, the sleeping pills—two of which Naima had crushed and stirred into Darvin's orange juice.

"Factor in the jet lag and he'll be out for twenty-four hours," Marva had assured her daughter back at the Hôtel Doucette, where they had hatched their plot.

Pauline Ficelle was sitting through the second straight showing of *Le Fabuleux Destin d'Amélie Poulain,* a movie she had already seen twice before. It was the hit of the summer in France, the whimsical tale of a shy young waitress in Montmartre who manages to bring disparate lonely people together and find true love for herself.

Sitting in the theater in the somewhat seedy Clichy district of Paris, Pauline Ficelle knew that, on some level, she identified with the doe-eyed innocent portrayed by Audrey Tautou on the big screen. She was doing what she was doing for love—and a deep concern for other people. Just like Amélie.

Monsieur Semple had given Pauline a very precise message to give to another man. He had written it down for her to memorize word by word. She was to say nothing more or nothing less. And she was not to deliver the message until exactly three o'clock.

"But what if I go to the office of this Monsieur Oldcorn and he is at lunch?" Pauline Ficelle had asked.

"He won't be," Cleavon Semple had replied.

Monsieur Semple gave her these instructions at eight-thirty in the morning. What was Pauline supposed to do with herself until three?

"I don't know," Monsieur Semple had responded irritably. "Whatever you would want to do. Just don't do it anywhere anyone you know would see you. Be discreet."

"And after I deliver this precise message to Monsieur Oldcorn?"

"Go back to Mulhouse. You'll be back by eight thirty tonight. Dinnertime, more or less. Like I promised you."

"And when I come back to Paris next Sunday?"

"We pick up right where we left off."

"I still don't know what to do until three o'clock."

"Well, figure it out. Go shopping. Go to the zoo. Go to the movies."

Pauline was hurt by Monsieur Semple's angry impatience. But she would do what he wished. She knew there was some danger attached to it, but that only aroused her more. She decided to go to the movies before her mission. Two helpings of *Amélie*. Then she would deliver the message that Monsieur Semple had assigned to her. At exactly three o'clock. She wished Monsieur Semple had been a bit more forthcoming with her. After all, she had given him her dead husband's police uniform—and his gun. No (or at least very few) questions asked.

"This is crazy," Hassan said, staring at his nearly clean-shaven pate in the hotel bathroom mirror. His long locks had been reduced to a thin layer of fine, light brown hair.

"Put on the glasses," Marva said.

Hassan carefully looped the wire hooks around his ears. His eyes grew large and strange behind the lenses.

Marva held up the passport photo in the looking glass.

"You're Darvin!" she shrieked happily.

Hassan maintained a serious expression as he stared at his—that is to say, Darvin Littlefield's—official image staring back at him.

"No careful customs official would fall for this," he said.

"And that's what I'm telling you," Marva retorted. "There *are* no careful customs officials during tourist season, let alone at the end of August, on Paris–New York flights. All you have to do is say 'Hi' to the official at JFK airport."

"Ai," Hassan said.

"They're gonna glance at your passport photo and as long as you're a tan-skinned man named Darvin Littlefield who looks a little bit like that caramel-colored cutie in the photo, ain't gonna be no problem. They got a long line of folks behind you. All you gotta do is say 'Hi.' "

"Ai," Hassan said earnestly.

"No, baby, you gotta aspirate that 'H'!"

"Ai!" Hassan repeated even more earnestly. "Ai, ai, ai! . . . Hai!"

"Say that again," Marva said.

"Hi!"

"By George, I think he's got it," Marva sang.

"Hi," Hassan said, flashing a winning grin and extending a hand.

"No need to shake hands. A simple, enthusiastic 'hi' will say enough. After all, you've already passed through a metal detector, so they know you're safe."

"You're right. I'm just scared."

"Then relax."

"Will you relax with me?"

Marva didn't know how to respond. "Okay," she said finally, "but only for an hour."

"I really can't thank you enough, Mr. Dukes."

"Please, Naima, call me Archie."

They stood in the center of the parlor of the Hôtel Doucette, amid the shrouded furniture, surrounded by the stripped-down walls. "I just spoke with Marie-Christine again," Naima said. She handed Archie a scrap of paper with the address and phone number of Madame Rghada Zebouni in Montreuil. Marie-Christine and Xavier were staying with her. Through an old contact in the upper echelons of a certain airline, Archie had wangled a first-class seat for Mademoiselle Pinchot and child on a 6:00 P.M. flight, Paris to New York.

Archie had also managed to get an economy-class seat for Darvin Littlefield on the same flight. And now he had offered to go and pick up
Marie-Christine and Xavier and drive them to the airport.

Archie handed Naima keys to the front and back doors of the
Hôtel Doucette. If anything went wrong, she could hurry back to
safety here.

"I've also confirmed with Charisse Bray that she will lead a tour
group to the Fontaine Saint-Michel at four o'clock sharp," Archie said.

"You're amazing," Naima said.

"What's amazing will be if this all goes off without a hitch."

"Please thank Charisse for me."

"You can thank her yourself when this is all over."

"Any news of my father?"

Archie frowned. "Not that I've heard."

"Do you think he's still alive?"

Naima blurted out the question and was as startled by her candor
as Archie clearly was. After a moment, he grasped her shoulder and
squeezed. *"Bon courage."*

Marva and Hassan lay side by side on the hotel-room bed, both of
them fully dressed, in other people's clothes. Marva wore a striped
pantsuit that once belonged to her dear friend Ernestine Dukes. Hassan was dressed as Naima's boyfriend, wearing Darvin Littlefield's
khaki pants and Lacoste shirt. Hassan was fast asleep, Marva wide
awake, her mind spinning in silent prayer.

Dear Lord, I know I'm not exactly in a position to make de-
mands right now. And I ain't demandin' nothin'. I'm plead-
ing with you, Lord, to let this all work out. I know I'm a
sinner. Hassan and I both sinned in the most terrible, selfish
way. But you've made us pay, Lord. You took Jeremy and that
is something I'll have on my conscience forever. I'm going to
have to face Jeremy's people soon and beg their forgiveness

for whatever part my sins had to do with his death. And you've taken Ramzi away from Hassan. You see how Hassan suffers from his cousin's death. You took Web Janes and I suppose you had your reasons for that.

What I'm begging, Lord, is that you don't make anyone else pay with their life for all this mess. I don't understand it all, Lord. I'm so scared and confused right now. I don't understand my own husband. I don't know what's come over Loïc, where he is or what he's doing. Maybe you've already taken Loïc. I guess I could see why you'd think I deserve that. But if Loïc is still alive, please let him stay alive, Lord. If not for me, then for our daughter.

Thank you, Lord, thank you so much for Naima. Maybe I haven't thanked you enough for her, not lately anyway. I know I don't deserve her, Lord, but thank you for bringing her to me twenty-three years ago and thank you for bringing her to Paris, to this hotel, to help me today. She's figured it all out, I think she's found the right solution. She's gonna save us all. Hassan will be reunited with Marie-Christine and their little boy. Marie-Christine told Naima that she knows people in New York who can help them. Maybe it will work out for them there and maybe it won't but please, Lord, I'm beggin' you, just let them all get to New York safely. Hassan, Marie-Christine and Xavier. Naima's worked it all out so carefully. Thank you once again for my daughter, Lord. She's so smart and brave it makes me wanna cry.

And thank you for Prunella and Archie and Charisse and thank Ernestine for me in heaven. Maybe I'll see her there someday. Maybe not. I know it's your call, Lord, and my case might be right on the line. But please don't punish me anymore right now, Lord. I wanna make things right. Please don't take my family away from me. Spare Loïc. Protect Naima. Let us get through this ordeal intact—as a family. Thank you, Lord.

"Mmm, ghrrrrr, brrmrr," Hassan muttered and stirred beside Marva on the bed.

See, Lord, we resisted temptation. We've come to our senses, Hassan and me. We're ready to recommit to our true loves, our true lives. Please just give us the chance. Please, Lord. Please.

Juvenal stood near the back of the art gallery he owned near the Place de la Bastille, hands on his hips, staring at the floor. He had maintained that posture the whole time that Naima explained to him all that had happened since he'd left her apartment after Darvin's arrival that morning. She spoke in a hushed rush. The gallery was closed and she and Juvenal were the only people in it, but Naima still bristled with paranoia. She had barely noticed the array of sculptures and paintings, every work created by an artist of the African diaspora, all around her. She was focused on one thing: persuading Juvenal to help her in the plan she and Marva had designed.

"What I need from you," Naima said evenly but urgently, "in fact, all I need from you is for you to drive up to the Place Saint-Michel, near rue Danton, at four o'clock. Just wait there on your moto. I will bring the passenger to you. He'll put on the helmet, hop on the back and you're off. Take him to the appropriate terminal at Charles de Gaulle. You don't have to talk to him. Hell, you don't even have to look at him. Just him give him a ride and then you're free. No risk to you at all."

Juvenal continued to stare at the floor, hands on hips, saying nothing.

"Are you listening to me?" Naima snapped.

"It is not risk to myself that raises doubt," Juvenal said. "It is the question of whether we should not leave this whole matter to the professionals. Maybe we're helping someone who does not deserve our help." Juvenal had still not looked up.

"You'll be helping me," Naima shot back. "You'll be helping my mother. Do we not deserve your help?"

Juvenal finally raised his head, fixed Naima with his laser gaze. "You know I will do anything you want."

"Thank you."

"And after I take this ... this ... Darvin ... to the airport ... what happens with us?"

Naima, still wearing her baseball cap and dark glasses, smiled. "As we say in America: We'll jump off that bridge when we get to it."

The offices of Carmichael Associates were located on the Avenue George V, in a building of such stately beauty and elegance that it might have been the embassy of a small but spectacularly wealthy nation. Pauline Ficelle felt weak and insignificant as she entered the company's glittering lobby and approached the scowling receptionist.

"Who?" Pauline heard an angry American voice snap over the intercom after the receptionist had announced her name to Harvey Oldcorn. Cleavon had told her to be prepared for such a reaction.

"Please tell him I am the concierge of Monsieur Semple."

"I heard that," Oldcorn's voice barked. "Send her in."

Pauline passed through a set of mahogany double doors and entered a plush, high-ceilinged, sun-drenched chamber whose towering windows looked out on a meticulously manicured garden. Harvey Oldcorn remained seated behind a massive, gleaming desk.

"Bon-JER," he said gruffly, gesturing for her to take a seat in a slick leather armchair. "I assume you have a message for me from your boyfriend."

Oldcorn's rudeness cured Pauline of her insecurity. How dare this vulgar man speak to her in such a manner? She had been worried about freezing in front of Cleavon's American enemy. She had wondered, while sitting in the movie theater earlier that day, if she might bungle the message. Maybe even break down in tears and not be able to say what Cleavon had instructed her to say. But now, insulted by this vulgar man, she delivered the message with the same fierce and steely intensity that she knew Monsieur Semple would have displayed himself.

"Mission accomplished," Pauline said. "Our mutual acquaintance has completed the job for which you hired him. The physical proof will emerge quite soon. He would like to meet you to collect the rest of his fee."

"Hmmph," Oldcorn snorted. With his bulbous nose, plump cheeks and wispy white hair, he reminded Pauline of a certain character in an American movie. But she could not recall exactly who it was. She stared severely at Oldcorn as he knitted his brow. "When and where?"

"La Fontaine Saint-Michel. At four o'clock."

"That's less than an hour from now. I hope he's expecting the physical proof to emerge before then!"

Now Pauline realized who it was Oldcorn resembled: the Magician of Oz. The projected image of the charlatan: a huge head, the voice that was booming and cruel. But Pauline could also see in Oldcorn the magician after he is exposed, once the curtain is torn away and he's revealed to be a bumbling fraud.

"Our mutual acquaintance," Pauline said, following Cleavon's instructions precisely, "has come into possession of something that you want: a compact disk."

"Son of a bitch," Oldcorn growled. "How much?"

"His fee for the job. Times five."

"Tell him to go fuck himself."

Cleavon had prepared Pauline for that response. In fact, the entire conversation had gone exactly the way he had said it would. She was merely reciting verbatim the lines he had written for her. Including: "You can tell him yourself. At Saint-Michel at four o'clock. He'll have the CD. He'll take the entire payment in cash."

Oldcorn shook his head and chuckled. "What balls."

Pauline was waiting for Oldcorn to dismiss her. She would then deliver the last line Cleavon had written for her, leave the office, return to her car—parked just a few meters away on rue Quentin—and drive back to Mulhouse. She would not, under any circumstances, try to contact Monsieur Semple by telephone. Nor would he contact her. They would wait until she returned to Paris on Sunday and speak face to face.

Harvey Oldcorn stared at Pauline in a strange, cloudy way, as if he were looking through her, or past her. Then he said something Cleavon had not said he would say: "Madame Ficelle..., what exatly do you know about me anyway?"

Pauline was caught completely unprepared. She could no longer look directly at Oldcorn. She looked down at the intricately patterned, undoubtedly expensive rug and did not reply.

Oldcorn reached across the vast and shiny surface of his desk, lifted a picture frame and turned it around. Pauline glanced up and saw the black-and-white image of a strong-featured, unmistakably American woman with a jutting chin, a jolly smile and a stiff, sticky-looking hairdo.

"That was my wife. A lifetime civil servant. Devoted to understanding foreign cultures and extending American values wherever she could. We were married for forty-three years. We had no children. That good woman was my whole life. She was working in the American embassy in Nairobi when it was blown up by terrorists. Three years ago last week. Now I don't know what your boyfriend has told you about me or what anybody else has told him about me, but you ought to know, *madame*, even if he doesn't, that my wife did not die in vain. I will see to that. I will see to it that my wife did not die in vain. I will grieve for any other person, any other American, who might end up sacrificing his life or experiencing the loss of a loved one in the war that is to come. But it is a war that must be fought. Tell your boyfriend I'll bring him his money. But tell him he ought to know that I'm doing what I'm doing for something more important than money. Tell him I believe in what I'm doing. Then ask him what he believes in."

Pauline felt as if she were shrinking in her leather chair. She could feel her lower lip quivering. She said nothing to Oldcorn. And she was not going to say anything to Monsieur Semple. Not today. She was going to follow his instructions and get back to Mulhouse. She only hoped that her hands, which were beginning to tremble uncontrollably in her lap, would be steady on the steering wheel during the five-hour drive.

The console on Oldcorn's desk buzzed, and Pauline heard the receptionist's voice: "Inspector Lamouche calling."

"Put him through," Oldcorn said, his voice and demeanor instantly softening. "Well, bon-JER, Inspector," he boomed jovially.

"Good day to you," a French voice wheedled in English, over the speaker phone.

"Any news?"

"Yes. I have for you some questions regarding ze murder of Jeremy Airston."

Oldcorn laughed abruptly. "Him? I was hoping you were going to tell me you'd found Hassan Mekachera. Certainly, he's the one who killed Jeremy Hairston. He's probably killed Loïc Rose by now, too. And God only knows what's happened to poor Marva Dobbs. You'll most likely find her chopped up in pieces somewhere soon."

"Ah bon?" Lamouche said.

Oldcorn let out another sudden seal's bark of a laugh. "Well, I'm just speculating."

"Mais oui. But regarding ze Airston murder, we have found some interesting forensic evidence zat we would like to discuss wiz you."

"Forensic evidence?"

Pauline Ficelle looked directly at Harvey Oldcorn for the first time in several minutes and saw the color drain from his face.

"Ye-e-e-e-ssss," Lamouche wheedled over the speaker phone. "Hair and fiber. Zat sort of zing. Perhaps you could come up to my office in ze *mairie* of ze Eighteenz Arrondissement, tomorrow morning at nine. Feel free to bring your attorney."

Oldcorn seemed to have aged ten years before Pauline's eyes. "We *are* on the same side . . . aren't we, Inspector?"

"I am afraid I do not know what you mean."

"No, of course not. You're French."

"So I see you tomorrow zen?"

"Yes," Oldcorn said, reaching for a button on the console.

"*A de*—" Lamouche's voice was abruptly cut off the speaker phone.

Oldcorn looked at Pauline as if he'd forgotten she was still there. "What?" he snarled.

Pauline practically leapt from her chair and hurried toward the double doors. Suddenly remembering the last line Cleavon had scripted for her, she turned back to Oldcorn and said, "You and I never met."

Nineteen

EVERYBODY ARRIVED EARLY. NAIMA was the first of the schemers to get to the Fontaine Saint-Michel. At 3:50 P.M. she was leaning nonchalantly against a granite pedestal, with one of the fearsome bronze dragons just above and behind her. The vast square in front of the fountain was typically lively for an August afternoon, filled with camera-toting tourists and an international collection of attitudinizing youth: males and females in their teens and twenties, of all shapes and hues, sporting cornrows and tattoos, multiple body piercings, shaved heads and unruly, tumbling manes of hair. They were chattering into cell phones, hauling backpacks, gliding by on skateboards or rollerblades or sitting and sunning themselves; or standing in clusters flirting, joking, smoking cigarettes, trying to look cool.

Naima, in her black T-shirt and baggy cargo pants, her baseball cap and shades, fit right into the scene. No one noticing her would have guessed that she was getting ready to execute the handoff of a fugitive to his getaway driver. Naima herself was surprised by how utterly calm and focused she felt. Maybe it suited her, she mused, this life of danger and chaos she'd been living the past two days.

Naima was facing north. In the distance, she saw Charisse Bray emerge from the rue de la Huchette, on the east side of the Place Saint-Michel, her tour group close behind. It was only 3:52. While it would take a minute or so for the group to walk up to the fountain, Naima was worried that they were too early. Juvenal was still nowhere in sight. Charisse must have been nervous. She was about to lead the group across the street, not noticing the DON'T WALK sign, almost stepping right into the path of a dark blue van that came zooming down the Boulevard Saint-Michel. One of Charisse's African-American tourists pulled her out of harm's way at the last second. Naima watched the van roll up to the next corner and stop in the tow-away zone just in front of the Café Le Départ. She thought she saw the silhouette of a police officer, wearing his cap, in the driver's seat. Shit. The last thing she needed was for a suspicious cop to appear on the scene.

Charisse's group began crossing the street, obscuring Naima's view of the van. That was when she noticed the tall, elegant and elderly black man who seemed to have appeared out of nowhere. In fact, he must have arrived from the west side of the Place Saint-Michel and now stood a few feet in front of the other bronze dragon. Dressed in a beret and nicely tailored charcoal gray suit, he definitely did not seem like a tourist. He regarded Naima briefly with a cold and scrutinizing eye.

As the old man turned away from her, Naima checked out Charisse Bray and the approaching tour group of twenty or more African Americans. From a distance, the creamy coffee-colored young man with short hair and glasses, overnight bag slung over his shoulder, looked exactly like Darvin Littlefield. But he seemed a bit unsteady on his feet, lumbering forward awkwardly, reminding Naima of a drunken frat boy trying to act sober. This was not a good sign. Hadn't Marva and Hassan rehearsed his walking around in Darvin's spectacles back at the Hôtel Doucette so that he would look as natural as possible? Naima saw her mother beside Hassan, unrecognizable as Marva Dobbs, in the straight-haired, reddish brown wig and oversized, heavily tinted glasses. It was the seventies-era pantsuit that really made the disguise. Marva Dobbs would never wear multicolored stripes—certainly not in the twenty-first century. Marva kept a light grip on Hassan's elbow, guiding him along as if he were half blind. Definitely a bad sign.

It was not yet 3:54 but everything was in motion. The ball was in play. Where the hell was Juvenal?

Naima saw an old white man dressed in the aged preppy clothes of an Ivy League provost pass by in front of her and walk directly toward the elegant old black man. The white man carried a battered brown satchel, which he laid on the granite tiles of the plaza. The old black man greeted him but they did not shake hands. They stood face to face in front of the fountain, only a few inches apart. Though they were both dignified senior citizens, Naima sensed something confrontational, almost feral, in the way they faced each other. Naima thought of nature films she'd seen, of two lions, or bears, or baboons, who were about to tear each other apart. The old men were speaking but she could not hear what they were saying over the whooshing and splashing jets of water in the fountain.

In the distance, Naima saw the cop emerge from his dark blue van, parked in front of the Café Le Départ. Where the hell was Juvenal?

"This is a very historic spot," Charisse Bray said as the tour group arrived at the edge of the fountain. "A sort of crossroads of many communities in Paris, including African-American expatriates."

Charisse continued talking but Naima wasn't listening. Naima saw Marva spot the two old men standing just outside the circle of tourists, then quickly look away. That was when Naima remembered the two old spies her mother had mentioned. The one Loïc had had dinner with at the restaurant a couple of months ago, and the other one, the "very sad old black man" Archie Dukes had spoken to. Naima could not remember their names but she wondered what they were doing here at this precise moment. Marva, in her disguise, stared straight ahead, into the bubbling fountain. She did not acknowledge Naima. She let her hand slip from Hassan's elbow.

At exactly 3:55, Juvenal pulled up to the Place Saint-Michel, stopping on the west side of the square, beside the tangle of motorcycles, bicycles and scooters chained to metal barriers. Naima finally left her post beneath the dragon, maneuvering her way into the group of tourists. She took Hassan by the hand. He calmly looked down at her and Naima smiled. Oh, yes, with his hazel eyes magnified by the Coke-bottle lenses, he was a dead ringer for her boyfriend. While Charisse continued to talk history, Naima led Hassan away from the group. Marva did not acknowledge them, staring resolutely straight ahead. Hand in hand, Naima and Hassan walked right past the two old spies who were still absorbed in quiet confrontation. Naima was relieved to see that Hassan's gait was more normal and steady as they approached Juvenal on his moto.

"Hurry," Naima said, opening the black case attached to the back of the seat and handing Hassan the spare crash helmet.

Juvenal kept the visor of his own helmet down. He did not look at Naima or at Hassan. His gaze was focused straight ahead, down the rue Danton. While Hassan fumbled with the helmet, Naima turned around and glimpsed the cop wending his way through the crowd of tourists and young people gathered on the square. All she really saw was the uniform. All she feared was that the cop was headed her way. She turned back to Hassan. He'd strapped on the helmet and was mounting the seat, wrapping his arms around Juvenal. Naima touched Juvenal's shoulder.

"Godspeed," she said.

Juvenal nodded, then revved his engine and roared away, Hassan clinging to him. Just as the moto disappeared down the rue Danton, Naima heard the horrific scream and the gunshot behind her.

Loïc Rose, wearing a dead policeman's uniform, sat behind the wheel of the used van Cleavon Semple had bought that morning, trying to concentrate on the task at hand but feeling profoundly frightened by the confluence of bizarre circumstances in which he found himself. He glanced at his watch: 3:53. He observed, through the rearview mirror, a large group of African-American tourists walking toward the fountain. Barreling down the Boulevard Saint-Michel, he had almost run over their leader—he recognized her, Charisse Bray—a minute ago. Crazy. Here he was preparing to kill a white man in cold blood and he nearly killed a black woman by accident.

"Oldcorn must die," Cleavon had said to Loïc over and over again. "That is the only way to deal with a man who wants you dead and has the power to make it happen. You have to kill him first."

There was, Loïc reluctantly admitted, a compelling logic to this argument. Hassan, Cleavon said, could not be saved. But if Loïc wanted to save Marva, Oldcorn must die. Harvey believed that Loïc had told his wife all that he knew about the plot against Webster Janes, the framing of the Mekacheras, the WORTHEE bombing. If Oldcorn had hired Cleavon to kill Loïc to prevent the truth from coming out, then certainly he would hire someone else to kill Marva. Therefore, Oldcorn must die.

"Once he's taken out," Cleavon said, "all orders he gave are null and void. Your old pals in the Authority who thought you were insane to challenge him will bow down to you once they see that you fought him and won."

"Perhaps," Loïc had countered. "Unless, of course, I'm in jail."

No matter, Cleavon said. Oldcorn must die. Hassan could not be saved. Maybe Marva and Loïc could not be saved. But think of Naima. Once Harvey learned that Cleavon had not killed Loïc, he was sure to go after the Frenchman's daughter as a way of getting

Loïc to hand over the incriminating audio evidence. If Harvey had gone so far as murdering Jeremy Hairston to send Loïc a signal, what was to stop him from kidnapping Naima, maybe even . . . ?

"Don't say it!" Loïc had snapped at Cleavon.

"You see my point, then?" the old man asked.

Yes, Harvey Oldcorn must die. But Loïc did not know if he was prepared to do the killing himself. He had never shot anyone before. He was not sure he even had the technical capacity, let alone the *sangfroid*, for such a thing. Years ago, he and Marva had taken a few sessions of target practice together and she was a much better shot than he. Cleavon tried to reassure Loïc: "You'll be firing from very close range." But that hardly calmed Loïc's nerves. Maybe for Cleavon, assassinating a man point-blank in the back of the head was no big deal. Loïc found the very idea sickening.

Now, sitting in the van, sweating in a dead cop's clothes, Loïc realized that Cleavon's whole scheme, this outrageous plan he had agreed to under duress, was sheer madness. Staring into the rearview mirror, he couldn't even spot Cleavon Semple in the crowd of people in front of the fountain. Yet he was supposed to wait until Harvey Oldcorn showed up, then step out of the van—leaving the motor running—walk up behind Oldcorn and put a bullet in his brain. In the resulting pandemonium, Loïc's cop disguise would make him invulnerable. He would yell at people to calm down, move away. He would run back to the van and drive to Cleavon's building. The old spy, having hurried from the scene of the crime, would meet him there. Cleavon would take command of the vehicle. Loïc would hide in the back of the van, change out of the police uniform and into his civilian clothes. Cleavon and Loïc would then drive to the countryside, hide out somewhere and plan their next move.

This was madness, Loïc realized too late. Sheer madness.

He was sweating copiously now, acutely aware of the weight of the dead man's cap on his head, the dead man's silver badge hanging on his left breast pocket, the dead man's gun in its holster on his hip. Everything frightened Loïc. He was frightened of the crowd on his right, all the merry people sitting at the sidewalk tables of the Café Le Départ. He was frightened that someone might approach him and, believing he was an authentic police officer, ask him for assistance he could not provide, thus exposing his masquerade. He was frightened that an authentic police officer might approach him and ask what the hell he was doing parked there, thus exposing his masquerade.

He was frightened by the memory of October 17, 1961. For nearly forty years, he had traversed the Pont Saint-Michel in a mindless fog of forgetting. He always remembered the *Libération* of 1944. He remembered the student riots that roiled this *quartier* back in 1968. He even remembered standing on the Place Saint-Michel and explaining the statues on the fountain to his daughter in 1985. But until very recently, Loïc Rose had blotted out the memory of the protest, and subsequent massacre, that had taken place here forty years ago. Now, sitting behind the wheel of the blue van, wearing a dead policeman's clothes, facing the Pont Saint-Michel, awash in brilliant August sunshine, Loïc remembered the cops in their helmets and black leather jackets, surging into the crowd of peaceful, mainly Algerian demonstrators, swinging their billy clubs, firing their pistols. He remembered the sight of young men, badly wounded but still alive, being tossed into the churning waters of the Seine. He remembered begging the cop who had already smashed his camera into pieces to stop hitting him as the nightstick came down again and again and again, until he was beaten unconscious.

And now, more frightened than he'd ever been in his life, Loïc saw, in the rearview mirror of the van, Harvey Oldcorn crossing the Place Saint-Michel, brown satchel in hand. Time to kill. Loïc stepped out into the street, slamming the door of the van behind him. The keys were still in the ignition, the motor running. Loïc walked toward the square knowing that this might be a suicide mission. Knowing that he might never see Marva or Naima again. The people he loved most, his wife and daughter, might never know what exactly he had done to set this crisis in motion or to try to resolve it. They might never understand, never forgive him. That was what frightened Loïc most.

. . .

"The devil ain't the devil cuz he's smart," Marva's Alabaman grand-mother used to say. "The devil is the devil cuz he's *old*."

Those words popped into Marva's mind as she stepped onto the Place Saint-Michel and saw, through the crowd, standing beside the fountain, the oldest devil she knew: Cleavon Semple.

"What the fuck?" Marva muttered.

"Huh?" Hassan asked.

"Nothing."

They were in the middle of Charisse's group. Ernestine's wig was making Marva's scalp sweat and itch and Hassan was walking a bit strangely, having trouble keeping his balance in Darvin's glasses. Marva held on to him by the elbow and wondered how the hell he was going to manage at the airport by himself. Though the amber lenses of Ernestine's old glasses were scratched, Marva could see just fine. She located Naima standing beneath one of the fountain's dragons.

"Is everybody here?" Charisse Bray called out as the whole group moved toward the fountain, maneuvering around all the other tourists and young people who crowded the square. Charisse was ob-viously on edge, so nervous she'd almost walked straight into the path of a van that had been speeding down the Boulevard Saint-Michel. Marva, however, had maintained a stony calm all day—until she saw Cleavon Semple in his beret, loitering with intent, slyly scanning the crowd. As the old devil turned his attention to the tour group, Marva looked away, certain he would not recognize her in Ernestine's clothes. All the same, she clutched her dead friend's handbag more tightly, feeling through its alligator skin the shape of the revolver hidden inside. She didn't know what the fuck Cleavon Semple was doing here but she would not hesitate to shoot him if he tried to mess with her plan. Moving closer and closer to the fountain, Marva tried to keep her gaze focused on the statue of Saint-Michel, waving his sword victoriously, the figure of Satan crumpled at his feet.

"This is a very historic spot," Charisse Bray said, stopping at the edge of the fountain. Marva could barely hear her over the shooting jets of water. She glanced at her daughter, who looked just like any other young person hanging out on the Place Saint-Michel on a lazy summer's day. Then, taking a quick look to her right, she saw Cleavon again. Only now he was talking to Harvey Oldcorn.

"Motherfucker!" Marva screamed inside. At least she hoped she had only screamed inside. Since no one turned to look at her, she was fairly certain the cry of rage had not burst from her mouth. She struggled not to look again at Cleavon and Harvey. Why were they here? Had someone tipped them off to Marva and Naima's plan? The only person who could have told them was Archie Dukes. Why would Archie have betrayed her? What the fuck was going on? Were they all, Hassan and Marva and Naima, about to be arrested? Or killed?

Naima walked up to Marva and Hassan. As her daughter took her lover by the hand, Marva stared straight ahead into the bubbling fountain. She did not want any meaningful last look with Hassan. She just wanted him gone, on his way, out of her life.

Charisse Bray was talking but Marva didn't hear her. She heard only the splash of water in the fountain. She stroked the alligator skin of Ernestine's handbag, felt the outline of the gun inside it.

Marva glanced back at Cleavon and Harvey. She had thought they'd be checking out the tour group but instead they stood face to face, ignoring everyone around them. They were obviously having some sort of intense discussion but Marva couldn't hear a word of it. She saw, several yards behind Cleavon, Naima standing on the curb with Hassan, who was strapping on a motorcycle helmet. Marva saw the moto and driver—this would be Juvenal—next to them. She looked again at Cleavon, who was now holding a CD in his hand, waving it, tauntingly, in Harvey Oldcorn's face. Wondering again what was going on, Marva noticed Cleavon glance anxiously at some-one standing a few feet behind Harvey. Only at that moment did Marva see the cop.

"So v-v-very rich in his-his-history," Charisse Bray said loudly, her voice shaking. "This sp-sp-spot on which we—"

What was this bizarre sight before Marva, this loose-limbed police officer hovering near the fountain, looking worried, fidgeting, rocking back and forth on his heels, reaching tentatively for the gun on his hip, then jerking his hand away as if the butt of the pistol had burned his fingertips? Had Marva completely lost her mind? Was she only imagining, in some delirium of angst, that this was her husband disguised as a cop?

Juvenal roared off, away from the Place, with Hassan hanging on behind him. Marva saw Harvey Oldcorn turn around and look directly at the cop. Now Marva saw the cop's bright blue eyes, wide with fear, saw the silver hair beneath his lopsided cap.

"Son of a bitch," Harvey Oldcorn said.

Marva didn't hear him say it. But it was easy to read his lips. As Harvey reached beneath his jacket, Marva unzipped Ernestine's alligator handbag.

Loïc stood perfectly still, hand poised over the gun in its holster. He stared directly, helplessly, at Oldcorn. As Marva pulled the revolver from Ernestine's handbag, she saw Oldcorn pull a long black pistol from his inner jacket and point the gun at Loïc. She grasped her weapon in both hands and aimed it at Oldcorn's head. She could see that his right arm was fully extended. She saw that a silencer was attached to the barrel of his gun. Loïc remained frozen in place, like a prisoner before a firing squad, waiting to be executed, with no blindfold. Marva figured she had barely enough time to shoot Oldcorn first. Just as Marva was about to fire, a white kid with cornrows glided between her and Oldcorn, on his skateboard. The scream exploded from her involuntarily as she squeezed the trigger.

"MUTHAFUCKAAAAAAH!"

Cleavon spotted the black girl right away, as soon as he arrived at the lip of the fountain. She was doing her best to look nonchalant in her cap and sunglasses but she was obviously an undercover cop—or an assassin. So this was Harvey's gambit. To meet with Cleavon but to have him killed on the spot. Cleavon doubted that Oldcorn suspected the same thing was in store for himself. Or maybe he had. And the young black chick was there for Harvey's personal protection. Whatever the black girl's deal was, Cleavon didn't like the looks of her. He could see she was a stone-cold killer. "Takes one to know one," he muttered to himself.

And what did Cleavon see next? A group of black tourists moving across the square. Cleavon didn't recognize anyone in the group, though one woman did remind him of Archie Dukes's dead wife, Ernestine. Far off in the distance, past the approaching tourists, Cleavon saw the blue van parked in front of the Café Le Départ. Good. Loïc hadn't managed to fuck that up. Now Cleavon had to hope that the Frenchman had the stomach to go through with the next step of the plan. Loïc had been so nervous all day, Cleavon was beginning to regret not having killed him last night. But no, he needed Loïc right here, right now. Cleavon felt the slightest twinge of guilt because, if all went according to plan—to Cleavon's own secret plan—Loïc was going to end up dead any minute now. And once it was discovered whose uniform Loïc was wearing, Madame Ficelle was going to have a lot to answer for. But, by then, Cleavon would be far, far away.

Cleavon spotted Harvey Oldcorn arriving several minutes early, brown bag full of cash in hand. Boy, did he look pissed off. The tiny firecrackers started bursting in Cleavon's brain.

"Where do you get the balls?" Oldcorn said, setting down the satchel.

"Oh, they come from my daddy's side. He was one of them Western Negroes. Born in the Colorado territories. He was a cowboy when he was young. Bet you didn't even know there was black cowboys, didya, Harvey?"

"Save it for your memoirs." Harvey was breathing hard, sweating. His whole head was turning a sickly shade of pink, almost purple. "Your girlfriend said you had physical evidence."

"I believe what she said was that the physical evidence would emerge shortly."

"Yeah, right. That's why I only brought you half of what you asked for."

"Half?!"

"You'll get the other half when that physical evidence . . . emerges."

Cleavon was not disappointed. This was exactly what he had expected. He would still walk away from this whole episode with two and a half million francs. Not a bad two days' work. About 350,000 American dollars to spend—if Cleavon decided to return to America. "Unfair enough," he said.

"So what exactly did Frenchy tell you?"

Come to think of it, where the hell was Loïc? Wasn't he supposed to be coming up behind Harvey about now? "Oh, something about America needing a new Pearl Harbor."

Cleavon suddenly noticed, out of the corner of his eye, the black girl walking toward him. She was holding hands with a light-skinned guy in thick glasses, a travel bag slung over his shoulder. So maybe she wasn't an assassin after all. Or maybe the guy in the glasses was? They walked right past Cleavon. Were they planning to turn around and shoot him from behind? Where the hell was Loïc?

"Pearl Harbor," Oldcorn snorted. "In the form of what?"

"He mentioned the U.S. embassy in Paris."

Oldcorn shook his head and chuckled. "Loïc always did think small."

And there he was now, several meters behind Harvey, in the uniform of Madame Ficelle's dead husband. Loïc was the most jittery-looking cop Cleavon had ever seen.

"So you have a CD for me?"

Cleavon reached into his inner jacket pocket—his hand brushing against the pistol in its shoulder holster—and pulled out the disk, holding it up for Harvey to see. "You sound great in stereo."

"Where are the original tapes?"

"With the owner. You'll find him and them . . . badly burned up."

Cleavon tried to look Harvey straight in the eye but he kept glancing at Loïc, standing in front of the fountain, fidgeting like a frightened schoolboy. Loïc had failed, just as Cleavon had known he would. The Frenchman didn't have the nerve to draw his weapon and fire.

"*Ah bon?*" Oldcorn said, smiling, however faintly, for the first time. The idea that Loïc and the tapes had been incinerated obviously pleased him.

"You'll be hearing about a nasty fire in the *banlieue.*"

"Well, Cleavon, for a decrepit old nigger, you aren't totally useless."

Cleavon was still waving the CD in the air. He let his gaze linger on Loïc, who was standing frozen in front of the fountain, as if waiting to be killed. He knew Oldcorn would turn to see what he was looking at—and he did.

"Son of a bitch," Harvey growled. As Oldcorn reached beneath his jacket for his gun, Cleavon slipped the disk back into his own jacket pocket.

Oldcorn was already aiming his pistol at the bridge of Loïc's nose as Cleavon took hold of his own gun in its holster. Cleavon looked at the back of Harvey's big fat head, the pink flesh covered here and there with cottony wisps of white hair. If his timing was right, he would be able to kill Oldcorn in the instant after Oldcorn killed Loïc. Whether Cleavon would then be able to make it to the blue van and get away clean was open to question. Then, just as he was about to whip out his weapon, Cleavon heard the scream: "MUTHAFUCKAAAAAAH!"

Oldcorn's head exploded in a shower of blood. The Place Saint-Michel turned into a sort of war zone—not for the first time. As Oldcorn's body fell to the right, his pistol fired. Cleavon saw Loïc's cop cap fly off as the impostor was propelled backward. A blast of high-pitched screaming erupted like an air-raid warning. Cleavon glimpsed Loïc falling backward, with a huge, blood-streaked splash, into the fountain. There were people running in every direction. Cleavon's hand was still inside his jacket, clutching the butt of the gun he had not had time to use. He looked down and saw Harvey Oldcorn sprawled at his feet, half his head a mass of blood, muscle and tissue that inevitably reminded Cleavon of the calves' brains on which he had so often feasted at his favorite neighborhood brasserie. He looked up again and saw, standing stock-still in the frantic, swirling crowd, the shooter, holding her gun in both hands. The woman he had thought resembled Ernestine. Of course, he now realized, it was Marva Dobbs. If he'd recognized her earlier, he might have been afraid that she would shoot him. He might have shot her by now himself. But Cleavon could see that Marva was in a state of shock. It was clearly her first time killing a man. But she had crossed the line Loïc could not, finished the job her husband was unable to complete. Cleavon was confident that Marva did not even see him. He picked up the satchel and began to walk calmly through the still swarming, screaming crowd. About five seconds had passed since Marva shrieked and fired.

The black girl in the baseball cap and shades—the woman he had thought might assassinate him—bolted across Cleavon's path, weaving her way around the terrified, flailing people, grabbing the gun from Marva's hands, ripping it away before Marva even realized what was happening, and plunged into the churning horde on the east side of the square. Now he realized who she was—the daughter, Naima.

Cleavon was walking calmly but briskly through the chaos, clutching his satchel full of money, getting closer, step by step, to the dark blue van. The getaway vehicle was surrounded by onlookers now. Customers had risen from their sidewalk café tables to try to see what was happening. The two-tone whine of police sirens pierced the air. Cleavon took one last look back. He could see the top of Marva's reddish brown wig, bobbing in a mob of people. There was no sign of Naima at all. Oldcorn's body lay motionless on the granite tiles, and Loïc was floating on his back, the water in the fountain bubbling, pink.

Cleavon returned his attention to the path ahead. Suddenly there were cops everywhere, running out of every side street, whipping around every corner, charging toward the action. Cleavon opened the door on the driver's side, slipped into the van. He waited as several police cars came roaring across the Pont Saint-Michel. Honking his horn only once to clear his route, Cleavon turned onto the Quai des Grands Augustins and sped away from the scene of the crime. The satchel full of cash lay in the passenger seat. The van was loaded with his most important possessions: his clothes and mementos, his favorite chair, his notebooks and unpublished manuscripts, his IBM Selectric. Cleavon Semple did not know where he was going. He only knew he would never return to Paris.

He hoped Madame Ficelle would not miss him too badly.

Twenty

"IT'S GOT TO BE you," Juvenal told Naima. "It has to be clear that this is your statement. You have to show your face. Only then will they leave you alone."

"They" meant the media horde outside the walls of the Hôpital Decoust. Naima sat with Juvenal, Archie Dukes and Prunella Watson, sealed off from the rest of the world in a second-floor waiting room. Through the locked glass doors, Naima saw a crowd of uniformed police officers, their backs turned discreetly away from her and the three friends of her family. It was nearly eleven o'clock, seven hours after the shootout on the Place Saint-Michel. Naima was feeling rattled again. She had been so cool and alert for so much of this day and night. But now here she was in the same hospital her

mother had checked out of, fugitive lover by her side, two nights earlier. Pru had written a public statement for Naima to deliver. Naima
wanted someone else to read it, maybe Juvenal. She was afraid that
she would break down in front of the cameras when she had to tell
the world that her father was in a coma.

"Juvenal is right," Pru said. Archie nodded in agreement.

"*D'accord*," Naima said, rising wearily from the waiting-room
couch. She would follow their advice. She only wished she were back
in the zone.

As an accomplished athlete, a star in both volleyball and middle-
distance running in high school and college, Naima knew what it
was like to be in that state of heightened performance known as the
zone. She had experienced the exhilaration of knowing that every
ball she smashed over the net would be a point scored. She had rev-
eled in that intoxicating sense of certainty, coming off the final turn
in a race, that she would overtake the leaders and cross the finish line
first.

On the Place Saint-Michel, just before four o'clock that afternoon, Naima had been in the zone. After watching Juvenal and Hassan disappear down the rue Danton, she heard her mother's scream
and the gunshot. Naima whirled around and saw the old black man
in his beret, standing ramrod straight. Viewing him from behind,
Naima could see that his right arm was bent, that he seemed to be
holding his hand to his chest. Then she saw the preppy old white
man sprawled on the ground at the black man's feet. The white
man's head had been blown open and he was clutching a gun in his
hand. A millisecond later she saw the policeman fall backward into
the fountain, water and blood splashing onto the granite tiles of the
square. She did not see his face, only his cop's uniform. In the ensu-
ing pandemonium, Naima maintained her calm. She was in the zone.

Naima spotted her mother in the crowd of running, shrieking
people. Marva just stood there, in her wig and shades, clutching the
revolver in both hands. With the new set of instincts she seemed to

have acquired in the past day or so, Naima knew she had to get the weapon away from Marva. Naima did not know who had shot whom. She saw the old black man casually pick up the brown satchel the white man had been carrying and begin walking away from the fountain. For a moment, Naima worried that the old man was going to shoot Marva. But she quickly realized—again, instinctively—that he was calmly fleeing the scene. In the next instant, Naima was scrambling through the crowd, then ripping the gun from her mother's hands. Marva let out a little squeal of surprise as Naima seized the weapon, then scrambled away, managing to tuck the revolver into one of the big pockets of her cargo pants as she plunged deeper into the frantic crowd of people. Naima, thriving in this new zone she'd discovered, knew that even if her mother had committed a murder, it would be hard to convict her without a murder weapon.

Once she hit the rue de la Huchette, Naima stopped scrambling and switched to the sort of calm and easy gait she'd seen the old black man display on the Place Saint-Michel. She made her way to the Hôtel Doucette, entered through the back door. Using one of the rags in the parlor, Naima scrubbed all fingerprints off the gun, then dumped the weapon in a bucket of white paint and tightly sealed the lid. She exited the hotel, took a looping amble through the neighborhood, winding her way back to the building on the rue des Saints-Pères, then used the relatively secret passageways to get back to her parents' apartment.

She checked in on Darvin: still unconscious, snoring. Naima tore off her black T-shirt and cargo pants, took a quick shower, then switched into a floral-printed, knee-length and ladylike dress she'd owned since high school. At 4:45, Inspector Lamouche called. Naima expected to hear that her mother had been picked up on the Place Saint-Michel. Instead, Lamouche told her that her father had been shot. Surgery to save his life was just getting under way. Lamouche told Naima a police car was waiting outside her building to take her to the Hôpital Decoust. Naima was amazed by the way the media horde on the Boulevard Saint-Germain parted to clear her way to the police car. Only when she arrived at the hospital did she learn that the cop she had seen get blasted and fall into the fountain was her father wearing a bizarre disguise. The bullet had only grazed the left side of his head. But there had been a massive loss of blood flowing to the brain.

And that was when Naima started to rattle. Soon after her arrival, Inspector Lamouche joined her in the chamber outside the operating room. He sounded genuinely sympathetic. "I am so sorry, *mademoiselle*, about ze misfortune zat befall your fahzer."

"Thank you, Inspector, but if you don't mind—"

"Yes, yes, I know zoperation continue. But ze good news is, ze police, we have your mohzer. She is alive and well in a prison cell. Her lawyer, Olivier Matignon, arrive soon, at the prefecture. He will contact you here."

"Thank you, Inspector."

"Iz good news, no?"

"Yes, thank you but—"

"I leave you now."

Not long after Lamouche left, Prunella, then Archie, then Juvenal arrived in rapid succession, having heard the news. The police took them all to the second-floor waiting room. The cop in charge said it was for their protection. Naima sat there with her three co-conspirators, each of them trying to reassure the others, none of them, while under the watchful protection of the police, able to say all that they knew, or surmised. At ten thirty, the doctors came to tell Naima that Loïc was alive but in a coma. It was impossible to know when or if he would emerge from it.

Half an hour later, a small phalanx of cops escorted Naima to the main courtyard of the hospital, where a podium was set up in front of the mass of reporters, satellite trucks, blazing lights and cameras. Standing in the media lightstorm, Naima could feel herself slipping back into the zone. Poised yet clearly vulnerable, she read the statement, racing through the text, hearing her own words only as frag-

ments echoing in the courtyard: "Father in a coma . . . mother coop-
erating with police . . . whereabouts of Hassan Mekachera un-
known . . . a full press conference at a later date . . . family in crisis . . .
please respect our privacy . . . taking no questions tonight . . . at this
difficult time."

Naima turned away from the violent glare, hurried back to the
second-floor waiting room. The police remained on guard outside
the glass doors. Archie and Prunella had departed. Only Juvenal was
there, sitting on a shiny orange couch. Naima collapsed in his arms.

"You okay?"

"I'm not gonna cry," Naima said.

"I know." Juvenal gestured toward the television suspended from
the ceiling in the corner. It was turned off. "I watched you out there.
You were fantastic."

Naima buried her face in his shoulder. *"Merci."*

"Do you want to go home?"

"Not yet."

"So let me ask you. The package I sent off to New York . . . how
will we know when it arrives safely?"

"We won't. Probably not for a while."

"Can I ask you another question?"

"You mean about us?"

"Yeah."

"I'm thinking about it, Juvenal. Really, I'm thinking about it."

"I must say," Inspector Lamouche said, "zis case is most bizarre. And
so are you, Madame Dobbs."

It was nearly midnight and Marva was seated in a metal chair
that was bolted to a cement floor in a dank interrogation room somewhere in the bowels of Paris's central Préfecture de Police. She was
still wearing Ernestine Dukes's striped pantsuit, but the wig and sunglasses and alligator purse had all been seized by the cops. In the
eight hours since she had been taken into custody by the cops who

swarmed into the Place Saint-Michel after the shooting, Marva had been locked in an underground cell, released to discuss her case with Olivier Matignon (who showed up at the prefecture without her even asking to see him) in a secluded waiting room, placed back in her cell, released again to answer questions from high-ranking police officials—in the presence of her attorney—then placed back in the cell and finally told, by Matignon, that she would be allowed to go home. But first she would have to sit through another interrogation, this one by a detective from the Eighteenth Arrondissement, regarding the murder of Jeremy Hairston.

Marva was already exhausted. She had managed to keep her composure these past eight hours. She wanted desperately to get to the Hôpital Decoust to see her comatose husband and her courageous daughter. So she resented being delayed by a grilling from La-mouche. He had requested to meet with her alone, no lawyer present. Matignon advised her to do it, to stick by her earlier statements, show she had nothing to hide. The oily little cop sat behind a bare metal desk in the interrogation room. He wore a crimson polyester suit and black-and-red checkerboard necktie. Flipping through a dossier and shaking his perfectly round head, he said, "You are truly bizarre, *madame.*"

"Kiss my ass," Marva replied.

Lamouche looked up, smiled his sickly little smile, then returned his attention to the dossier. "According to zis record, you said earlier tonight zat after leaving ze hospital wiz Hassan Mekachera, you and him went to a café. You told him to run for his life. He leave the café and you never see him again. Correct?"

"Listen, Lamouche, I know what I said. I really don't need to have you redo an interrogation that your superiors have already done."

"Ah, yes, of course, you are right, *madame.* You have dealt tonight wiz peoples far more superior to me. In fact, you have been given rahzer special treatment for someone who may be guilty of multiple crimes. And me, I am just a lowly cop from ze lowly Eighteenz Arrondissement. But I am trying to discover who killed your good friend in your very restaurant. So please, I ask only a bit of cooperation."

Marva sighed impatiently. "You've got it."

"So: Hassan leave you and you go alone to your house in Normandy. And zere, you sleep for ze next day and a half."

"Yes, I was very tired and I may have suffered a concussion from my car accident. If I had known my daughter was in town, I would not have stayed out in Gisors so long."

"And you no worry about your husband during zose zirty-six hours?"

"No. I thought he might join me out there."

"Right, but zen you decide to come back to Paris and go on a tour, dressed in a disguise."

"Incognito," Marva said sternly, "not disguised. I had these old clothes in a closet in Normandy and decided that if I were going to return to Paris I didn't need people coming up and harassing me about Hassan. I was planning to tell the police what I knew but first I wanted to think things through on my own and unwind a little."

"Unwind on zis tour?"

"Yes."

Lamouche smiled cryptically and shook his head again. "Bizarre. *Alors,* so only on ze Place Saint-Michel do you see your husband. Like you, he is incognito, unwinding, I suppose, in ze costume of a police officer. Are you two fond of ze masquerade balls?"

Marva did not respond. She just stared stonily at Lamouche.

"And zen you see Oldcorn wiz your husband. You see Oldcorn shoot your husband and so you shoot Oldcorn."

"I've never shot anybody in my life."

"Yes, yes, zis is a fascinating bit of confusion here. Witnesses say zey see a black woman wiz a gun. But zey describe four or five different-looking black women holding zis gun."

"I've never held a gun in my life."

"And ze gun which fire ze bullet which kill Monsieur Oldcorn has not been found. Zere was also mention from a witness of a black man at ze scene."

"There were lots of black men at the scene, Lamouche. I was with a black tour group, for Christ's sake."

"Zis was an old black man in a beret. Nobody in ze tour group fit his description."

"Well, I've got nothing to say about a man I didn't see. Now, if you don't mind I'd like to go visit my husband at—"

"Yes, just a couple more questions. Regarding your husband, zis policeman uniform he was wearing. Do you know when, or where, he got it?"

"Nope."

"We have run a check on ze badge number he wore. It was ze uniform of an officer from a city far from Paris. An old badge number also, not in circulation for ten year or more. Unfortunately, we do not yet have ze name of ze officer. Zere is a problem wiz database in zat particular city. Ze technological person who can solve ze problem will not return from holiday until Monday."

"I thought you wanted to question me about the murder of Jeremy Hairston."

"Yes. In fact, I zink I know who murder your Jeremy. It was ze late Monsieur Oldcorn."

"Ah bon?"

"You don't seem very surprised."

"Jesus Christ, Lamouche—"

"I know, I know, you are important woman wiz somewhere to go. Your husband is important man. So is your lawyer. So was zis Oldcorn who show up in my office Monday to ask what I was doing to help track down Hassan Mekachera. All you important people. I am not so important. I am a lowly cop trying to find ze truze. You important people. You can get away wiz what you need to get away wiz. But you know, *madame*, Hassan Mekachera, he is not so important. He don't have important people to protect him."

"Can I go now? Am I being charged with anything?"

"I zink zat people more important zen me are trying to figure out what exactly to charge you wiz, *madame*. And, yes, you may go now."

Marva rose from the metal chair. *"Au revoir."*

"One final question, *madame*. What do you zink happen to Hassan?"

Marva struggled to maintain a neutral expression, shrugged her shoulders. "I have no idea."

Inspector Lamouche leered. "I have idea. I zink he already dead."

In his first minutes in America, Hassan Mekachera tried to walk like an American, striding purposefully down the exit ramp of the plane. After staying awake all through the flight, managing to watch movies and read magazine articles through Darvin Littlefield's glasses, he could see reasonably well in them. Hassan Mekachera lined up with the Americans at the passport control station. He heard English all around him, understanding words here and there. The whole swirl of familiar yet weird sounds, the rhythms and dissonances, the music of the language—or this particular version of it— made Hassan feel as if he had just stepped into an American movie. One with no subtitles.

The officer behind the glass reminded Hassan of an American football coach he'd once seen on TV. Ruddy, still trim and fit but a bit haggard around the eyes. He wore a steel gray crewcut. Hassan smiled and slapped down the passport. "Hi!"

The officer slid the passport through the slot in the glass, regarded it carefully, then glanced up at Hassan and scowled. Hassan had continued smiling, just as Darvin Littlefield was smiling in his passport photo. The officer studied Hassan's face, then looked back down at the photo. He abruptly snapped shut the passport and slid it back to Hassan. "Welcome home," he said flatly.

Hassan rode the escalator to the baggage claim area and waited

several minutes beside a carousel before he saw Marie-Christine enter the space, wheeling Xavier, slumped contentedly, fast asleep in his
stroller. Hassan had actually seen them both in the first-class section
as he had boarded the plane in Paris and headed toward his
economy-class seat. Xavier had been squirming in Marie-Christine's
lap. Marie-Christine had actually glanced up at Hassan, practically
looked him in the eye, and not recognized him in his disguise. Now,
in the baggage claim area, Marie-Christine looked about uncertainly,
only recognizing Hassan when he came striding toward her through
the crowd. They threw their arms around each other but Marie-
Christine quickly pulled out of the embrace. "There are some friends
of mine waiting for us outside," she said. Hassan was almost startled
by the sound of French. "They'll take us to Brooklyn."

Hassan squatted to look at their little boy. Xavier gurgled softly
in his sleep.

"He's been like this for the whole flight," Marie-Christine said.
"Who would have guessed? Airplanes relax him."

Hassan kissed his son's chubby little cheek, fought the urge to
cry. He stood up, looked at Marie-Christine in wonderment.

"So—whaddya have to say for yourself?" she asked, switching
into English, speaking in an exaggerated nasal accent.

Hassan held her face in his hands and replied in Arabic: "Praise
be to Allah."

"So that bucket of paint I mentioned to you?" Naima said to Archie
Dukes.

"I've already disposed of it," Archie replied.

They sat together in the living room of Naima's parents' apartment. The shutters and windows were wide open, the sunshine pouring in. It was noon, Thursday, August 30, 2001. To Naima's surprise,
the media had obeyed her request from the night before. Nobody was
staking out her building.

"You know, you showed incredible presence of mind yesterday."

"Thank you, Archie."

"Where's your mother?"

"In her bedroom, still sleeping. We're going to go by the hospital together later today to see Papa."

"Have you met with Olivier Matignon yet?"

"He's coming by in an hour to brief me."

"Good."

"Is there nothing you want to tell me, Archie?"

"You should talk to Matignon first."

"Well, here's one thing. Our whole plan to meet at the Fontaine Saint-Michel . . . Was it just a coincidence that Papa and this Oldcorn guy had planned to meet at that exact same place at exactly the same time?"

"I suppose you could call it a coincidence," Archie said with a wry smile. "Or you could say that you and your father are a classic example of great minds thinking alike."

Naima appreciated the compliment but, at the moment, it was the state of Loïc's mind that worried her most. "Do you think there's going to be a trial?" she asked Archie.

"Hard to say. That's something you'll have to discuss with Matignon. A lot will depend on Loïc's condition, his capabilities, once he comes out of his coma."

"You mean if."

Archie took Naima's hand in his and squeezed. "Keep the faith, my dear."

After Archie left, Naima slipped into her bedroom to check on Darvin. He was already sitting up in bed, groping the nightstand. "Where are my glasses?"

"Darvy, you're awake!"

"What time is it?"

"About noon."

Darvin rubbed his eyes. "Wow, you mean I've only been sleeping for an hour?"

"Something like that."

"Feels like much longer. Jesus, I gotta pee really badly."

"Here, Darvy, let me help you to the bathroom."

Naima pulled her boyfriend up on his feet, wrapped her arm around his waist and guided him toward the door.

"Thanks, honey," Darvin said, yawning. "Anything happen while I was asleep?"

Getting Darvin a new passport took only two hours. Getting him to accept the reality of the situation he and Naima were in was proving much more difficult.

Friday, August 31, 11:30 A.M. Having left the U.S. embassy on the Place de la Concorde, Naima and Darvin walked slowly up the Champs-Elysées. Unlike the lovers all around them, they were not holding hands or strolling arm in arm.

"Why are you withholding information?" Darvin asked.

"I'm not," Naima protested. "I've already told you there's a lot I don't know myself. Marva and her lawyer have told me that I'm better off not knowing. So you and I are in the exact same situation."

"Not true! I've just gone to the American embassy and lied. That could be a serious offense!"

At Naima's behest, Darvin had told the authorities that his passport and wallet had been stolen while he napped on a bench in the Jardin du Luxembourg. He hadn't mentioned his glasses, since he was wearing contact lenses and such a theft would have made little sense. What galled Darvin was that Naima had still not told him why she had wanted him to lie. In the past twenty-four hours, he had not seen Marva, nor had he been allowed to visit Loïc in the hospital. Naima pleaded with him to be understanding . . . and supportive. In order to please her, he had booked a flight back to New York, scheduled for Saturday morning. Darvin would be returning home alone.

"You're just going to give up the movie shoot?" Darvin asked as they made their way up the grassy, tree-lined stretch of the gigantic boulevard.

"I talked to the director yesterday. She wasn't happy about it. But what else can I do, Darvy? My father's in a coma, my mother's about to be put through a judge's inquiry. I have to stay here with my family."

"And film school?"

"I really haven't thought about it."

"Have you thought about us?"

"Please, Darvy, you just have to be patient with me. Everything is in flux right now. I don't know what's going to be happening tomorrow, let alone in the next few months."

"And Juvenal?"

"I told you nothing happened between us."

"But while I'm back in New York, you'll be here with him smoking cigarettes and sipping cognac!"

Naima let out a loud, raucous laugh. "Ah, yes, Parisian decadence!"

Darvin finally laughed, too. "I'm sorry, baby, it's just that I love you, you know."

"I love you, too."

They walked in silence for a while. Naima finally remembered something positive they could discuss. "Congrats, again, on the new job." Darvin had learned the night before that he had been hired by an important statistical analysis firm.

"Thanks."

"See, it's better that I won't be there with all these family worries, distracting you."

"It's just a job," Darvin said. "It's not as meaningful to me as our life together."

"Oh, Darvy."

"Did I tell where the office is?"

"I don't think so."

"The World Trade Center. Ninety-ninth floor."

"Cool! When do you start?"

"Two weeks from Monday. September seventeenth."

. . .

Pauline Ficelle had felt sequestered in Mulhouse, completely cut off from the rest of the world during the day before, the day of and the day after the wedding festivities. She had not watched any television, had not listened to the radio, had not read a newspaper. She had spoken only to family and guests. Just as she had expected, no one, not even her older sister, who knew of Monsieur Semple's existence but was too busy being the nervous mother of the bride, had asked Pauline why she had had to rush back to Paris on Wednesday. Pauline cheerfully fulfilled all her family duties Thursday, Friday and Saturday. She left Mulhouse at dawn Sunday, managing to avoid the worst of the *rentrée* traffic on the A6 superhighway. Arriving at her building on the rue de Latran, she rode the elevator up to the fourth floor, tapped lightly on her lover's door.

"Monsieur Semple?"

No answer. She rang the doorbell. After three rings, still no reply. She pulled out her collection of tenants' keys and opened the door, her heart pounding. As soon as Pauline stepped into the darkened apartment, she sensed something bizarre but she didn't know what it was. "Cleee-*vohn*?" she called out.

She rushed into the bedroom, then to the kitchen, the bathroom. Only when she returned to the living room did she realize what had changed. The bookshelves were completely empty. No boxes of papers, no notebooks and unpublished manuscripts. The sturdy wooden armchair in front of the desk had disappeared. So had the electric typewriter. That was when the reality hit Pauline like a fist in the throat. She crumpled to the floor and wept. Monsieur Semple was gone. And he wasn't coming back.

"I don't know if you can hear me, Loïc, but, boy, have we really fucked things up this time."

Marva sat at her husband's bedside, midday Sunday. It was just the two of them, surrounded by bleating, blipping machines. The top portion of Loïc's head was bandaged. An oxygen mask covered the lower portion of his face. His eyes were closed. Fluid was running through tubes, in and out of his body. Marva had been told that comatose states were very mysterious. No medical expert was certain of what Loïc was absorbing from the world outside his dormant consciousness. Marva decided she would just talk to him, the way she always had—only a little more honestly than of late.

"First I wanna say I'm sorry. I know I've said it before but I still don't know what's registering with you. I've been apologizing a lot lately. To you. To Naima. I met a planeload of Jeremy's people from Arkansas Friday. That was hard. Apologized to all of them, too. At least we know who killed Jeremy and we know that Oldcorn got what he deserved.

"I've talked to Olivier Matignon every day since Wednesday and he's filled me in. At least as much as he's wanted to fill me in. Jesus, Loïc, what happened to us? After thirty-nine years together? I guess we both went temporarily insane. Me first, then you. I hope you can find it in your heart to forgive me, baby. I've already forgiven you . . . so you might as well."

Marva laughed and, for a while, couldn't stop laughing. When she finally settled down, she thought she noticed Loïc's eyelids fluttering. She decided she had only imagined it. But she kept staring. "Loïc, my love?"

The eyelids were flipping like mad now. Then, after a few seconds, Loïc was staring right back at her, his blue eyes wide open.

Marva was about to start screaming with joy, was ready to burst from the room and alert the doctors. But then . . . Loïc winked.

Perhaps it was just an involuntary ocular muscle spasm. But no. Loïc kept one big blue eye open as the other closed in an obviously conspiratorial squint. Both eyes opened wide again. Then both eyelids closed, like a heavy stage curtain slowly dropping.

. . .

Loïc floated in a long, long dream. He was in a rowboat with his father, in choppy waters, under a pewter sky. Erwan, in his black wool cap and stubbly beard, was doing all the rowing. Loïc, in this long dream, was six years old, dressed in an oversize policeman's cap and uniform, clumsily clutching a gun in his tiny hands. A hard rain came down. The waves grew wild, carrying the boat aloft, tossing it from side to side, water splashing everywhere.

"Hold fast, my son!" Erwan screamed above the battering waves. "It's not your time yet. Not yet!"

This same damned dream seemed to go on forever.

So Loïc knew quite well when he was awake. Eternity was a dream from which you never woke up. If it was a pleasant dream, you were in heaven. If it was not such a pleasant dream, well . . . Loïc hadn't known where his eternal dream was leading. He was just damn glad to be awake.

Loïc knew that he was awake when he saw Marva's lovely, smiling face.

"Can you hear me?"

These were the first new words Loïc heard. Spoken in English. By the beautiful Marva, who was beginning to cry even as she continued smiling.

Loïc saw other figures now, standing around his bed in the brightly lit room. But he still felt the pull of the rowboat behind him, sucking him back into the violent, battering waves. He could just barely hear his father's voice, crying against the waves, urging him to hold fast.

When he looked at the scared but hopeful faces of the young white-coated doctors standing beside Marva, Loïc realized that the earthly realm was winning.

Then he saw Olivier Matignon. The criminal lawyer. The lawyer who was practically a criminal himself.

Loïc began to understand all of what was being said to him. He focused on Marva's smiling, crying face. It was the tears, and the joy behind them, that kept tugging him forward, away from death with Papa in the rowboat.

Olivier Matignon was asking him what he remembered of the past few days and weeks. Loïc remembered everything. Perfectly. Clearly. Especially what had happened on the Place Saint-Michel.

He had glimpsed Marva out of the corner of his eye—disguised as Ernestine Dukes, clutching the .38 caliber revolver she'd taken from the armoire in Normandy—firing, with deadly accuracy, at the head of Harvey Oldcorn.

Two seconds earlier, Loïc, unable to pull the dead policeman's gun from its holster and kill Harvey Oldcorn, saw Cleavon Semple reach into his own jacket pocket as Harvey Oldcorn reached into his.

Two seconds before that, Loïc had recognized his daughter, Naima, in a baseball cap and sunglasses, standing beside two black men on a motorcycle. He didn't know what the hell was going on. He saw the mouth of Oldcorn's pistol in his face, was blinded by the white light of its firing.

He remembered everything up until that moment. Remembered it all with perfect clarity. But when Olivier Matignon leaned into his face and asked him what he remembered, Loïc knew to smile benignly and say: "Fishing with my papa."

Marva, Loïc noticed, was now not just smiling but laughing through her tears. He wondered if she was in on his ruse. No matter.

"You have been in a very deep coma," one of the young, frightened-looking doctors said.

Other medical staff began pouring into the room. Loïc fell asleep. But only for a dreamless few minutes. When he awoke again, he saw Marva, a young doctor, Matignon and the cop from the Eighteenth Arrondissement, Denis Lamouche, surrounding his bed. He felt the tug of his veins in the crook of his left arm, sucking in the liquids being poured into his body through clear plastic tubes.

"Loss of blood flowing to the brain," the young doctor said.

"In a coma for three days," Olivier Matignon said.

"Permanent memory loss," Marva chimed in.

"Monsieur," Inspector Lamouche said, leaning on the metal rail, putting his face very close to Loïc's. "Do you remember what happened at the Place Saint-Michel?"

Loïc forced a weak smile. "We went fishing with my father . . . ?"

Just as Lamouche turned away in obvious disgust, Naima exploded into the room. Next thing Loïc knew, Marva and Naima were both in his arms, convulsing in laughter and tears, reminding him why he would not allow himself to die. At least not yet.

"Maman, it's delicious!" Naima said, taking a bite out of a second juicy, crispy drumstick.

"So glad you like it, baby," Marva said, thrilled to be pleasing the toughest culinary critic she'd ever had. "I've been trying out some different spices."

They were sitting together in the breakfast nook, eating dinner early Sunday evening. Marva had prepared her daughter's favorite meal: fried chicken, mashed potatoes and black-eyed peas. Marva had already told Naima how Loïc had come out of his coma, how Marva had seen him wink.

"A deliberate wink," she repeated.

"Maybe, Maman," Naima said, taking a sip of chilled Brouilly. "I'm just glad he's alive and responsive."

"I know you don't believe me," Marva huffed. "But never you mind. I think we just have to accept that from now on, Papa is going to be suffering from a severe case of—what to call it?—selective amnesia!"

"If you say so, Maman," Naima said in that judicious yet non-committal tone of her father's, a tone that had always bugged Marva.

"Okay, okay. You'll see what I'm talking about. Finish up now so we can get back to the hospital to see him."

Naima, at the moment, was clearly blissing out on her meal. Digging into a chicken breast, she said, "Maman, you're at the summit of your art."

Marva shrugged, helplessly flattered, squirming happily in her chair. "It's just home cookin', baby."